HVZA 2

Hudson Valley Zombie Apocalypse

Written by

Linda Zimmermann

For videos, blogs, podcasts, and information on HVZA and the HVZA graphic novel go to:

www.hvzombie.com
and
http://drtruesdale.wordpress.com/
http://voiceofthehudson.wordpress.com/

HVZA logo by Big Guy Media and Ryan Browne
Special FX flesh on cover created by Michael Worden

Eagle Press
ISBN: 978-1-937174-24-8

Chapter 1

"If anyone finds this, please bring it to West Point, if you can, so the people I care about will know what happened to me. I've lost a lot of blood from the bites and head wound, I'm all alone with very few supplies, and I don't know if I'll survive."

The woman was writing in a black and white college ruled notebook with a green pen that had a bank logo on it. The boy who originally owned the notebook, Dylan, had most likely died in the house, along with the rest of his family, about a year earlier. As a doctor, Rebecca "Becks" Truesdale, was all too familiar with the various stages of human decomposition, and since the start of the zombie apocalypse in June of 2012, she had plenty of corpses to examine. In fact, she had witnessed enough death, and *undeath* for that matter, to last a lifetime.

When she broke into the house on Sparrow Lane, Becks wasn't exactly thrilled to find five corpses, but with her ammo dangerously low, it was infinitely better than running into five hungry zombies. Her wounds had been too severe to allow her to dispose of the bodies at first, so she had to be content to spend a couple of weeks recuperating to get enough strength to toss the father, mother, and three children out the dining room window. Fortunately, the corpses were completely dehydrated so they weren't terribly heavy. But they were rather brittle, so a few limbs, ears, and fingers broke off here and there as she was dragging them through the house and pushing them through the window, but she eventually disposed of all the bits and pieces.

Becks didn't see any signs of bites or self-inflicted wounds on the bodies, so the cause of death for Dylan's family was not immediately evident. However, it was just one more painful reminder that death came in many forms, especially after the government collapsed and everyone was left to fend for themselves. Perhaps it had been the flu, pneumonia, food poisoning, or carbon monoxide from the large kerosene heater in the middle of the living room. Becks favored the latter; as it appeared the family all passed peacefully in their sleeping bags huddled around that heater.

"If I don't make it and I'm found someday, a first-year med student will be able to determine my cause of death in a heartbeat. There's an ugly

1

gash in my scalp and a probable fracture of the left parietal region (that's a cracked skull for you laymen). Then there are about a dozen bites on my hands, arms, shoulders, and legs. Hopefully, I had enough Eradazole that I won't be going zombie, but several of the wounds are still infected from those bastards' filthy mouths.

"I'm going to have to try to find more antibiotics in the other houses in the neighborhood, but I'm still too weak and dizzy for any serious fighting. I'm just going to have to take my chances, though, because if these wounds go septic, I'm screwed.

"And the worst part of all this, is that *I'm stranded somewhere in New Jersey*! Oh, the horror…"

"There's a term my parents used that really disturbed me—'snug as a bug in a rug.' As a rather fastidious and medically inclined child, I recoiled at the thought of disease-carrying insects taking up residence in our carpeting. My mother was always so pleased that at a young age I took it upon myself to vacuum the entire house on a regular basis. But she never realized—and I never told her—that I was only doing it to suck all the little vermin into oblivion.

"However, as troubling as that phrase was to me in my youth, as I look back to the last year and a half at West Point, safe and secure from the outside world of the zombie apocalypse, those words are the first things that come to mind about my peaceful existence there during that time. I was, indeed, snug as a bug in a rug—albeit a highly fortified, military rug.

"There was no fear for my personal safety. I was well fed, with excellent accommodations (in other words, hot showers, flush toilets, and a soft bed), my lab was state-of-the-art, and I was working with my old friend Dr. Philip Masterson, and a host of other talented scientists and doctors. Granted, many of the people I loved, including my ex-husband and best friend, Cam, were still 'out there' fighting the good zombie fight, but the Hudson Valley of New York was becoming more secure every day, so my anxiety level on their account was minimal.

"Most importantly, we were making great progress in the war against the ZIPs (Zombie Infection Parasites). We had a new formulation for Eradazole that now made it effective for up to one month after getting infected. The QK series of drugs—which had saved my life, but almost killed me—were being phased out and replaced with the Triton series (so named as the parasites originated in the ocean), which finally managed to eliminate mature parasites in the mid-phase stage of infection without causing severe harm to the host. However, we still didn't have anything that would help the poor victims of full-blown, end-stage infection. A bullet to the brain was still the best course of action in those cases."

Becks put down her pen and notebook so she could gingerly readjust her position on the couch. Her head was throbbing and a lot of the bite wounds were inflamed and very painful. However, the thing that bothered her the most was the memory of how she received those wounds. Perhaps "haunted her" would have been a better term.

"Becks, you're going to be jealous!" Phil Masterson announced in a sing-song voice as he practically skipped into the lab early one morning in October of 2014.

"Did you get the last of the frozen strawberries?" she asked, craning her neck to see him without removing her arms from the biosafety cabinet in which she was running some samples.

The farms that had been created at West Point had produced such an abundance of fruit and vegetables that much of it had been frozen— something that was possible because the military post had a variety of solar and alternative energy solutions that literally made it a bright beacon in a very dark world. It also made it the last bastion for ice cream thanks to its freezers, and the dairy cows that grazed on the parade field.

"Better than that," Phil said with a genuine wink, not just one of his involuntary eye twitches that were rare these days, now that his son had mostly recovered from the ordeal at the family farm. Life was as good as it could get, under the circumstances.

"The only thing better than strawberries is chocolate, and if you are holding out on me with a chocolate bar, or even an expired box of Count Chocula, then you and I are going to have a problem."

"Even better than chocolate," Phil whispered, as if the walls had ears.

That made Becks stop what she was doing and spin around in her chair to face him with a puzzled expression.

"Come on, stop torturing me. Spill it," Becks demanded, gesturing with her gloved hands for Phil to come out with it.

3

"I have just two words for you—road...trip," Phil said, practically bursting at the seams.

"What! No...n-no way!" Becks stammered with excitement. "Where are you going? When are you going? Can I come, too?"

As wonderful as life had been inside of West Point, they hadn't been off the base in months, and only then it had been on official business to help set up a lab and clinic in the Albany area. It was one of the rules to which they all agreed before signing on to the project. Everything in the world of the zombie apocalypse had a price, and the price for safety and security was your freedom.

Of course, this wasn't the typical American freedom everyone once enjoyed—you were still free to go anywhere, but now scavengers were also free to rob and murder you, and zombies were free to eat you. Still, there was a certain level of adrenalin that Becks missed from her days of fighting to survive. It may sound crazy, but living on the edge was quite a rush; as long as you were able to keep alive, of course.

"Sorry, Becks, it's just me, some scientists and techs from other departments, and about a two dozen army personnel. They're setting up some labs for research, and Eradazole and Triton manufacturing, at the Picatinny Arsenal in New Jersey, and they need someone to get them up and running."

"You lucky bastard!" Becks shouted, tossing a box of Kimwipes at his head to get that smug expression off his face. Phil dodged the awkward projectile and then looked even twice as smug.

"Hey, cut that out or I won't bring you back a nice, shiny, new gun," Phil said, waving a finger as if to a disobedient child.

Before the apocalypse, the arsenal had been the headquarters of the United States Army Armament Research, Development, and Engineering Center. As insurgents and terrorists were beginning to be replaced by the undead as the biggest threat to national security, rumor had it USAARDEC started developing all kinds of anti-zombie weaponry, not the least of which was some sort of sonic disruptor rifle that literally blew apart the nexus of zombie parasites that formed throughout the human nervous system. It supposedly sounded and looked like something out of Buck Rogers, and everyone who had heard the rumors was just itching to get their hands on the futuristic technology.

"And no, I'm not bringing you back a disruptor," Phil added, as if reading Becks' mind.

"You're no fun anymore," Becks said, extending her lower lip in an unmistakable gesture of pouting.

Despite her disappointment, she was more than happy to help Phil get supplies together and compose some protocols for the various stages of manufacturing and research. Of course, standard procedures were already documented in a manual, but things changed so rapidly that last week's data and operating procedures were often ancient history. They worked late into the night before Phil was scheduled to depart, but everything was finally ready to go and packed into the transports. Becks' pillow felt particularly good as she settled down and fell asleep almost immediately.

"Wake up! Becks, wake up," a voice said in the fog of her sleep-deprived brain.

Even months of security behind the walls of West Point couldn't erase the ingrained fight-or-flight response of the outside world, and when she realized a hand was on her shoulder, Becks reacted as if a zombie was attacking. Fortunately, the jab from her fist just glanced Phil's jaw and he staggered back in time to avoid the thrusting foot that threatened a very sensitive area of his anatomy.

"Becks, for Christ's sake, it's Phil!" he yelled, as he stepped all the way back into the hall until she came to her senses.

"Phil, what the hell?" Becks said, rubbing her eyes. "You scared the crap out of me. What's wrong?"

Giving it another few seconds to make sure she was fully awake, Phil gingerly took a few steps back inside her room.

"It's Phil, Jr. Last night I told him I was going away for about a week and he freaked out. I've been trying to calm him down, but I'm afraid he's going to have a relapse," Phil replied, referring to the catatonic state in which the boy had been after witnessing his mother, sister, and grandparents slaughtered and eaten at the farm. It had taken a very long time for his son to even speak again, and longer still to start acting in any manner approaching normal.

Phil's twitch had also returned, and Becks could see the anguish and fear in his face.

"Do you want me to go to your quarters and stay with him?" Becks asked, placing a consoling hand on his shoulder.

"No, I want you to go to the arsenal instead of me. They're leaving in an hour."

Becks was showered, dressed, packed, and standing by the transports at 0430, a full half hour before they were scheduled to pull out. To say she was excited was an understatement—it was like the last day of school, the first day of vacation, and Christmas all wrapped into one. And damn, but didn't it feel good to strap on her faithful Smith & Wesson Model 629 again, full of those hefty .44 Magnum cartridges that made Cream of Brain Soup when she plugged a zombie in the head. Not that she needed the relatively little pistol when traveling with the mighty army convoy, but old habits do die hard.

The convoy consisted of two large trucks full of supplies, a smaller truck with scientists, techs, and heavily armed soldiers, and four armored Humvees—two at the front and two in the back—each with one of those lovely .50 caliber machine guns. Becks missed driving her own Humvee with its potent .50 cal, but as she wasn't going to need it at West Point, she had given it to Cam, who would definitely be putting it to good use.

Sweet-talking her way into the passenger seat of the lead Humvee, Becks trembled with nervous anticipation as they left the gates of West Point. There wasn't much to see before dawn by the headlights on the wooded sections of highway, but as they descended Route 6 with its commanding view of the former Woodbury Commons shopping center, Walmart, and all the other retailers clustered in the area, Becks saw the faint flickering of campfires. It appeared that survivors had made the parking lots into base camps, with large numbers of RVs formed into circles, like the wagon trains of the old west.

It made sense, as this was the point where two major highways met—the New York State Thruway running north and south, and Route 17 from the west—and the driver explained that these camps had become bartering stations for food, weapons, tools, and whatever was left to loot out of the stores. Consumerism was not dead, even in the midst of the zombie apocalypse!

As they headed south on the Thruway, she wondered if they would see the large packs of zombies that used to clog the roads, but she didn't see even a single straggler. Becks was beginning to wonder why they needed all that firepower in the convoy, until they came to the Suffern checkpoint. Where cars once zoomed onto Interstate 287 at the border

6

with New Jersey, now stood a heavy steel wall with guard towers. Becks looked at the driver with a shocked expression.

"New Jersey is pretty much a no-man's land, ma'am," the smooth-cheeked, twenty-ish Sergeant Tim Colaneri said. "We are hoping to start pushing south next spring, while the troops at the arsenal start moving north and east. But right now, it's worse here than it ever was in the Hudson Valley."

"I guess that makes sense, given the population density," Becks said as her palms began to sweat. Trying to lighten her own mood she added, "Then again, I always thought New Jersey was just one step away from an apocalypse on a good day."

They both laughed, but it didn't help allay the rising fear in her gut. *What was she thinking?* Had she completely forgotten about the endless days and nights of terror? Had she forgotten what it was like to literally run for her life, to watch others die horrible deaths, or to be so close to a zombie that you could smell its stench? Perhaps leaving the safety of West Point wasn't the smartest thing she could have done. There was something to be said for being a bug in a rug.

Interstate 287 was zombie-free, as military patrols drove its length from Suffern to Route 80 in Parsippany at least once a day. Just off the highway was another story entirely. Stately homes that once housed affluent New York City commuters were now burned-out shells, vandalized and left to the elements, or boarded up and reinforced like small forts.

Last year, Becks had seen messages scrawled on cardboard and bed sheets hanging from apartment windows in Manhattan—desperate cries for help that never arrived—and now she watched, heartbroken, as they passed more homes and businesses with similar signs, tattered and weather-beaten.

"CHILDREN INFECTED, PLEASE HELP!"

"WIFE IN LABOR, NEED DOCTOR."

"SURROUNDED BY ZOMBIES, FOR GOD'S SAKE SOMEONE HELP US!"

"NO ONE LEFT BUT ME, IS ANYONE OUT THERE?"

There were a few, however, that had a morbid sense of humor.

7

"HAD I KNOWN, I NEVER WOULD HAVE PAID MY TAXES."

"ANNOYING NEIGHBORS ALL TURNED ZOMBIE. 3 CHEERS FOR THE APOCALYPSE!'

"MOTHER-IN-LAW ATE WIFE...BEST DAY OF MY LIFE!"

After a while, Becks stopped reading the signs and concentrated on looking for signs of life, and the undead. She thought she saw a pickup truck driving on a local road under the highway, but she couldn't be sure, as she only caught a glimpse. She was sure of one thing, though; just about every town and road was thick with packs of zombies.

"Isn't anyone fighting them down here?" she asked Colaneri.

"No, ma'am, at least not so as it's had any real effect on the dirty scummer population," the young driver replied, eyeing a distant pack with contempt.

"Say what?" Becks asked in amusement. "Pray tell, what is a scummer, and when did we start using that term?"

"Oh, sorry, ma'am," the sergeant apologized, as if he had just used a four-letter word. "Don't exactly know what it means, but we had a British instructor at the Point who kept calling the zombies 'dirty scummers,' and me and some of the boys just picked up on it."

"You were a cadet?" Becks asked in a more serious tone.

"Yes, ma'am!" he replied, sitting up straighter in his seat. "All I ever wanted to do since I was a kid was graduate from West Point, like my dad and grandpa. And I was only a year away from my dream when the scummer shit hit the fan—oh, excuse my language, ma'am. Could have kept taking classes, but there comes a point where Duty, Honor, and Country are best served with a gun."

"Amen to that!" Becks said as she lovingly patted the holster that held her revolver.

Becks admired his dedication and youthful zeal. She was also envious of his seemingly boundless energy—energy she used to possess before the scummer shit hit the fan. Had she grown so much older in just over a year? The mirror in her quarters certainly indicated that was the case.

For the remainder of the drive, Becks and Sergeant Colaneri talked about their lives BZA (before the zombie apocalypse), which inevitably led to discussing the fate of their respective families. Becks considered concealing the fact that her parents had taken an overdose of sleeping pills when they discovered they were terminally infected. However, as they did it to prevent being a burden to her, she relayed the event as it happened, and spoke with love and pride at their ultimate sacrifice.

After Colaneri wiped away a few tears, he told his own sad story. He was at West Point when the infection spread to his small hometown in Kansas. His father was retired military—a colonel in Special Forces, no less—so Cadet Colaneri had every confidence his family would be safe and secure. His father turned their home into an armed fortress, but neglected one small detail—he had unknowingly become infected while helping local law enforcement eradicate a herd of zombies that had wandered into town.

With windows nailed shut and doors barred, Colonel Colaneri quietly switched late one night, turned over in bed and proceeded to kill and devour his wife. After having his fill of her, he next attacked his 10-year-old daughter when she got up in the morning to pour herself a bowl of cereal. She at least had time to scream, which alerted his 15-year-old son, who was able to barricade himself in his bedroom. It was at this point that Sergeant Colaneri received a frantic call.

"I told my brother that our father would expect each of us to do his duty," the sergeant stated with a cold, steely demeanor that shouldn't have come so easily to someone so young. "I told him to take the hunting rifle he kept over his bed and put down the enemy that had killed our father and taken over his body. I told him to be a man, and to do his duty. Then I got off the phone and cried like a baby."

"Did your brother survive?" I asked, almost in a whisper.

"He was on his own on the road the last I heard from him, before communications went down. He said he would meet me at West Point, but that was so long ago. But he's a tough kid, and if anyone can make it, he can," he said, fighting back more tears. "Our dad would be proud of him."

"Your dad would be proud of you, too," Becks added, taking the liberty to give the man's arm a reassuring squeeze.

"No ma'am, I haven't earned that honor yet," he said with visible shame. "The closest I've come to the enemy is driving by them all safe and secure in this armored Humvee. Not exactly boots on the ground, ma'am."

Becks felt like telling the young soldier to be careful what he wished for, but she understood the anguish and guilt he felt about being in a relatively safe environment while the ones you loved were fighting for their lives in this hellish world.

As they drew close to the Picatinny Arsenal, they went through a series of checkpoints similar to those at West Point—except a few of these soldiers had some weaponry Becks had never seen. Being stationed in a weapons research center obviously had its perks.

Becks wasn't quite sure what to expect when they finally entered the grounds of the arsenal, but if she had to make a list of ten possible scenarios, children riding bicycles and skateboards would not have been on that list.

"We try to create as normal an environment as possible," the sergeant explained. "At least for the kids."

"Are they all from military families?" Becks asked, as she braced herself for a sudden stop as the convoy had to halt for a little girl chasing a soccer ball across the street.

"At first, the policy was military personnel and their families only—absolutely no refugees—like at West Point. Then one day one of our patrols came upon a couple of kids in a wrecked minivan, surrounded by scummers.

"They had lived in Hawthorne, and their parents had decided they would ride things out in their home, rather than go to a refugee center. Those centers were awful, as you know, so it seemed to be a good idea at the time, as the government kept insisting this was a 'temporary situation.' When they ran out of food, they decided to make a run for it, but by then it was too late. They got as far as their driveway when they were attacked by dead neighbors, and their parents were torn apart right in front of them.

"Somehow, this 8-year-old boy managed to get his 5-year-old sister into the van. He actually drove several miles and got onto 287, where he lost control and went off the road. Our patrol cleared all the filthy scummers away from the van, and when they opened it, they found this trembling little boy clutching his sister, with both of them still covered in their parents' blood.

"The refugee policy was amended that day."

The sergeant explained that while they didn't have the manpower or resources to conduct active search and rescue operations, whenever they encountered people in distress they took them in. He described at least half a dozen other cases of people being trapped in the most awful and terrible

10

circumstances, only to be rescued at the last minute—something with which Becks had personal experience.

"And it would break your heart to know just how many of those refugees were *zeeohs*," the sergeant added.

"Were what?" Becks asked.

"Z, Os: zombie orphans. You know the military. They have to name everything."

Becks had been so absorbed in the sergeant's stories, she hadn't paid much attention to their surroundings until they stopped in front of what looked to be a Cold War-era blockhouse in the middle of the woods. She also hadn't noticed that the rest of the convoy was gone.

"Well, ma'am, this is it," the sergeant said, gesturing toward the structure that had probably looked just as bad 50 years earlier. Seeing Becks' expression, he added, "And don't let appearances deceive you. Here at the arsenal, the good stuff is often hidden in the plainest packages. And the best stuff can kill you without you seeing it coming."

"Good to know!" Becks said laughing, as she got out of the Humvee and stretched her legs.

The sergeant retrieved her bags and brought them to the rusty metal door of the building.

"Been a pleasure ma'am," he said, as he was about to get back in the Humvee. "Best of luck with your work, and when you need a ride back to West Point, feel free to request me as your driver."

"Will do, Sergeant, and best of luck to you!"

After he pulled away, Becks went up to the door of the windowless building and raised her fist to knock, but the door started to open before she made contact. A very tall young man—15, maybe 16 years old?—with close-cropped blond hair, wearing a sharp-looking uniform she didn't recognize, greeted her. She imagined this was what Cam probably looked like in high school, although you could never have paid Cam enough to get into a uniform. It had been tough enough on the rare occasions that called for him to wear a suit and tie.

"Allow me to escort you to the commanding officer of the project, Captain Lennox," he said formally, without introducing himself.

As Becks followed him down a dimly lit hallway flanked by plain, cookie cutter offices, she couldn't resist getting personal.

11

"No offense, but aren't you a little young to be an officer? In fact, aren't you a little young to even be in the army?"

"Army ROTC Cadet, ma'am. We can all do our part regardless of our age," he said with an unpretentious combination of pride and determination.

"You are absolutely right," Becks replied, thinking back to how often people didn't take her seriously because of her youthful appearance. She really didn't get that treatment any longer, as more than a year of a zombie apocalypse had a way of maturing, if not outright aging, some people.

"Sir, this is Dr. Rebecca Truesdale," the young man said as he ushered Becks into a slightly larger and marginally less plain office at the end of the hall.

"Thank you, Ronan," the forty-ish officer said as he stood to warmly shake Becks' hand. "And would you please see that the doctor's quarters are prepared immediately?"

"Already done, sir. And all of the status reports have been updated and are awaiting your review," the ROTC Cadet said a moment before turning as if executing a drill maneuver and heading back down the hall.

"Don't know what I would do without that boy," the captain said just loud enough for Ronan to overhear. He then lowered his voice to a normal level and invited Becks to sit. "That young man led his family and a group of neighbors through hell to get them to safety after the Hudson Valley Quarantine ended last year. But I guess I don't need to tell *you* what conditions were like then."

As he spoke that last sentence, he tapped his index finger on a file folder in the center of his desk. Becks leaned forward just enough to see that the folder had her name on it. She had not been extended the same courtesy of a file on Captain Jeffrey Lennox, but if he were not graying at the temples of his chestnut-colored hair, Becks would have sworn he just stepped off of a Harvard rowing team. He had that blue blood, privileged look about him, but he also possessed an easy charm that eliminated any taint of snobbery. For a brief moment, she regretted that he wore a wedding band, but then she quickly refocused on the task at hand.

Becks was pleased that Lennox had an excellent working knowledge of the projects, and was even more pleased that he seemed to be the type of leader to let the experts do their job with minimal interference. On his part, Lennox was relieved to find someone with a combination of

12

expertise, independence, and guts—not the "helpless egghead" he had feared West Point would send him. After going over the basics of what needed to be accomplished in the next week or so, Lennox offered to have her taken to her quarters so she could freshen up and rest for a while, but Becks insisted on going straight to the lab and getting started right away.

Driving a short distance on a narrow road through the woods, they came to a small clearing with another nondescript box of a building. The sergeant told her she shouldn't judge a place by its exterior; but realistically, how good could the interior be?

After descending five floors of concrete staircases with cold, unpainted, metal pipe railings, the captain ran his ID through a card reader. After a soothing, green light was illuminated, a panel marked "A2" slid open in the wall. Only after a successful retinal scan, voice recognition, and fingerprint imaging did Becks hear a series of clicking and whirring that released a host of locks on the massive steel door. It looked like they would need four men to help open the door, but a gentle tug with two fingers was all the captain needed for the hydraulic assist mechanism to swing open the portal to the cosmic candy store of military weapons research labs.

"I don't even know what I'm looking at in here!" Becks exclaimed with wide eyes as she tried to take in row after row of lab benches full of monitors, test equipment, and exotic weapons components that looked like something out of a science fiction novel. As they passed through the long lab, she saw teams of researchers measuring, recording, and tweaking strange pistols, bizarre and deadly-looking helmet attachments, and long cylinders that resembled rifles, but had neither open barrels nor any type of magazines for ammunition.

"Oh, this is just some old technology we are trying to adapt specifically for the zombie threat," the captain said with a dismissive wave of his hand. "The really good stuff is in another building."

"Damn, I'll take your leftovers and hand-me-downs any day!" she exclaimed, pausing in front of an unattended work station, and struggling to resist touching the object that looked like an unholy cross between a Gatling gun and a bassoon.

"No, no, no! Please step back, Dr. Truesdale," the captain said with urgency, jumping forward and thrusting his arm in front of Becks to push her back a foot or two. "That's one of the nastier devices, and it can be touch activated."

"Okay, just looking," she replied, instinctively raising her hands in the air and backing away another few feet. "I know enough to not mess with anything."

That was sort of a lie, because she wanted to run around the lab and mess with *everything*. And she couldn't swear that she *wouldn't* have touched the Bassoon-o-Matic Deathray, or whatever the hell it was.

Deciding it would be prudent to put her hands in her jacket pockets, they proceeded to the back of the lab, where the captain had to go through the same security routine to open a somewhat smaller, but more sophisticated steel door. As soon as it started to open, Becks recognized the telltale seals and air filtration systems of a biohazard lab. After one more air lock, she expected to enter another high-tech fantasy land of everything a scientist's heart could desire. Instead, the third door opened to a brightly lit, huge, but completely empty white room.

The captain noted Becks' look of disappointment and quickly offered, "*Tabula rasa*, I'm afraid. But look on the bright side, you can fill in this blank slate from the ground up with whatever you need and want."

It was a bit of a shock to find that nothing was set up yet, but Becks never backed away from a challenge. And within the hour, she was already in conference with the staff of two dozen military and civilian scientists and techs who would be running the research and manufacturing. Within 24 hours, the skeleton of the lab was established, and day-by-day it was fleshed out, until by the fifth day, everything was fully functional and bottles of Eradazole and Triton were already being filled on the assembly line.

Becks' next project was to start culturing the various types of ZIPs that proved so effective in her meat grenades. The idea behind it was to introduce slightly different zombie infection parasites into the zombies' system (by way of them eating the infected meat delivered by simply tossing glass jars that would break in front of a crowd of hungry zombies). These different ZIPs created a deadly competition—deadly for the zombie that died once and for all because of the parasites fighting amongst themselves. And once another zombie ate the infected dead zombie, it began a domino effect that could eliminate a sizable herd in a couple of weeks without firing a shot.

While this co-infecting parasite scheme had initially been Becks' idea, other scientists had greatly improved upon it. And once the Picatinny Arsenal started making their own infected meat grenades, they could start doing some serious damage to the swarms of zombies that packed New Jersey roads tighter than summer weekend traffic on the way to the shore—at least BZA, that is. However, growing parasites was trickier business than simply manufacturing drugs, so she would need to work extra hard with the staff to make sure they got it right.

"You need a break," Captain Lennox said, early on the sixth day as Becks prepared for another meeting with the research staff regarding the new parasite project.

"Can't. Busy," she replied mechanically, not even looking up from her notes.

"Not an option," he replied with authority, slapping closed her notebook. "You've barely eaten or slept all week, and I'm not about to get my ass chewed out by the powers-that-be at West Point for abusing you."

"But we have a staff meeting in 15 minutes," Becks weakly protested, recognizing that this was a battle she would not win.

"No, ma'am, you do not. I have dismissed the entire staff for a day of R&R, as it seems that someone has been running them ragged for several days and nights."

Though his voice was stern, there was a thinly-veiled smile across his lips and a twinkle in his eyes.

"It appears I am outranked, and outmaneuvered," Becks said in surrender. "I will go to my quarters and relax for a while."

"No, you will not," he stated with a wide grin, as he offered his hand to help her stand. It was not so much of a gentlemanly gesture, as it was getting a hold of her in case he had to drag her screaming and kicking from the lab.

With his arm lightly positioned around her waist in case there was any resistance, he guided Becks up the five flights of stairs and outside into the first sunlight she had seen since her arrival almost a week earlier. The air was cool, but the sunlight felt warm on her face. With her eyes closed and her head back to soak in the rays, she didn't notice what was standing just ten feet away, until a loud snort made her almost jump out of her skin.

"What the...horses! One of those isn't for me, is it?"

15

"Yes, ma'am," Lennox replied, taking up a position next to a sleek, black stallion, and interlocking his fingers to give her a leg up on the saddle.

"Not on him!? Don't you have anything smaller—preferably something coin-operated, or on a carousel?" she asked, only half-kidding as she eyed the enormous, snorting beast.

"Don't tell me the highly capable and ultra-confident Dr. Rebecca Truesdale has never ridden?" he asked as if throwing down a gauntlet.

"Of course, I've ridden. I used to ride every summer," she replied, putting on an air of self-assurance while striding toward the intimidating creature. What Becks didn't say was that her only riding experiences were with the ponies a neighbor would have at his annual 4th of July parties when she was a kid.

Placing her foot in the offered hands, she hoisted herself up into the saddle. It was hard and uncomfortable, and she was not thrilled by how high off the ground she was. She watched Lennox effortlessly mount his steed and take hold of the reins—she would have bet anything he had been a polo player at whatever fancy pants country club his family had belonged to BZA—and then she tried to copy his grip and posture as if she knew what she was doing.

What ensued was a curious mixture of exhilaration and torture. Becks could not get the hang of preventing her butt from repeatedly being pounded against the saddle, causing extreme discomfort all the way up her spine to her neck and shoulders. Yet, the beauty, strength, and magnificence of the proud animal were something to behold. She envied Captain Lennox's fluid motions, as if he was one with the horse, and was transported to a higher state of consciousness as a result. Unfortunately, Becks was in a state of chaos and pain, wishing for *un*consciousness.

"Isn't this just what the doctor ordered?" Lennox shouted, beaming with joy, as he mercifully stopped after about 20 minutes.

"Yes, a doctor does come to mind," Becks replied, gingerly rubbing her back and neck. "It's been fun, but I should really get back to work."

"We're just getting warmed up!" he said with a devilish grin, moments before a subtle movement of his hands and feet made his horse spin and take off at a gallop. Beck's horse was clearly the alpha male, and with no urging on her part he took off like it was the start of the Kentucky Derby.

Terrified, yet elated, she held on for dear life, but quickly realized that the faster her horse went, the less pounding her body took as his entire motion changed. After a swift and incredibly adrenaline-charged sprint across a field and up a hillside, Lennox again came to a halt, but this time she was almost sorry to stop. Almost.

"I thought you would appreciate if we combined a little business with pleasure," the captain said with an enigmatic look, a moment before he pointed down to a large open area adjacent to a lake.

Prodding her horse forward a few more feet, Becks instinctively reached for her pistol—which she was not wearing—when she looked below and saw zombies; dozens and dozens of them staggering in all directions. She was about kick her heels into the stallion to send him back into a gallop, when Lennox grabbed the reins of her horse.

"Hang on, those scummers are contained in an electrified fence. Look, over there!"

He pointed to a small child who shuffled over to the 8-foot-high metal fence, and the instant her hand made contact there was a sharp buzzing sound. Her little body shook for a few seconds, then went totally limp and she hit the ground.

"Is she dead? I mean, for good?" Becks asked, her mind reeling with the sight of the large herd. She hadn't been this close to that many zombies since going to West Point in the spring.

"No, the ZIP network is just temporarily disrupted. She'll be up and around in about 10 minutes. But we very well could have upped the voltage and put her down for good, but we would lose too many test subjects that way. These scummers are so stupid, they never learn."

As if to emphasize his point, four or five other zombies got up off the ground and stumbled right back into the electrified fence, dropping again like sacks of potatoes. Apparently this went on all day and night.

Becks was all too familiar with the ZIPs that brought on the apocalypse, and how electric shocks affected them. At ParGenTech, where she conducted her initial research on the parasites, she used a stun rod to subdue her test subjects, which she rather enjoyed. If outposts of survivors were able to generate enough electricity, these fences would work wonders for their security—especially dialed up to lethal levels.

"So tell me, what exactly do you test on these...scummers?" Becks asked, deciding to employ the local lingo.

"Would you like to find out for yourself, Dr. Kilzombie?" Lennox asked with a self-satisfied smirk. Apparently, someone at West Point had told him about the nickname Cam's men had given her in the early days of the infection outbreak, when she had to shoot three zombies in a restaurant in Cornwall.

"As my reputation precedes me, need you ask?"

Forgetting that she didn't know what she was doing, Becks prompted her horse to take off at a gallop down the hill. She almost fell off, twice, but somehow managed to stay in the saddle. Fortunately, the horse had apparently been to this facility many times before, and he knew to take her right to the entrance of a large, concrete building, where he stopped without needing to receive a command from his hapless passenger.

The ground felt *so good* beneath her feet as Becks stepped down onto terra firma. Slowly bending and twisting ever so slightly, she hoped to surreptitiously readjust her misaligned and battered anatomy.

"Riding a horse really makes you feel alive, doesn't it?" Lennox asked, giving Becks a slap on the back.

Makes me wish I was dead, she thought, but nonetheless managed a smile and a nod.

Becks followed Lennox past a pair of saluting guards at the door, and they entered the nondescript building that was made of very thick, reinforced concrete walls. She now knew that outward appearances meant nothing at the Picatinny Arsenal, and she fully expected another high tech wonderland of labs and test equipment inside. Instead, bare concrete walls were faintly illuminated by the occasional light bulb hanging from the ceiling. Except for a couple of tables and chairs, the long room had no other furniture. What it did have, however, were rows of heavy steel cabinets with sophisticated security locks.

Captain Lennox sauntered over to the second row to a cabinet labeled SBX-170A. Placing his palm on a screen set flush into the door of the cabinet, there was a *beep* and a *clank*, and the massive door swung open in a wide arc. When it opened far enough for Becks to see inside, she thought her eyes would pop out of her head. She had no idea what it was, but it was the most beautiful and elegant weapon she had ever seen. It was as long as a rifle, but had no moving parts or an open barrel. There was a laser scope mounted on top, but other than that it looked more like a white ceramic lighting fixture than a weapon.

"Is this a magic wand or a gun?" Becks asked, raising her hands to indicate she was clueless.

"A little bit of both," Lennox replied, cradling the object in his arms and running his fingertips down it in what could only be characterized as a caress. "The SBX-170A is the culmination of high intensity infrasound technology, utilizing rapid pulse acoustic emitters to either propagate widespread non-lethal bursts, or initiate focused waves that inflict tissue damage—*with extreme prejudice*."

"Oh, cool! The Sonic Disrupter!" Becks gushed like a kid on Christmas morning.

Lennox tried to look dismayed at her science fiction reference, but he couldn't help but appreciate her enthusiasm. And it really was like something out of movie.

"If you must give it a name, we call it the Whale Bone," he said, then realized that needed some further explanation. "Whales use infrasound to communicate over long distances. They also use intense bursts of sound to stun their prey. And, the white composite material kind of looks like bone, hence the nickname."

"Yeah, yeah, that's all fascinating," Becks said with a dismissive wave of her hand. "Now, are we going to stand around chattering all day or are we going to take this baby out for a test drive?"

Becks could barely contain herself as they went outside to the holding pen, but her exuberance was knocked down a few pegs as they approached the fence and the stinking, rotting occupants all surged toward them. She stopped in her tracks and reached for her gun again, and for a moment felt panic that she was unarmed—until a few of the closest zombies hit the electrified fence and dropped to the ground. Even though in her head she knew she was safe, in her heart and stomach she couldn't suppress that old fear. Fence or not, this many zombies eyeing her as dinner just a few yards away was simply too close for comfort.

"Steady, Doctor," Lennox said, placing a reassuring hand on her shoulder. "They still creep the hell out of me, too. I never get used to these filthy scummers. Let's give ourselves a little breathing room, shall we?"

Sliding back a small panel in the center of the weapon, Lennox swiftly ran his fingers across a touchscreen, pointed the "Whale Bone" at the closest zombies, and within a second or two at least a dozen of them hit the dirt twitching. Becks wondered how far her jaw had dropped.

"But, but, I didn't hear anything!" she exclaimed in amazement.

"The early prototypes made a buzzing noise just to let the user know it was working," he explained as he hit the touchscreen a few more times, "but we decided it was best to keep it silent so as not to attract any attention. Now, watch this and start counting!"

Raising the Whale Bone to his shoulder, a red laser spot appeared on the forehead of a short, adult male with a round head and big eyes. Becks had just said "three" when those eyes turned bright red as capillaries began to rupture. At the count of five, blood trickled from his ears and nose. At seven there was a gush of blood and jellied tissue from his eye sockets, nose, mouth, and ears, and the zombie was dead as a doornail before he keeled over.

Of course, Becks immediately had to try the weapon herself, but after she sonically disrupted the head of the fifth zombie, Lennox clamped his hand over the control panel and protested that she needed to leave them at least a few test subjects.

They went back into the concrete building and Lennox showed her the contents of some of the other cabinets. Truthfully, Becks didn't understand a lot of what the Lennox was telling her about the various high tech weapons and ammo, but she was so fascinated that she listened for almost an hour. Few people ever truly impressed her, but Lennox was definitely one of them. And she had been mistaken about his Ivy League education—he was the son of a Boston iron worker, and had graduated from West Point with a degree in systems engineering, specializing in weaponry.

"So how did someone with your background get to lead this project? Aren't there any medical staff that could have done it?" she asked, wondering why such a brilliant engineer was "slumming" on zombie drug manufacturing and ZIP farming.

"Ah, good question," he replied with another of those devilish smiles she had glimpsed on occasion at meetings. "While I applaud your innovative delivery system for the infected meat, I felt that glass jar grenades could use a slight upgrade. I have plans for some rather unique biological agent delivery systems. Those scummers won't know what hit them."

Try as she would, Lennox wouldn't divulge any of his plans for getting the co-infecting ZIPs into the zombies' bodies, but he said that if

20

she attended a little dinner party at his quarters that evening, he might share an idea or two.

"That's blackmail," she stated without malice.

"But blackmail for your own good. You'll be leaving in a couple of days and you should relax at least one night. And there are some people I want you to meet."

Becks really wanted to get back to work, but one night off might be fun. She agreed on the condition that Sgt. Colaneri and Ronan join them. After an even more painful ride back, she actually slept several hours before the party. The day off definitely did her good, and when she arrived at the captain's quarters, she was looking forward to the evening.

Becks was greeted by Mrs. Lennox, who looked just as blue-blooded as her husband. She had been a hotshot corporate attorney BZA, but as there wasn't much call for lawyers these days (at least there was something good to be said about the zombie apocalypse!), she had been running one of the zeeoh daycare centers and schools. Their own two children—a little boy and girl who could have been blueblood poster children—made a brief and polite appearance in their cute little footed PJs, then were ushered off to bed.

Quite an eclectic group of military and civilian personnel were in attendance, and the topic of conversation was clearly skewed to a subject near and dear to Becks' heart—every way possible to kill a zombie—from primitive clubs made from sticks with rocks duct taped to them, to multimillion dollar missile systems. After dinner and several rounds of drinks, the "war stories" began circulating about everyone's most harrowing and outrageous zombie encounters. Becks noticed that the sergeant sat in awkward silence during the telling of these stories—as he had none to share. Ronan also did not share any stories, but it couldn't have been because he didn't have a long list of zombie kills and narrow escapes. Becks assumed it was a combination of modesty, and a reluctance to relive some painful memories.

It was late when Becks got back to her quarters. Even though she hadn't worked at all that day, she was exhausted. She wasn't used to socializing—or horseback riding—and it all seemed to take more out of her than an 18-hour shift in the lab. But she was very glad she had been blackmailed into going to the party—although she had completely forgotten to ask Lennox about his plans for the ZIPs delivery systems. It had been good food, good company, and the last time she would be able to kick back and have fun for a long time. Perhaps it was even the very last time.

Chapter 2

Due to the highly-skilled and competent doctors and scientists on staff, it only took Becks another two days to get everyone up to speed on how to grow healthy, competitive ZIPs. She could have stuck around a few more days to make sure the first few batches were successful, but they did have phone and video chat capabilities with West Point, and there was no reason she couldn't come back if any of the procedures needed tweaking.

Also, the base meteorologists said there was a 30% chance of a coastal storm developing that night, so they suggested that the supply run to West Point leave by mid-morning to avoid any bad weather. Becks got word to Sgt. Colaneri, and even though it was his day off, he volunteered for the assignment.

At 8am, as Becks was saying her goodbyes to Captain Lennox and the project staff, the first raindrops already started a staccato beat on the roof, and a steady breeze swirled the fallen leaves into mini twisters. By 9am, as she finished packing equipment, the sky had turned an ominous greenish-black and a steady rain was coming down at a sharp angle in the stiff wind. At 10am, as she climbed into the front seat of the Humvee driven by Sgt. Colaneri, she questioned whether or not they should head out in this intensifying nor'easter—which obviously *was* developing, and a lot sooner than predicted.

"Orders say we go," the sergeant replied. "And the lead Humvee is carrying some new exotics the boys at the Point have been jonesing to get their hands on."

"Exotics? Are we talking exotic fruit? Exotic dancers?" Becks asked, having no clue what the sergeant was talking about.

"I wish!" he replied with a little too much enthusiasm, and then actually blushed. "No, ma'am, we are talking explosives. They call them exotics because they are so unique—and so dangerous."

"So, this isn't your father's nitroglycerine," Becks said trying to make a joke, but not feeling particularly amused, given the fact that they were about to drive into a storm right behind a vehicular bomb.

The short stretch of Route 80 wasn't too bad, just a lot of heavy rain. But as soon as they got on Interstate 287 and started heading north, Mother Nature unleashed her fury.

"This is their idea of a 30% chance of a storm developing later on tonight?" Becks complained as she rocked from side to side in the buffeting winds. "Good to know that there are some things that the apocalypse didn't change—meteorologists still suck at predicting the weather!"

As experienced as Sgt. Colaneri was behind the wheel of the formidable Humvee, he and the other driver soon slowed down to a snail's pace. Debris peppered the hood and windshield, from fine grit and leaves, to sticks the diameter of a pencil. Undaunted, the mini convoy kept creeping slowly northward, until branches the size of a linebacker's arm started flying through the air. Over their radios, the sergeant and the driver of the other vehicle decided to stop and call West Point.

"Picatinny convoy, be advised that we are getting our asses kicked here by the weather," a static-garbled voice from West Point replied. "We have reports of flooding, downed trees, and extremely limited visibility. Suggest you return to base, ASAP."

After checking in with the arsenal, they got the okay to turn around and head back, but it was already too late. The fierce winds had brought down huge limbs and entire trees so that the road ahead was blocked. Fortunately, they were near an exit ramp, so the two drivers decided to take "a short detour" on local roads and get back on 287 further south, where hopefully the highway was clear.

Becks thought back to all of her parents' antiquing adventures when she was a kid. Her dad was notorious for his "short detours," which on more than one occasion necessitated getting a motel room for the night once they discovered just how far from home they had wandered. She hoped the Army personnel had a better lay of the land, but she feared that Y chromosomes predisposed men to roam far afield.

Another strike against them was that they were now entering the No Man's Land of unpatrolled and unsecured streets. Actually, it immediately became clear it was Zombies' Land as several large herds caused a series of additional "short detours." Between avoiding the masses of rain-soaked zombies and the almost zero visibility, within 15 or 20 minutes they were hopelessly lost.

Driving down a typical New Jersey suburban street, bumping into the occasional wandering scummer, the two drivers argued about where they were, what direction to go, and whether or not they should stop and wait out the storm. Becks was starting to get very anxious.

"Everything is under control, right?" she said, more trying to convince herself than pose a question.

"Yes, ma'am. Don't you worry, we'll be out of here in no time," the sergeant lied unconvincingly.

He started to say something else, but the words never had a chance to leave his lips.

At first, amidst the blinding downpour and howling winds, Sergeant Colaneri and Becks thought that a big mass of leaves was blowing straight down just ahead of them. An instant later, they realized those leaves were attached to an immense oak tree that had just uprooted and was plummeting toward the lead Humvee like a hammer to a bug. It was all so surreal, like watching a horror movie in slow motion, and no matter how hard you tried, you couldn't push the OFF button. However, a heartbeat later it was like someone hit the ignition button on the main engines of a Saturn 5 rocket.

As the huge oak crushed the explosive-filled Humvee, a deafening concussion tore through the air and an orange-red ball of flame expanded like a supernova. The last thing Becks remembered was their Humvee lifting off the ground and spiraling sideways as it broke apart, as if a petulant child had thrown his little toy truck into a wood chipper.

Was she at the bottom of a deep, dark well?

Becks felt disconnected from her body and was unable to open her eyes. There was a high-pitched ringing and muffled buzzing in hers ears, and they felt like they were stuffed with cotton soaked in molasses.

The next second of emerging consciousness brought pure, unadulterated pain.

Had her skull been cleaved in two by an ax? Was there a swarm of rats feasting on her corpse? It was all like some terrifying nightmare where sleep paralysis prevented her from moving or speaking. She was completely helpless and could only experience pain.

Suddenly, a loud blast pounded against her already damaged eardrums, startling her back to her senses. Her eyes popped open and the first thing she saw was Sgt. Colaneri on his back in the middle of the road about ten feet away, with his pistol pointed in her direction. Why would he be pointing a gun at her, she wondered?

As he squeezed off another round, Becks fully expected to feel the additional agony of a bullet wound. Instead, the searing pain in her left arm subsided. Blinking rapidly, she turned her head to see the young female scummer—who had been chewing on Becks' forearm—fall backward and to the right, while the fragments of her skull blew off to the left.

Still blinking her eyes again and again to try to focus in the wind-whipped rain and the fog of injury, Becks finally realized that this was worse than any swarm of rats. Far worse. These were the unclean, unrelenting, unholy, undead, and they were in the process of trying to make a meal out of her. Finding her voice again, she screamed as she had never screamed in her life. Adrenaline pumped through her like a fire hose and she started punching and kicking at the four remaining scummers latched onto her, but her thrashing only seemed to make them sink their filthy teeth in deeper.

The sergeant fired several more rounds, and even though he was obviously badly wounded, he was able to take down each of her attackers with devastating headshots, splattering her with the foulest smelling gore in the process. For a moment, she was glad of the heavy rain that almost immediately washed away most of the blood and lumps of brains.

Springing to her feet, the universe suddenly spun out of control and Becks dropped to her knees in a wave of pain, nausea, and vertigo. Placing a hand on either side of her head—as if that would help to steady her thoughts and clear her vision—she found that her hair was soaked in her own blood from a long gash in her scalp. But her injuries were nothing compared to the scene that began to resolve itself in front of her.

About 40 feet away, the lead Humvee was a flaming, scattered pile of parts—both mechanical and human. Whatever they had been carrying created an explosion of such force that the largest piece of anything that existed was half of one of the armored doors and some smoking tire rims. You can imagine what that meant for the flesh of the four occupants.

What was left of Becks' Humvee was lying on its left side, but she had no clue how many times it flipped over before stopping in that position. She didn't know at what point she had been thrown from the vehicle, or how long she had been lying in the street unconscious, or even how long the filthy scummers had been chewing on her. Head spinning, heart pounding, she managed to crawl over to Sgt. Colaneri. They would need to help each other to get to safety, as dozens of scummers were staggering down both ends of the street towards them. It wasn't until she was right next to the sergeant, however, that she realized he was beyond help.

At first, Becks thought his legs were just pinned under the Humvee, but there was a gap of almost three feet from the edge of the massive vehicle and his thighs. His legs were gone! Blood was spurting out of the two stumps at a furious pace, and she grasped at the hot, gooey masses of flesh to try to stem the flow. She knew it was a futile effort, but still tried clamping down on the slippery arteries squirting out the remaining seconds of his life.

With his last bit of strength, the sergeant dropped his gun, grabbed Becks' wrists and told her to stop trying to help him, and save herself.

"Run!" he whispered between gasping, raspy breaths. "Take my weapons and run!"

The scummers were closing in fast, and for a brief moment the blood and pain and horror of the scene was too much and she gave up, resigned to just letting the undead bastards kill her and get it all over with. But then Becks looked into the sergeant's eyes, and his look burned into her soul. It was a look of sadness, fear, and agony, for sure, but there was also something else, something good and pure and unmistakable—the look of fierce defiance, even in the face of certain death.

"Tell my brother I'm proud of him, and that I went down fighting," he said in a strong, clear voice, a moment before a gush of blood erupted from his lips. Two choked gasps later, and Sgt. Colaneri lay still and peaceful—his life's burden lifted.

Her life seemed inconsequential at that instant—except for the purpose of honoring the memory and request of the man who saved her life, the man who rested in bloody pieces on the pavement, the man who had yearned for a chance to be a hero, and paid the ultimate price for that honor.

The scummers were so close now that Becks could smell them, but she took the time to straighten the sergeant's hair, cross his arms across his chest, and kiss him gently on his cheek. Then as fast as she could, she grabbed the pistol he had dropped, and tried to unfasten his belt which held another sidearm, ammo, a canteen, and other equipment, but her fingers were so slick with blood and rain she couldn't unlatch it. Finally, she just yanked down as hard as she could, and pulled the belt off over the stumps of his legs.

As Becks tried to stand, a former clergyman with half his face missing and the other half swarming with maggots, lunged for her. She managed to barely roll out of the way, and his head hit the pavement just a foot from hers. Instinct kicked in, and before she even realized that she had raised a pistol to the side of his head, she pulled the trigger. The concussion blew some of the maggots off his face and into her hair, but she had no time to pick them out as it looked like the clergyman's entire congregation was almost in arm's reach of her.

Trying to bolt forward toward the nearest house, after just a few steps the vertigo brought her splashing down into a big, cold puddle. She tried again, but still only made it another ten feet to the edge of the muddy lawn. Her body convulsed a few times and she vomited; the force of which felt like a hammer blow to what she realized must be a fracture in her skull.

A tiny Asian girl carrying a half-eaten squirrel grabbed at her leg and Becks raised her pistol, but with everything spinning she realized she was just as likely to hit the squirrel, or her own leg, as hit the girl. She decided not to waste precious ammo and opted to kick the little girl right in the teeth, which completely yielded in her soft, decaying gums beneath the sole of Becks' boot.

There was no longer any more time to waste; she knew if she fell again she would be dead meat—literally—so with all her strength and determination, Becks got to her feet and raced forward, somehow managing to go the twenty or thirty feet to the side of a modest Cape Cod style house. The windows were not boarded up, which most likely meant one of two things—the occupants evacuated when the outbreak first

27

began, or they all turned and never left the house. Still, facing one zombie family was better than facing an entire neighborhood of scummers.

Grabbing a decorative stone which once helped frame a little flower garden, she bashed away at a side window. The window was just above eye level, and her chewed-up arms and legs didn't have the strength to hoist her through the opening she had created. Plan B wasn't exactly an elegant solution, but beggars can never be choosers during a zombie apocalypse.

Waiting until the nearest scummer was about ten feet away, Becks raced forward and grabbed the moldy collar of his velour jogging suit— *Really, people still wore those in the 21st century?*, she thought—and yanked him up against the wall of the house. Pressing the pistol against his forehead so she wouldn't miss, she blew a good portion of his brains out, and then directed his falling corpse so that he landed doubled over, not flat. This grisly stepping stool of flesh gave her just enough height to get her arms and shoulders over the window sill. Squirming and pulling herself forward, she let gravity do the rest and she fell forward onto the hardwood floor of a dining room with a jarring and excruciating thud. But she was inside, and she prayed that was a vast improvement on her previous situation.

Dirty, rotting hands grabbed at the window sill, and one extraordinarily tall woman—was she standing on the human step stool?—had her chin on the inside sill, snapping her broken, green teeth at Becks. Still deciding to conserve bullets, in case she was not alone in the house, she pistol-whipped the Amazon bitch and slammed down the upper section of the window, crunching quite a few fingers in the process. But it wasn't until the third time that she raised and slammed down the window that the sill was finally clear of grasping hands. She hefted up one of the dining room chairs to wedge into the gap above the window, just in case some clever scummer tried to lift it open, and then pulled the curtains closed, hoping that "out of sight" was "out of mind" for the horde of her pursuers.

Now, she had to make sure the house was secure. She would need to do a slow and careful room by room search. Becks still had one of the sergeant's pistols clutched in her right hand, and with her left, she pulled out her faithful Smith & Wesson, which she hadn't needed to use in many months. It felt like an old friend in her hand, and she was suddenly

28

confident that she could handle anything this house had lurking in the shadows. Unfortunately, her wounds and the ensuing shock got the better of her, and before she could even take a step, the deep, dark well opened up again and swallowed her whole.

When the storm moved off and the skies cleared the next morning, a search and rescue helicopter took off from the Picatinny Arsenal. With so much debris from the storm, and so much human carnage from over a year of apocalyptic chaos, it wasn't easy finding the wrecked convoy. But the helicopter's FLIR camera finally picked up the heat signature of the huge explosion and resulting fire that was still smoldering despite several inches of rain.

Passing overhead a few times and taking photos, it was clear that the lead Humvee and its passengers were blown to bits. The second Humvee was less damaged, but that was a relative term as it was just in larger chunks. Also in chunks were the bloody remains of Sgt. Colaneri and the scummers he had shot, which the rest of the neighborhood scummers were now feasting upon. At least one of the recognizable pieces of body appeared to be from a female. There were no signs that anyone had escaped the blast or the ensuing raw meat orgy.

The official conclusion was that everyone had been killed, and there was no reason to risk inserting a search team into such a heavily infested area.

When word reached West Point, Phil sank to his knees and wept. When Cam got the news, it was like his heart had frozen in his chest—but some small voice in his head told him not to completely give up hope, yet.

To the unconscious, lone survivor bleeding on the dusty floor of the suburban New Jersey house, the roar of the helicopter engine and the emotional turmoil of the people she loved were all unknown to her. She was blissfully ignorant, in a near coma-like state. It would only be when she awakened that the real nightmare would begin.

The next thing Becks knew was that there was a terrible taste in her mouth and her tongue and lips were as dry and parched as paper. Her eyes flickered open to see that her right arm was glued to the worn hardwood floor in a dried puddle of her own blood and pus. Prying her arm free, which started it bleeding again as the massive black scab stuck to the floor, she used both shaky arms to push herself to a sitting position, which only started the Merry-Go-Round spinning again in her brain. The resulting nausea made her heave, but she was so dehydrated that nothing came up.

It was daylight, but which day was it? From the scabbing and swelling of her wounds, she had to have been unconscious for at least 24 hours, but more likely it was closer to 48. Her head was splitting, and she was so, so weak from lack of food and water and blood loss—but on the bright side, she hadn't been chewed on any more, so she assumed there weren't any scummers roaming freely through the house. Becks held her breath for a moment to listen carefully, and when she didn't hear any sounds, inside or out, she also assumed the crowd at the window had given up and wandered off.

Just as she was about to breathe a sigh of relief, it hit her—infection! Not the infection caused by all the bacteria in her wounds, which looked bad enough, but infection from the zombie parasites! Her bloodstream must be swimming with eggs. She needed an Eradazole tablet, and she needed it ASAP. Even though she foolishly didn't travel with a backpack of supplies, she always, *always*, had a small pouch of Eradazole on a Velcro strap around her left wrist. It was against regulations at West Point to *not* carry the life-saving, ZIP-killing medication with you at all times, and thank god that was one regulation she didn't ignore.

Carefully peeling back the torn sleeves of her jacket and shirt, she got a much better look at the festering bite marks in her forearms. They would need immediate attention, but first things first. She yanked open the zip lock of the little pouch on her wrist, and tipped it over to let the half-dozen tablets drop into her right palm, but nothing fell out! Panicking, she tapped the bottom of the pouch harder and harder. Something did finally fall out—a single lump of blood-soaked tablets. Then she noticed that the waterproof pouch must have gotten torn in the accident, and when she was trying to stem the flow of blood from the sergeant's stumps, his blood must have filled the pouch and drenched the pills.

"Think, Becks, think!" she said out loud.

Would the medication be ineffective now? Would the compounds in the blood or the moisture deactivate the precious and delicate chemical structures that kill the ZIPs? Using her fingernail, she scraped off the bloody outer crust of the lump and saw some flecks of mint green—the color of untainted Eradazole. Were there enough of those flecks to stop the infection? There was only one way to find out.

Like some macabre act of communion, Becks popped the entire congealed lump into her mouth, pulled the sergeant's canteen from his belt, and took several big gulps. The coarse mass scraped the length of her dry esophagus and she could feel the cool water when it hit her stomach— her very empty stomach. She remembered the Hershey's bar that Captain Lennox had given her as she was leaving, and she fished around in her jacket pockets until she found it. She downed it in two big bites.

She would need a lot more food and water, as well as something to clean her wounds, and some heavy doses of antibiotics. Walking was still out of the question, so she kind of pushed and pulled herself with her hands and feet and slid across the smooth floor to an open doorway that looked like it led to a living room. Every few feet she paused to catch her breath and listen for any sounds, and bit by bit, she inched her way onto the dirt-matted shag carpet of the next room. As she pushed her way past a grimy, tan, faux leather sectional couch against the wall, she had her answer as to the fate of the former occupants.

There were five sleeping bags of various sizes arranged in a circle around a kerosene heater in the center of the room. Cautiously dragging herself forward, it was soon evident that the desiccated bodies were no threat to her. Tins of chips and cookies, and a couple of bottles of Gatorade, sat on a nearby coffee table, and she pushed her way past the corpses and ate and drank as much as her stomach could handle. The exertion of crawling just that short distance was exhausting, and she stretched out across the floor and either fell asleep immediately, or passed out again.

This time it was night when she awoke, and the faint moonlight probed the empty eye sockets of the nearest corpse, which seemed to be staring right at her. By its size and lack of hair, she assumed it had been the father of the household—World's Greatest Dad, if the macaroni picture on the wall was to be believed. Groping for the flashlight on the sergeant's belt, she was relieved to feel the cool cylinder of metal between her fingers.

By flashlight and with more crawling, she moved on to the kitchen, the floor of which was thick with mouse droppings and dead ants and roaches. That didn't bode well for the food supply, and sure enough, chewed up and empty boxes of crackers and pasta covered the countertops. She considered herself lucky that the food in the living room had been in metal tins.

Using a chair to help herself get up to unsteady feet, she fought the vertigo long enough to open some cabinet doors, and was rewarded with a feast of things such as canned veggies, canned spaghetti *with* tiny meatballs, no less, and a blessed family-sized jar of crunchy peanut butter. Thank god those little bastard mice hadn't chewed their way into the cabinets!

As tempted as she was to eat as much as she could possibly cram into her belly, she realized that she didn't know how long this food had to last—which was an entirely different subject, which she didn't want to even contemplate at this point. If she didn't treat these infected wounds soon, it wouldn't matter how many rescue squads the Picatinny Arsenal and West Point sent to find her. And now that she thought of it, she wondered why a patrol hadn't located the wrecked Humvees yet...

After she finished eating—like an animal, she had to admit—she made her way into a bathroom. Under the sink she found a bottle of rubbing alcohol and some bandages. However, her hopes of finding antibiotics in the medicine cabinet above the sink where dashed by tubes of suntan lotion, toothpaste, and some poison ivy cream. At least there was one bottle of iodine and a small bottle of aspirin. She would have to try the upstairs bathroom for some real medicine, but she knew she was still too weak and dizzy to tackle the stairs.

Using a pair of scissors she found in a kitchen drawer, and holding the flashlight in her mouth, she carefully cut open her pants to expose the various bites on her legs. The BDUs and boots had offered some protection, but not enough that she didn't have eleven infected wounds of various depths, mostly in her lower calves, just above the boot tops. At least no large chunks of flesh were missing. She must have spent an hour squeezing out pus and screaming into a balled up towel she stuck in her mouth as she poured alcohol and iodine on the wounds, and then carefully bandaged them.

Her left arm had a big hunk of skin and a flap of flesh peeled back, but she doused it in alcohol, pushed it back in place, and put in a couple of stitches with blue thread from a travel sewing kit she found. Her right arm and hand were worse, as a few bits of flesh had definitely been torn off and swallowed by the scummers—an image that made her feel sick to her stomach to even contemplate. She did her best with the alcohol and bandages, and then turned her attention to the crusty gash on her scalp.

Becks had to use the scissors and a Bic disposable razor to gingerly clear the hair around the 4-inch wound on the left side of her head. It was a jagged tear, and didn't she have fun putting a few more blue stitches into her scalp to try to hold the torn flesh together. She almost passed out, but managed to get through her Frankenstein transformation.

She was beginning to feel feverish, and prayed that it was from bacteria and not parasites. She needed more sleep. Crawling back through the living room and over some of the dried corpses, she made it to the couch and found a soiled, orange and 1970s green, crocheted afghan to cover her. The house was cold at night, and maybe an hour later she awoke shivering. God help her, but she unzipped the World's Best Dad's sleeping bag and rolled out his body. Turning it inside out at least, she tried not to think of the former contents and what caused all the staining as she snuggled inside the sleeping bag for warmth.

The next day she had one important mission—get upstairs and find antibiotics. Her wounds were seriously infected and she needed heavy doses of amoxicillin or ampicillin, or anything she could find. With a family of five—three of whom were boys—there must have been plenty of need for antibiotics, and she was counting on the fact that a substantial number of people never finished the full course of their prescriptions because they were feeling better or just forgot. With the average attention span in the digital age being about 60 seconds, or less, a 10-day course of medication was often too much to ask of a patient!

Forgetting she had a fractured skull, she made the mistake of trying to stand, which only made the room start spinning like a centrifuge and she fell back onto the couch. Giving herself a few minutes to regain some equilibrium, she slid down onto the carpet and began crawling to the staircase leading to the second floor. It was covered with the same nasty, dirty shag carpeting as the living room, only most of the shag was worn down to nubs in the centers of the steps from years of kids going up and down.

Becks could just picture the three brothers racing down the stairs, two at a time, the morning they all took that trip to Disney World. (She wasn't psychic; there was a framed collage of photos on the wall.) She could also picture them dragging their feet down the staircase on the first day of school every year, and reluctantly heading up the stairs when their mother told them to stop playing video games and go to bed. But she couldn't dwell on the memories of this family, as she was in very real danger of becoming a memory, too.

Lifting her butt onto the first stair, she grabbed onto the railing overhead like she was riding the subway. Using both her arms and legs, she raised herself up to the next stair, and slowly but surely lifted and sat her way up. Fortunately, the bathroom was right at the top of the stairs, so she turned onto her hands and knees and made her way into the small room with fixtures that were even more outdated than the carpet.

Starting with the cabinet under the sink—as it was at eye level—she found more rubbing alcohol, Ace bandages, gauze bandages, athlete's foot cream, and Costco-sized bundles of cheap shampoo, soap, and cleaning supplies. Then she carefully and slowly raised herself high enough to sit on the toilet, which she then used as a platform to help lift her rear end onto the sink, so she could reach the medicine cabinet without having to stand. Unfortunately, her hopes of a treasure trove of medications were once again dashed, this time by tubes of toothpaste and Clearasil, Pepto-Bismol, Imodium, children's aspirin, and eight half-empty bottles of a variety of cough medicines.

Becks was incredibly disappointed and scared at finding nothing to fight the infections, but then it dawned on her. Where were the tampons? Where was the Midol, the mascara, the lipsticks, and eye shadow? There must be another bathroom in the master bedroom where the mother of the household kept all of her cosmetics and personal items—and hopefully all the family's drugs.

Crawling back out of the bathroom, she saw that the bedroom at the end of the hall to her right was the only one that didn't have piles of clothing on the floor, so she assumed it had been the parents' room. She was correct, and she was also correct in assuming it had another bathroom. And to her great relief, the large, double-doored medicine cabinet in that bathroom was a small pharmacy of Walgreens' prescription bottles.

You name it, and someone in this family had at one time been prescribed it—including no less than seven different bottles of antibiotics, all of which still had anywhere from two to six capsules or pills left. Didn't anyone ever take the full ten days of medication as prescribed? Not that she was complaining, as their inability to follow their doctor's orders just might save her life.

As Becks looked over the labels, she saw that two of the bottles were for doxycycline and had been prescribed in June of 2012—prime tick season—so she suspected that Dylan Serviss and his brother Bryan (the names on the labels) had both showed symptoms of Lyme's Disease, which had almost been running as rampant as the ensuing ZIPs infection. Two other bottles had been prescribed for their mother, Betty Serviss, both of which were for 250mg of Ciprofloxacin—commonly prescribed for urinary tract infections.

As Becks dry-swallowed 500mg of Cipro, she gave thanks to the disease-carrying ticks and Mrs. Serviss' compromised bladder that made her salvation possible. There were no guarantees this would be enough antibiotics, but it sure beat nothing.

After stuffing all the drugs she could find into a bag, she crawled over to the dresser and closet looking to find some clean clothes. She was smelling mighty ripe and her torn and chewed shirt and pants were still covered in her own clotted blood, and that of Sgt. Colaneri. Gently peeling off her clothes over her swollen and painful wounds, she used a couple of wash cloths and some scented body spray (which had a high alcohol content) to clean up a bit. What she wouldn't have given for a hot shower or bath!

Unfortunately, Mrs. Serviss was a very petite size 4, which was half of Becks' size. However, World's Greatest Dad had been short and trim enough that his sweat pants weren't too baggy on her, especially when she put on three pairs for warmth. And she even found a couple of NY Giants sweatshirts and jerseys which she also put on in layers.

While Becks was now warmer and more comfortably clad, and relieved that she now had some antibiotics in her system, the exertion had made her head pound and she was quite nauseated. Shaking some of the dust off the bed comforter and pillows, she crawled under the covers and slept a few hours. As soon as she woke up, she took another 500mg of Cipro. Then she slid back down to the floor and decided to explore the boys' rooms.

21st century boys' bedrooms: Video gaming gear, stacks of graphic novels, sports equipment, and posters of 21st century girls. While some of the boys' toys may change over time, testosterone is still testosterone in any century.

Apart from some stale candy, there didn't appear to be anything of use to Becks until she crawled onto a pair of upside-down football cleats hidden under a dirty t-shirt.

"Son of bitch!" she shouted as she rubbed her bruised knee.

It wasn't quite the apple falling on Newton's head, but the cleats on Becks' knee made her realize that all of these football and hockey helmets and pads could offer protection if she got in a close quarters fight with zombies, and baseball bats and hockey sticks could make great weapons— with a little modification. She remembered visiting the survivor outpost at the Ace Hardware store in Ellenville, NY the previous year—Fort Ace, they called it—and marveling at all the cool and highly effective weaponry they had made from tools, gardening equipment, and simple household items.

"Every home contains an arsenal, if you just get a little creative," one of the Fort Ace men had told her.

If Becks wanted to conserve ammunition and not attract attention from the undead, or any living scavengers who might be in the area, she would have to come up with some silent and deadly zombie killing weapons.

But that could come later. First, she had to heal enough to fight, and that meant sleeping, eating, and antibiotics. It also meant keeping warm as the temperatures at night were already dipping below freezing and there came a point where it didn't matter how many layers of clothing and blankets she had, she needed a source of warmth.

Until she could secure another house that had a fireplace, or preferably a woodstove, she would have to use the kerosene heater. As carbon monoxide from that heater had more than likely been the cause of death of the entire Serviss family, Becks was less than pleased that it was her only choice, but at least it was better than no choice.

Her excellent memory—which was a mixed blessing at times— brought to mind that carbon monoxide was absorbed by hemoglobin 210 times faster than oxygen. Unless a room was adequately vented to remove carbon monoxide from the air, death would come quickly and quietly as the body was slowly deprived of oxygen. Not a bad way to go when death by zombies was awaiting you at your doorstep, but Becks had too much fight left in her to cash in her chips now. And she *never, ever,* again wanted to experience the horror of something trying to eat her alive.

Every time she slept, she woke up at least once from a screaming nightmare—a nightmare that had been all too real and almost fatal. And not a single hour of the day passed without her thinking of the inexpressible terror of feeling the teeth of the undead tearing into her flesh in a frenzy of mindless hunger. She tried to put it out of her mind, but the infected bite wounds were a constant reminder. If she survived this ordeal, the scars would continue to haunt her every day for the rest of her life.

Two long weeks passed with Becks rarely getting out of bed. She had managed to get the kerosene heater—and two heavy containers of kerosene—upstairs and into the parents' bedroom. Using the kids' mattresses as extra insulation against the drafty windows, she made a rather warm "nest" in which to recuperate.

To vent the carbon monoxide, she used Dylan's hockey stick with a Ginsu knife duct-taped to it to cut some holes in the ceiling above the heater, which she kept in the doorway. She safety tested the arrangement for several hours before trying it while sleeping and found that all the fumes rose harmlessly into the even draftier attic where they were blown to the outside through vents on either end of the house. Probably a substantial amount of heat was being lost, as well, but *better that than waking up dead,* she told herself in an attempt at some zombie humor.

To pass the time, Becks piled a stack of the boys' comic books and graphic novels on the bed and snuggled under the covers to read by candlelight. She never had any interest in comic books as a kid—and quite honestly thought they were only for people with very poor reading skills—but she found herself getting into the fantasy world of superheroes and alternate realities. Given the seriousness of her current situation—wounded and alone in the zombie-infested suburbs of New Jersey—it was just what she needed to escape reality for a few hours a day.

The rest and antibiotics really helped. All but two of the wounds had closed up and were no longer infected. The others were still of some concern, but as soon as she could explore other houses she hoped to find more meds to mop up at last of the bacteria. Her head still hurt like a son of a bitch, but at least she was able to stand and walk slowly without waves of dizziness and nausea. And now that she felt able to function in at least a limited capacity, she could do two important things—make plans and make weapons.

Becks really liked her ceiling ventilating tool of the Ginsu taped to the hockey stick. Taking a few practice swings at the fake leather couch and a coat rack, she realized this could make a decent weapon for ventilating zombie skulls, as well, or at least for thrusting a blade through an eye socket or ear canal and into the brain to sever the ZIP nexus controlling the body. And there was not one, but two large sets of knives with which she could create her hockey stick and broom handle spears. Either Mr. or Mrs. Serviss got sucked into some late night infomercials, or they had received the knife sets as gifts from friends or relatives who had gotten sucked into some late night infomercials. In any event, God bless American consumerism where no one is truly happy until they have at least two of everything they don't need!

Using a small department store telescope that one of the boys had trained on a neighbor's bedroom window—could it possibly have been a woman's bedroom!?—Becks began checking out the surrounding houses. She used crayons and 11x17 sheets of printer paper to draw a layout of the neighborhood.

Red rectangles denoted houses with broken windows or busted-in doors that had most likely been stripped of supplies, or had become winter nests for small packs of zombies. Blue squares were houses that still looked intact, but didn't appear to have chimneys for fireplaces or woodstoves. They would be worth exploring for food and weapons, though. The most promising prospects were the two green squares that were both intact and had chimneys.

One of those green square houses was only three doors down across the street. Becks could just see the corner of a wood pile in the backyard. There was also an RV parked back there, which meant there was most likely a generator and a camp stove—unless someone else had already taken them. What Becks wouldn't do for a hot meal and some hot water to bathe in! When she worked as a nurse at Nyack Hospital and at ParGenTech in the biohazard labs, she usually showered at least twice a day. It had now been weeks without washing and she was beginning to gross herself out.

Between her pistols and the spears (for which she had used a wicker umbrella stand and backpack straps to make a quiver), she was good to go

38

on offense. But Becks also knew she had to do something about defense, as she had to make damn sure she didn't get bitten again. The blood-soaked Eradazole had apparently been sufficient to eliminate the ZIPs eggs from the bites, as she wasn't feeling those symptoms that she knew all too well. But there wasn't any more Eradazole, and she no longer had a safety net between her and full-blown zombie infection.

For protection, she used some of the boys' shin guards, elbow pads, and paintball gloves. She also created some primitive armor by duct-taping rows of silverware across Mr. Serviss' leather jacket and down the length of some thick denim jeans. She would challenge any zombie to bite through a cluster of soup spoons and salad forks! Dylan's hockey helmet fit just right, and would help protect her skull from further injury. And what zombie apocalypse survival outfit was complete without a surgical mask, which every household bought by the dozens in the early days of infection.

Of course, the best scenario would be to stealthily cross the street and get to the "green" house (which was actually covered in fake brick face) undetected by the dozen or so zombies that were shambling about. Unfortunately, even if she was perfectly healthy and able to run at top speed, stealth was not one of her strong points, but she would give it a try. Between the overgrown shrubbery on the lawns and the cars in the street, she would not have to be completely exposed for more than about 20 feet at a time. Before leaving the house, she went over her planned route in her head at least five times.

Taking a deep breath and rechecking her pistols for the tenth time, she opened the back door and took her first step outside in weeks. She chose to leave the house that way for two reasons—the backyard provided the best route through the neighbor's shrubs, and she wouldn't have to look at the shattered Humvees and stained bits of cloth and bone fragments that used to be Sergeant Colaneri and the four other soldiers.

Although able to walk fairly well, Becks was still very weak and out of shape, and she soon discovered that crouching down and then standing again made her head pound. However, she felt she could fight through the pain, and just prayed that the vertigo didn't return.

Her progress was much slower than she had planned, as a few of the filthiest scummers Becks ever saw, clad in torn and soiled matching ski jackets (had this been a family?) suddenly took an interest in the front lawn where she was hiding behind a holly bush. Although the leaves were fairly thick, she didn't dare move an inch for fear of attracting attention. After a few minutes of trying to remain in a squatting position, she started to get wobbly and ever so slowly had to shift to her hands and knees.

The ground was cold and squishy from a recent light snowfall that had quickly melted. She tried to adjust her position to put her knees on some leaves to prevent getting her pant legs too wet, but the rustling sound was just enough to attract the shortest of the ski-jacketed scummers, who began shuffling her way.

If she fired one of her pistols, she would have at least twelve hungry assailants converging on her, with no doubt hundreds more in the neighborhood being alerted to her position. As quietly as possible, she pulled the Bauer hockey stick from the wicker umbrella stand quiver on her back. On the straight end, she had secured a 10-inch slicing knife for close quarters and for accuracy. On the curved end, was a heftier 12-inch chef's knife for long, arcing swings that wouldn't be very accurate, but should pack quite a penetrating punch.

When the lone zombie got within ten feet, Becks determined it was an adolescent, but due to filth and rot, she couldn't tell if it was a boy or a girl. The kid's left eye was swollen and bloody, and it was probably blind in that eye, which was why it still hadn't detected Becks when it was only a few feet away. Becks looked upon that eye as a big, red bull's eye target, and spun her hockey stick around so the 10-inch slicing knife was raised and ready.

"Hey, Shithead," Becks whispered softly.

The zombie stopped shambling and turned slowly toward the sound, leaning down and baring its brown and yellow teeth in anticipation of a meal. With one short thrust of the hockey stick, the razor-sharp blade easily sunk five or six inches through the damaged eye, which burst like a rotten grape. Becks would have sworn that the knife only stopped because the tip had reached the back of the skull. Twisting the stick back and forth a couple of times just to make sure the ZIP nexus was sufficiently disrupted, she backed away a few feet, pulled out the knife, and watched as the twitching adolescent of undetermined gender fell face first in the cold muck of the unkempt suburban front lawn.

Becks watched in fascination as the stream of deep, crimson blood poured out, accompanied by some sickly greenish strands of zombie parasites. As if conducting an experiment, the scientist in her took over and she actually checked her watch to time how long the blood gushed in spurts before the heart stopped beating. She even took a stick and poked around in the puddle of blood to examine the size, color, and relative health of the pieces of the parasitic network that had killed this child—and the rest of its family—and turned them all into mindless, savage predators.

The snap of a stick beneath the feet of the two other ski-jacketed zombies jolted Becks back to reality. She drew in closer to the holly bush and held her breath while she assessed the scene. Apparently, the other two zombies hadn't noticed the death of their former family member, but they were still too close for Becks to make a run for the next clump of shrubbery. Grabbing the nearest rock, she threw it as far as she could in the other direction, and was fortunate enough to hit an overturned metal garbage can. The can resounded from the hit, and then noisily rocked back and forth a few times, drawing the attention of not just the ski-jacketed zombies, but all the others on the street.

It took a few minutes for them all to stagger over to the garbage can. The cold weather, lack of food, and visible decay, were clearly having an effect on the zombies' speed and maneuverability, which was very good news, but then Becks was not up to speed, either. Waiting for the coast to be relatively clear, she got to her feet, but remained low, as she hurried to the long row of shrubs which ran the length of the front yard.

From this point, she would have to cross the street and just hope she wasn't noticed. In a sprint that made her lightheaded, she made it to the other side of the street and then hunkered down behind an SUV with all of its doors open. The interior was splattered with dark brown blood stains. Whoever had tried to flee in this vehicle obviously hadn't gotten very far.

Crawling along the curb, Becks stayed as low and as quiet as possible as she made her way inch by inch to the edge of the driveway of the house she hoped would be a safe haven. A row of thick hedges ran the length of the driveway to the garage, which was set back behind the house. After a careful scan of her surroundings, she felt confident enough to stand and walk the forty feet or so to the RV parked in front of the garage.

It was a Winnebago Class C, and apart from a year's worth of dirt, it looked pretty nice—and expensive. Becks and Cam had often talked about getting an RV and going cross country and up into Canada for a few months, but there was the small matter of time and money, i.e., a lack of both. Before life went to hell with the onset of widespread infection, Becks had still hoped to one day make enough money to pay off her mountain of medical school loans and get a decent secondhand RV to fulfill some of that dream a couple of vacation weeks at a time. Now, she had all the time in the world, and her pick of RVs, but unfortunately, the landscape had changed and the scenery wouldn't quite be the same.

Becks wished she could get this Winnebago up and running and find her way back to 287, but so many trees and telephone poles had come down in the storm that she would be lucky to be able to drive a couple of blocks without a major obstruction. If she was to get out of this mess, she was either going to have to be airlifted, or walk out. And as the weeks had passed, the cold, hard reality had set in that rescue teams were probably not coming. She knew she would have to go on foot, but not before she was one hundred percent healthy, and she had enough guns and ammo to shoot her way through the hordes of zombies that stood in the miles between her and the highway.

The RV was unlocked, and with her trusty Smith & Wesson in her left hand, she slowly pulled open the door with her right. It was always a good thing when nothing rushed out at you, but she was still very cautious as she entered. The first thing she noticed—other than a fortunate lack of zombies, humans, or corpses—was that the RV was filled with luggage and boxes of supplies. The owners were clearly ready to bug out, but never made it. Why? Becks would have to explore the house to look for answers, but there was a more pressing issue at the moment!

"MREs!" she practically shouted, before clamping a hand over her mouth.

Freezing in place, she waited breathlessly to hear if her outburst had attracted attention, and then carefully pulled back a shade to see if anything was moving her way. When the coast looked clear, she grabbed one of the cases of MREs, climbed onto the queen-sized bed at the back of the RV, and prepared to have her first hot meal in ages.

Becks was well versed in the practice of heating and eating one of the military "Meals, Ready to Eat," although she had told Cam on some of their camping trips that she would swear MRE actually stood for "Meals, Rarely Edible." Some of his military buddies also referred to them as "Meals Rejected by Everyone," "Meals Rejected by the Enemy," and a host of even less flattering monikers. But at this moment in time—

starving, scared, hurt, and alone—the beef ravioli MRE currently hissing and heating up in its pouch would be like a Christmas feast to her.

The first part of the MRE to be consumed was the chocolate chip brownie, which actually elicited several moans of delight. Then she sucked down the packet of cheese spread in one continuous squeezing action. The packet of applesauce and crackers didn't last long, either. Finally came the *hot* ravioli. Hot food! Even greater than the calories and nutrition, was the morale boost a hot meal gave her. Now, if she could only have a hot shower!

After scarfing down two more MREs—some chicken and noodle dish and some beef stew—she was ready to tackle the house. Even if the house was stripped of supplies, she could live for weeks on the food and water in the RV. She could also see if she could get the generator going for a shower splurge, although the noise would most likely attract way too much attention.

The yard was clear as Becks crept up to the back door of the house. Using the palm of her glove, she wiped away some of the grime from the storm door window, but could only see down a short hallway. There was a duffle bag and another piece of luggage in the hall, but no signs of life—or the undead. The latch on the storm door made far more noise than she had hoped, and the hinges and spring squealed loudly in protest, but at least it was unlocked. The wood and glass interior door was standing open, which seemed strange. It was like the owners were on their way out when something derailed their plans.

Before stepping inside, Becks grabbed her bladed hockey stick. It wasn't the proverbial 10-foot pole, but if any zombies were lurking in the house, she wanted to make sure she could keep them at a distance and dispatch them quietly. Becks had forgotten the adrenaline rush of entering a building in search of supplies, and never knowing what was around the corner. As terrified as she was, she had to admit she was also experiencing a twisted thrill.

Holding her breath, she went the few yards down the hallway, which went left toward a dining room, and right toward a kitchen. Choosing the kitchen first, on the closest countertop she found the keys to the RV, two cell phones, and a stack of cash—all of which were valuable BZA, but were now worthless. The other countertops had a variety of food stacked on them—mostly fruits and vegetables that had shriveled and blackened, but there were a few boxes of pasta and cereal, and some canned food which were all worth their weight in gold.

Becks then went into the next room, which was a den with a woodstove with a huge stack of logs and kindling! A pile of diamonds wouldn't have made a more welcomed sight. As tempted as she was to start a fire right that instant, she knew that nothing drew scavengers like the sight of smoke curling up into the air. Although she hadn't seen or heard any signs of other humans in the area during the past few weeks, she wouldn't take the chance. Darkness would fall soon enough and she could stoke the stove until it felt like a July heat wave—and maybe warm up some water for a bath, too.

But her wonderful plans would have to be put on hold, because the house wasn't as empty as she thought.

Chapter 3

A creaking floorboard sent a wave of panic through Becks as she backed against the woodstove and raised her makeshift spear in front of her. Tense seconds ticked by without another sound, and she hoped against hope that it was just a noisy old structure—until she heard that distinctive shuffling from the other end of the house, as well as upstairs.

The best course of action would be to retreat to the back door, prop it open, and hopefully lead the zombies outside. As she wasn't in top fighting shape, she could actually just let them go on their merry way, if possible. If not, she would have a better chance out in the open to kill them with her spear. Unfortunately, the best laid plans usually go to shit where zombies are concerned.

As she stepped back into the kitchen, two figures emerged from the shadows of the dining room and blocked the hallway to the back door. It was a woman around forty, as best as Becks could tell with all the facial decay, and a small male child, maybe four or five years old—both most likely zombies for a year, and both *very* hungry.

Becks lunged forward and thrust her spear toward the woman's eye socket, but the tip of the blade hit her cheek bone and slid back across the side of her face and ear. The sharp knife left a nasty gash, and split her ear in two, but it was not a fatal wound, and Becks needed some instant fatalities.

Her next thrust found its mark and the blade plunged deep into the woman's skull. She quivered for a few moments like a fish on the end of a hook, and then slid off the knife and fell in a heap. Out of the corner of her eye, Becks could see more figures coming down the staircase and entering the den; at least three adults. Two more older children were coming toward the kitchen from the dining room.

By this time, the first child had reached Becks and was trying to bite her left leg, but thanks to his small teeth and a row of teaspoons and a couple of butter knives duct-taped to her thigh, the child was having no success. Becks tried not to think about this once happy little kindergartner as she withdrew her hunting knife and buried it deep into one of his blue eyes until it gushed deep crimson.

Turning to assess the adult zombies in the den, she saw that there were actually five—three older adults, two males and a female, and two large, male teens. There were too many. She would either have to start shooting, or get the hell out of there. A couple of quick knife thrusts to the midsections of the other two children were enough to send them reeling backwards and allow Becks to step over the dead woman and into the back hall. As fast as she could, she opened the back door and slid the holder to keep it open. Then rushing back, she grabbed the wrists of the woman she had just killed and used all her strength to drag her out the back door, down a walkway, and half way up the driveway.

The stress and exertion made Becks head pound and a wave of vertigo swept over her for a second—threatening to bring up the three MREs she now regretted scarfing down—but she managed to stay on her feet and run back to the RV. Just as she got inside and locked the door, the adult and teen zombies started filing out of the house. They squinted at the sunlight and stumbled around for a few minutes on the patio, knocking into lawn furniture and each other, but then one of the teens started following the fresh blood trail. As he shuffled on, he made a beeline for the body in the driveway, and the others soon followed.

Becks tried not to look as the five zombies started feasting on the fresh kill—relatively speaking. In the early days of the infection, a zombie wouldn't touch another zombie until it had been dead for days and the parasites' pheromones had dissipated. Now, starvation drove them to eat one of their fellow undead the second it stopped breathing. Now, if only they would start *killing* each other!

Becks kept her eyes on the back door, waiting to see if anyone else came out. She was stunned to see one of the older children she had stabbed come crawling out about ten minutes later, slipping twice on its own blood and some internal organs that were sliding out of the huge gash in its abdomen. It made it as far as the driveway, where it keeled over and would become dessert for the adult zombies once their main course was complete.

When another ten minutes passed with no one else exiting the house, Becks dumped the clothes out of one of the pieces of luggage and stuffed it full of MREs and bottles of water. A quick scan of the contents of the other luggage uncovered some medical supplies and an enormous zip lock bag full of pill bottles—hopefully, some of which contained antibiotics. But she could go through those later. First she had to make her way back into the house before the zombies lost interest in their meal, or they realized there was fresher meat to be had.

Using the RV as a screen, Becks worked her way to the back end, and then darted ten feet to her left behind a bush, which got her past the corner of the house and the line of sight to the zombies. From there, she went straight to the back door, where she put her things inside, and then closed and locked both doors. Hockey stick spear at the ready, she made a room-by-room search, upstairs and down, and the basement, and found nothing but the dead younger child, and the one that clearly was about to expire with a few more labored, rasping breaths.

BZA, she would have been completely heartbroken by such a scene when she worked in Nyack Hospital, but now she was simply impatient for the child zombie to quit stalling and just die. There was already enough zombie food in the driveway, and Becks didn't want to draw a bigger crowd, so she wrapped the two little bodies in a shower curtain and put them in a large plastic bin in the basement.

"I feel like a goddamned serial killer," she said out loud in disgust, as she snapped the lid shut.

Her next chore was to get a big bottle of bleach from the laundry room and pour it on the puddles of blood to kill the ZIPs. She would mop it all up another time. And she would explore all the supplies this house had to offer—including a dining room table covered in guns—at another time, as well, because at this point she was so exhausted and in such pain that she had to rest. Curling up on a comfortable couch in the den, she slept deeply for several hours.

It was dark when Becks awoke, and although still very tired and sore, she found the energy to start a fire in the woodstove, and it felt glorious. Throwing the couch cushions in front of the hot stove and wrapping herself in some blankets, Becks drifted peacefully off to sleep, despite the sound of zombies in the driveway fighting over the last scraps of the woman and child.

By dawn, the zombies had wandered off, carrying away most of the bones so they could keep gnawing at them for days, hoping to eventually get through to the marrow. All that remained of the woman and child were some pools of congealed blood, clumps of hair, and scraps of clothing.

Becks began her morning with a vegetable lasagna MRE, but only one this time, as she had to think long term. Still, as this group of nine people had planned enough in advance to have emergency rations for all of them for at least a week, she could eat well for months, if necessary. Too bad they hadn't also planned on all being infected and turning zombie before they could get out of Dodge.

All of the previous day's activities had been physically too much for Becks, and she knew she would have to stay inside and take it easy for a few days. She began to inventory the food, beverages, weapons, clothing, and most importantly, all of the medications. Two big bottles of antibiotics were a sight for sore eyes, and her sore, lingering, infected bite wounds, as well. This would be more than enough to kill the last of the bacteria, with plenty more in case of other injuries.

There were also full prescription bottles for everything from allergies to anxiety, and attention deficit disorder to a king-sized box of sildenafil—the "little blue pill," because *God forbid you might have trouble getting an erection during a zombie apocalypse,* Becks thought, shaking her head. Unfortunately, the one thing that was missing was Eradazole; the one thing that could have prevented this group from getting infected, and the one thing that could save Becks' life if she got bitten again.

Curious to know more about the members of the group that were so well organized and prepared to hit the road to seek a safer place, Becks looked at all the holiday and vacation photos on the walls and refrigerator. It was apparent that the family that lived here had consisted of the woman

47

Becks killed, her husband (who was one of the adult zombies who ate her) and two of the children. The others appeared to have been from the husband's two brothers' families, although there were two women and several other children who were not in the house. Concerned that she had missed some zombies somewhere, Becks grabbed her pistol and spear to make another search.

She found her answer in a walk-in closet upstairs. Although on her initial search, Becks had used her spear to poke the racks of clothes in the closet to make sure no one was hiding in there, she didn't look down closely enough. She thought there were just piles of clothing and shoes scattered across the floor, but in the beam of a flashlight she saw the mixed skeletal remains of women and children—the missing family members.

Becks could only imagine the terror these people experienced, thinking they were moments away from all getting in the RV and taking off, and then witnessing their husbands, fathers, and children switching right before their eyes. The women must have grabbed the children and tried to hide in the closet, but their zombified relatives caught, killed, and devoured them. It was a chilling thought, and Becks suddenly decided she didn't need any of the clothing from this closet.

Needing to feel a little reassurance, Becks next took a look at the weapons piled on the dining room table. There were two .22 cal pistols and a .22 rifle, which didn't have the stopping power she preferred, but there were 200 rounds of ammo. Considering she only had a few dozen rounds left for her pistols, this was a treasure trove. There was also a 9mm pistol with a box of 50 rounds, which also put a smile on Becks' face. Then there were the two 30-06 hunting rifles which would pack a nice punch, but there were only two boxes of twenty rounds each available for them. All in all, it was a huge upgrade to her arsenal and Becks felt a little less vulnerable.

When night fell, she started another fire in the woodstove and heated a bucket of water—with some rose-scented bubble bath in it. Of course, there weren't any bubbles, but just the sweet aroma of roses was enough to transport her as she indulged in a long, long sponge bath, slowly going back and forth over every inch of her body. It was an almost erotic experience; except for when she ran the sponge over the ugly bite wound scars. She even washed her hair, or least what was left of her hair after shaving half her head so she could stitch up the gash she had received in the accident.

After a few days of eating well and sleeping by a warm fire, Becks was starting to feel like herself again. While she was safe in this house and had plenty of food and water, she obviously wasn't going to live here for the rest of her life—at least she hoped that was the case! She needed to start making her way westward to get back to Interstate 287, and wait for one of the daily army patrols. But not knowing just where she was and how far she was from the highway, she would just have to keep going west as directly, and safely, as possible. She had searched both houses and the RV for maps, but BZA everyone had relied on GPS units and digital directions, so no one seemed to bother with ancient paper maps anymore.

Her plan was to begin by establishing safe houses every few blocks. This way she could search for more supplies, check the lay of the land, determine where the concentration of zombies was the heaviest, and never be more than a few minutes' dash from a place of safety.

A three-inch snowfall delayed her first reconnoitering mission for a couple of days as she waited for it to melt. Then she donned her silverware armor over the hockey and football pads, strapped a 9mm on each hip, and her .44 in a shoulder holster, slung one of the hunting rifles over the other shoulder, grabbed her hockey spear, and put on the helmet and a fresh surgical mask. Even under these dire conditions, a look in the mirror made her laugh.

In a knapsack, she carried water, MREs, matches, a medkit, bleach (for any stray drops of zombie blood that might get on her skin), and antibiotics, just in case she couldn't get back to the house for a while. Her plan was to go west two or three blocks and try to find another house to break into. But Becks should have remembered what happened to plans during a zombie apocalypse.

Fortunately, the recent snowfall and cold temperatures had driven many of the zombies into sheds and basements to huddle together in packs for warmth, and made the rest rather sluggish. There were just a handful standing in the street, and they looked to be in a twilight state—the unique form of standing hibernation she had witnessed the previous winter. Of course, those that remained in the twilight state outside for too long froze to death, which was just fine with Becks. But rather than wait for that to

49

happen, she used her hockey spear to quietly dispatch the oblivious zombies in her path.

She quickly made it about six houses down Sparrow Lane to the south to the intersection of a larger east-west running road, crisscrossed with just enough downed trees to make it impassable by car—or RV. Small clusters of zombies stood shoulder-to-shoulder here and there, but just a few blocks up, the road curved to left so she couldn't see any farther. If she could make it to the start of that curve and clear a house, it would make good strategic sense. She would once again stick to the bushes and cars for cover and avoid confrontation if possible—let sleeping zombies lie. Little did Becks know a hornets' nest of zombies was about to be whipped into a frenzy.

Making good progress, she had quickly traveled the length of a long block without attracting any attention when she heard screaming. It was a woman, and she was screaming bloody murder at the top of her lungs, which immediately snapped all the neighborhood zombies out of their twilight state. Back in the direction she had come, and another full block further down, Becks spotted the woman desperately trying to fend off four zombies who were after her and the large baby stroller she was pushing! Rather than run, the woman was clearly ready to give her life for whatever was in that stroller, so Becks assumed it was something far more precious than canned corn.

"Shit, shit, shit!" Becks yelled as she abandoned her stealth mode and ran full tilt back toward the woman.

Zombies were starting to pour out of those basements and sheds and the streets were filling up fast. Becks used the blade on the curved end of her hockey spear and swung it like a baseball bat to take out a fat female zombie who must have eaten her entire family, and a distinguished, elderly, male zombie who had managed to keep his ascot neatly tucked into his smoking jacket even months after death. But there were too many zombies and too little time to stop and swing the deadly-bladed hockey stick. The woman and occupants of the stroller were running out of time as they were now surrounded by six very hungry predators, although two of them suddenly dropped after the woman thrust something at them. But the other four were just reaching out to grab her.

Despite the imminent danger Becks was in, she swung the hunting rifle over her shoulder and into position, and dropped to one knee. She hadn't practiced shooting in quite a while, but with the scope on this gun a novice couldn't miss. Four quick shots, four quick kills, giving the woman a little breathing room. Becks shouted for the woman to run towards her. Stunned by the sudden shots, it took the woman a moment to get her bearings, but then she grabbed the stroller and started running like a crazy person, zigzagging through the growing crowd of zombies.

Becks shouldered her rifle and drew both 9mm pistols. The woman would not make it far without help, so Becks ran towards her, picking off the zombies closest to the woman, and herself. The large, covered stroller was definitely slowing down the woman, but when Becks shouted at her to leave it, she screamed back, "My babies! I can't leave my babies!"

That's what I was afraid of, Becks thought, as she rushed forward to the side of the stroller and put a few rounds in the nearest group of mindless cannibals, but there were dozens, if not hundreds, more that would quickly take their place.

"This way, hurry! Hurry, god damn it!" Becks shouted, pushing the woman in the back to go faster.

Both 9mm pistols were empty by the time they reached Sparrow Lane. Pulling out her .44, Becks knew she would have to make each of those six rounds count. Fortunately, there was only one small group—the five former occupants of the house in which she was living. Unfortunately, they were more energized after their recent big meal of former relatives, and they were standing in the driveway of her safe house.

"Never let a zombie live another day, or they will come back and bite you!" Cam always used to warn her.

If she had the strength the day she cleared the house, she would have killed them all, but she couldn't change the situation. She would just have to deal with what was before her now.

As they ran up the street toward her safe house, which would take five of her six rounds to clear, Becks suddenly switched gears in her head. Realizing that she didn't know if this woman or her children were infected, she kept running past the house she had been living in the last week and headed for Dylan's house.

Wild with panic, just as they reached the front lawn the woman rammed the stroller into the curb, tipping it over. The zippered cover kept the little passengers from falling out, but there were strange and pitiful yelps of pain inside. Becks would deal with the injured babies, *after* they

51

got off the street. Picking the stroller up by its sides, she carried it to the back of the house, all the while yelling at the woman to hurry. Once inside, Becks put down the stroller and then made a scan of the entire house to make sure nothing had wandered in since she left.

The woman collapsed on the floor, clutching the front of the stroller in full-blown hysteria. Becks was very tempted to smack her back to her senses, but she was afraid she wouldn't be able to stop hitting her. Plus, the woman looked to be in her sixties and rather fragile.

So just what kind of an idiot takes their children for a stroll down zombie-infested streets, without any weapons, Becks thought. But she quickly corrected herself when she saw that the woman had used a knitting needle to kill two of the zombies, but that was pretty close to being defenseless.

"Lady, I'm a doctor. Move away so I can see if your children are okay," Becks said, slipping into the practiced calm demeanor she had cultivated from years of working in the emergency room of the hospital.

"My babies! My poor babies!" she shrieked, clutching the stroller even harder.

Becks tried to use soothing words and a reassuring touch, but when the hysteria continued—threatening to bring the entire neighborhood of zombies to their doorstep—she had no alternative but to slap the woman as hard as she could. The woman went tumbling to the floor, clutching her face in pain, but at least she shut up.

"Now, what is your name?" Becks asked, returning to the calm, controlled veneer.

"An—Angie," she replied, shaking like a leaf.

"Okay, Angie, we are safe now. Okay?" Becks said, starting to slowly unzip the stroller cover. "And what are their names?"

"My babies! Yes, my babies," the woman said, looking more relaxed and actually smiling. "Buttons and Smidgey."

"Buttons and *who*?" Becks asked in anger and disbelief, suddenly putting the pieces of the puzzle together—the woman was much too old to have young children, she did appear to be a bit insane, and the cries of pain from the stroller had not sounded human. "You have *got* to be fucking kidding me!"

As Becks finished unzipping the cover, she folded it back to reveal two trembling Shih Tzu dogs with pink ribbons in their hair. At the sight of her "babies" the woman pushed Becks aside and grabbed a dog in each arm, showering them with kisses, and getting licked all over the face in return.

For a rare moment in her life, Becks was utterly speechless. Sitting on the floor with her arms raised with a *what the fuck* expression, she thought she was going to blow a gasket in rage. Finally, she found her voice.

"Do you mean to fucking tell me, that I fucking risked *my* life and wasted *my* precious ammunition to save *you*, and *them*?" she shouted, seething with anger.

"But Buttons and Smidgey are my babies," the crazy old woman whispered, bursting into tears again, and then said between choked sobs, "They…are the only…children…I have left."

The black rage fled Becks' heart as swiftly as if a powerful laser had evaporated it. Who was she to judge this woman? Who could tell what horrors she had endured, how many family members she had lost, and what she had to do to survive in these conditions? So what if she had gone a little crazy—hadn't everyone to some degree and at some point since this all began? And if this poor woman found some tiny bit of solace and happiness with these dogs, then she was one of the lucky ones in this world filled with misery and despair.

"I'm sorry, Angie. I'm very sorry," Becks said in a genuinely contrite and soothing tone. "Of course they are part of your family. I completely understand."

After the dogs licked away her tears, Angie spoke in a steadier voice.

"I'm sorry you had to risk your life for an old fool like me," she said, actually sounding normal for the first time.

"That's okay, I'm glad I could help. But would you mind telling me what you were doing out there with only a knitting needle?"

"Well, Mr. Reggie said that my babies couldn't eat any more of our food supplies, so I thought I would just go to the store and get some proper dog food," Angie replied, jumping right back on the crazy train. But that's not what bothered Becks.

"Mr. Reggie? Is he your husband?" she asked, as she felt her anxiety level rise a few notches.

"Husband? Oh my heavens no," Angie said, giggling like an embarrassed school girl. "Mr. Reggie is our leader. He keeps all the bad people away and keeps us safe."

Over the course of about an hour, Becks coaxed as much information as she could out of Angie—who actually turned out to be 72 years old. The woman was guileless—as well as partially mindless—and told the long story of how Mr. Reggie's group—The Rovers, as they called themselves—had found her when they were scavenging for supplies. She was alone in her home—her family all dead—and they had brought her into their group, which occupied some of the larger homes closer to town. There were about 150 of them, and everyone earned their keep by doing chores. Angie was particularly proud of the fact the she had the *honor* to wash Mr. Reggie's clothes, and those of his inner circle.

When Becks asked what kind of man he was, Angie innocently replied, "Oh very fair. Very fair indeed! He only beats me when I deserve it. Yes, a very fair man."

As the rest of the story unfolded, it became apparent that the Rovers were the worst kind of scavengers. If they found you, they "rescued" you, took all your supplies and let you live if you basically became part of their slave labor force. Angie had never actually witnessed anyone being killed, but quite a few people "had gone missing" over the past year.

Becks' anger and fear continued to grow as Angie related stories of the younger women who had the *honor* to serve Mr. Reggie and his inner circle. Some of the less cooperative ones "had gone missing" from time to time, but Angie was sure those ungrateful women had simply run off. The children worked just as hard as everyone else, and discipline was swift if they didn't do as they were told.

Mr. Reggie and the Rovers Concentration Camp, Becks thought, as she realized she would have to accelerate her plans to reach the highway. She just considered herself fortunate that they hadn't "rescued" her yet.

"Well, you're out of that hell hole now, and you're free to stay here, with your babies, of course. There's not a lot of food, but enough for a while, and I can always find more," Becks said, deciding it would be wise for now to not mention the other house and all of its food and supplies.

"Oh, no! I must go back! What would Mr. Reggie do without me?" Angie replied, stunned at the mere thought of abandoning her great leader.

"I don't know, wash his own dirty underwear?" Becks replied with unmasked disgust.

"You don't understand. Mr. Reggie keeps us safe from the bad people," she said, as if speaking to a child.

"I keep myself safe," Becks replied, instinctively reaching for the grip of her Smith &Wesson. "And I can keep you, Buttons, and Smidgey safe, too."

Becks was about to add that if Angie stayed she would never be beaten again, but as she had recently smacked the woman to the floor, she decided to keep silent on that point. There were no guarantees that she wouldn't have to smack her again sometime.

"You're very sweet, dear, but Mr. Reggie needs me," Angie said in a tone that signaled that her scatterbrain was most definitely made up.

However, after Becks gave Angie two MREs—one for her, and one to split between her babies—her firm resolve softened considerably.

"Well, perhaps we could stay for a little while," Angie said, making sure her babies ate every last morsel on their plates, and then dabbed their mouths clean with a napkin. It was remarkable—Angie looked, and smelled, like a bag lady, yet her dogs were spotless and groomed as if they were about to enter the Westminster Dog Show.

It wasn't that Becks wanted Angie to stay—quite the opposite. It would be hard enough to get back to the highway on her own, let alone with a crazy lady and two dogs in a stroller in tow. And she certainly didn't need to have three more mouths to feed. But in good conscience, she just couldn't send this woman back to that monster so he could abuse her some more. Chances were, Mr. Reggie didn't even want her there, and was hoping she would wander off and get killed. Keeping Angie in this house was a short term solution, but until she could think of something else, or the situation changed, that's the way it would have to be for now.

Becks got the exhausted woman settled on the couch, with her babies, and as soon as they all drifted off to sleep, she headed back to the other house. It took some fast maneuvering, but she managed to lure the five adult zombies down the street toward the intersection, and then used the hockey stick spear to dispatch them all. She was getting pretty good at yielding her homemade weapon, although her pistol was still her favorite. But with all of the zombies having been whipped into a frenzy just a couple of hours earlier, she would try to refrain from agitating them any further.

News of Mr. Reggie's Rovers had inflamed Becks' paranoia, and with good reason. Having lived through The Reverend's army taking over Cam's compound, she knew that such people were worse than zombies, and shouldn't even be given the consideration of a headshot. No, a nice bullet to the abdomen was what they deserved, so they had plenty of time to know they were doomed.

With that cheery thought in her head, Becks went about splitting up and hiding all of the food and supplies, putting some in the shed under Christmas decorations and some in the attic in a trunk of baby clothes, among other inconspicuous places. She started down the basement stairs, but decided she didn't want to put any of her food near the plastic coffin which contained the two bodies of the children, who must be pretty ripe by now. But it did give her an idea.

Gathering up all the bones and bloody clumps of hair and clothing from the upstairs closet, she strategically placed them in the RV, yard, and at the front and back door entrances to the house. She also tossed things about, like emptying some of the luggage in the yard and driveway, to make it look like the entire property had been thoroughly searched by scavengers. Just in case the Rovers came calling, the body parts and ransacked condition might convince them that the place was uninhabited and already picked clean.

She also decided to *always* carry *all* of her weapons and ammo wherever she went. The threat level had just skyrocketed, and she just might be caught in a situation where she needed every bullet and every homemade spear.

Despite the activity of the day, Becks took the time and trouble to break into a garage of one of the houses that had a big dog house in the yard. For her effort, she was rewarded with several bags and a case of cans of dog food. She loved dogs, but she would be damned if Buttons and Smidgey kept wolfing down her precious MREs. She knew a lot of people who would have been thrilled to find dog or cat food for themselves, but fortunately, she had not had to stoop to that level, yet.

By late afternoon, the temperature was dropping, driving many of the zombies back to their "nests." If the cold remained the next day, she would try again to go west a few blocks to find a new place. As the Rovers were closer to town—which was to the southeast about a mile away

56

according to Angie—putting as much distance as she could between her and them was also an added benefit to her plan.

Angie was still fast asleep when Becks got back to the house, and continued to sleep though the noise of Becks dragging one of the boys' mattresses into the master bedroom so they could both spend the night near the kerosene heater. She would miss the woodstove, but at least the heater took the bite out of the air.

It wasn't until dark when Angie's babies had to go for "walkies" that she finally woke up. Becks nearly tackled the old woman when she started to open the front door.

"But they like to walk in the street," Angie protested, having absolutely no clue as to why Becks was upset. "They don't like damp grass and dirt."

"There are a lot of bad people out there," Becks said patiently, after counting to three to check her anger. "We have to go very quietly into the back yard so the bad people don't hurt your babies. In fact, you stay inside here, I'll take them out."

Becks wanted to avoid an unnecessary noise, and having to rescue Angie again if she wandered into the street. It was a cold, clear night, and with zero light pollution these days, the stars were stunningly beautiful, like jewels on black velvet. *If there are any astronomers still alive*, Becks thought, *they must think the zombie apocalypse is the best thing that ever happened.*

As Becks was lost in thought staring at the stars, while the dogs gingerly pussyfooted on real dirt, something rustled through a pile of leaves at the back of the property. It could have been anything—a raccoon, a deer, a rat—but when Becks shone her flashlight in the direction of the sound, it just so happened to be a cat.

Instantly, an explosion of high pitched yelping—poor excuses for a bark—erupted out of Buttons and Smidgey. It must have sounded like a pair of furry dinner bells to the local undead population. It took a lot to get nesting zombies out on a cold night, but immediately, everyone within earshot began to emerge into the bitter cold looking for a hot meal of "Shih Tzu on a leash."

Becks snatched up the hysterical canines and ran back into the house. A quick handful of kibble shut them up, but clearly this would be a problem going forward. After some negotiating with Angie, they agreed to turn the basement into the walkies area—as long as Angie promised to dispose of the waste on a regular basis. This was all going to be a lot more complicated than Becks initially imagined, and unless she could find some way to drive them all back to the highway, it appeared as if it would be impossible to quietly and quickly extract Angie and the dogs on foot.

That was the constant moral dilemma everyone faced who tried to do good deeds, post apocalypse. In short, as Cam put it, "You don't save someone for the moment, you save them for life."

Anyone with a conscience couldn't very well rescue someone from the jaws of zombie death and then toss them back into the fray—especially once you got to know the person's name and some things about them. It had led to the downfall and death of many a good person. "No good deed goes unpunished," as a clever playwright had once written.

On the other hand, as wacky as Angie was, it was just so nice for Becks to have someone to talk to again! As much of a loner as Becks was, she had realized that there comes a point where this Robinson Crusoe nonsense makes you a little screwy. And even though she preferred big dogs like German Shepherds, she had to admit that any wagging tails had the power to make her smile.

The next day brought sleet and freezing rain. There were no zombies out on Sparrow Lane, but one step onto the icy back deck—which almost resulted in Becks falling on her ass—convinced her to postpone her expedition. She actually spent a pleasant day chatting with Angie, while Buttons—or was it Smidgey, she couldn't tell—slept curled up in her lap.

She learned that Angie had been an elementary school teacher for 35 years, and her husband was a local politician who also ran several successful businesses. They both lived for their family, and they had three children and four grandchildren. The entire "clan," as she called them, got together every Thanksgiving, Christmas, and for at least a week at their Florida vacation home every year.

As Angie spoke about her family, the trauma of all the horrors she had endured since the infection began disappeared from her features, and she was not only lucid, but articulate—until she began relating the particulars of what had happened to each family member.

It was a story that had played out a million times across the country during those early days. The young children became infected at school, the parents secluded them in their houses to prevent them from being taken to

58

containment facilities, and they inevitably became infected themselves. Everyone had gathered at Angie's house for quarantine, and once the children began switching, no one had the heart to put them down, so they were all locked in the basement, until "they found the cure." No one realized in the beginning that for those who had switched, there was no cure.

When her daughter and youngest son switched, her husband and eldest son were badly bitten while fighting to try to get them into the basement. They died from their wounds over the course of the next week, leaving Angie all alone in her house with two corpses and a basement full of zombies that were once her entire world.

The dogs had belonged to a neighbor, who had never emerged from her house after quarantine, so Angie assumed her family had suffered a similar fate. Somehow, the dogs had managed to get out of the house and literally ended up on Angie's doorstep, whining pitifully and covered in blood—but not their own. The three of them survived for months on food she had stockpiled for "the holidays," until Mr. Reggie and The Rovers broke into her home and "rescued" her. In all fairness, she probably wouldn't have survived on her own much longer, but she had clearly been mistreated since going into their "care and protection."

When it came time for Becks to tell her story, she kept it comparatively brief. Her loving parents had become infected and took their own lives so as not to be a burden to her. The only thing she added was that Becks thought it was the most noble and selfless thing they ever did. They sacrificed themselves to give Becks the best chance to survive.

Before going to bed, Angie unexpectedly gave Becks a big hug.

"You know, it's only been a very short time, but you already feel like a daughter to me," Angie said, weeping gently. "Thank you for everything you've done for us."

That night, Becks cried as softly as she could until she drifted off to sleep.

The next morning was sunny and warmer, and Becks awoke with renewed determination to get them all to safety. In addition to safe houses, she would start looking for cars she might be able to get started. Even if she was only able to drive a few blocks at a time, it would be a way to take

Angie and the dogs with her. It would make her task immeasurably more difficult, but what other choice did she have?

When she sat up in bed, she was surprised to see that Angie wasn't there, but she just assumed they all went for walkies in the basement. She waited a few minutes, but didn't hear anything. A cold, sick chill shot through her as she grabbed a pistol and headed down the stairs two at a time.

They weren't in the basement. Running into the backyard in just her socks, she found that they weren't there, either. Racing to the street, Angie and the stroller were nowhere to be seen.

"*Son of a bitch!*" Becks shouted, as she hurried back into the house, determined to get her gear and go after the wandering, crazy, old woman.

She stopped short in the kitchen, when she spotted a piece of paper on the table near the door.

"Dear Rebecca," the note began, "I want what's best for you, my dear, and living on your own like this is no way for you to live. I've already lost one daughter, and I couldn't bear to see you hurt, especially on my account. You need to be safe, so I've gone to get Mr. Reggie, and the Lord willing, we will be back soon to rescue you."

Becks swore a blue streak as she quickly gathered her weapons and supplies. Slipping on her boots and jacket, she didn't even take the time to lace or zip them closed. There was no telling how long Angie had been gone. And if she had somehow managed to get back to Mr. Reggie, he and The Rovers could already be on their way. There was no time for stealth as she ran full speed down the street to her safe house—and not a moment too soon, as she could already hear the faint rumble of approaching engines.

Chapter 4

Winter had already come to Saugerties, New York, even though it was officially still a few weeks away. A couple of early snowfalls had blanketed the region, and Cam knew it would soon be time to hunker down in the compound for the winter. While he would have welcomed the safety and warmth of West Point, Cam and his decidedly independent-minded men politely declined the offer.

Unlike the previous year, they had a rather somber Thanksgiving dinner, even though conditions in the area had vastly improved. Thanks to the help of the Army, and a host of new anti-zombie weapons and medications to fight ZIPs infections in all but the worst cases, life was actually beginning to show small signs of returning to some level of normalcy—whatever the new norm would turn out to be.

The problem was, regardless of all the things to be thankful for, Becks was now "presumed dead"—a presumption that seemed to be reasonable, considering the accident scene photos the Army had taken from the helicopter. Indeed, reason and common sense told Cam that nothing could have escaped that terrible scene of carnage—the massive explosion, the horde of zombies, the few scraps of hair and bone that remained. But as the weeks passed, in his heart he just couldn't let go of the hope that Becks had somehow survived.

He also couldn't let go of the fear that she *had* survived, and was now hurt and alone in the zombie hell of the New Jersey suburbs.

When news of the accident reached the compound, The Monk, Smokin, and every man and woman who had known and fought with Becks—and even some who had never met her, but had heard the many stories—volunteered to mount a highly dangerous rescue mission into the heavily zombie-infested area where the incident occurred. But when Cam met with Phil at West Point on their way down to New Jersey, they were told that the military would not provide any support. Cam and his people threatened a small uprising, until they saw those accident scene photos. It was one of the hardest decisions Cam ever made, but they reluctantly went back to their compound.

There wasn't any chance the Army would have allowed the group to go through the Suffern gate and into New Jersey, anyway. Cam and his men had proven to be too valuable in the several joint campaigns they had waged to clean out strategic sections of the Hudson Valley, and they would be needed again in the upcoming northern New Jersey campaign in the spring. For the greater good, the Army couldn't allow such excellent fighters to get slaughtered on a pointless rescue attempt to try to save one person, even if that person was Dr. Rebecca Truesdale.

Phil had invited Cam and the others to stay to take part in a memorial service for Becks at the chapel at West Point. To a man, they all refused. It wasn't that they didn't care about Becks—quite the opposite. It was just that they felt that the finality of such proceedings would have forced them to let go of that slender hope that she was still alive.

Instead, The Monk officiated over a "Celebration of Hope" at the compound. It was his own bizarre concoction of spiritual ideas and ceremonies from around the world, that all focused on the theme of never giving up hope, no matter how desperate the situation may appear. The Monk read inspiring quotes from many of history's greatest religious figures and philosophers, but none resonated with Cam and his men more than the quote he read at the conclusion of the service.

"In the immortal words of Yogi Berra," The Monk shouted in his deeply resonating voice, "it ain't over, till it's over."

Chapter 5

By the time Becks was positioned by an attic window in her safe house, the first ATV in a line of five was weaving past fallen tree limbs and up over lawns on Sparrow Lane. Through the scope of the hunting rifle, she could see that the drivers were heavily armed men. And the second ATV also had a female passenger—Angie. In her well-meaning, but completely misguided, attempt to help, she had literally brought the threat to Becks' doorstep.

The ATVs all stopped in front of the Serviss house, and the men dismounted and brought their variety of military-style rifles into firing position. A short, chubby, bald man with very red cheeks and thick glasses said something to Angie, and then gave her a rough shove toward the house. Angie went inside for a few minutes, and during that time, the men shot a few zombies who had been attracted by all the noise. They made short work of them, but more were coming—many more.

The bald man shouted something—it sounded like he was telling Angie to hurry up. He waited another minute or two, and just as he was about to send one of the men inside, Angie came out the front door shaking her head, her hands raised in an "I have no idea" gesture. Apparently, this man had wanted Angie to coax Becks into being "rescued," and was not pleased that she had returned alone. Obviously not convinced that Becks was not in the house, he sent two men inside, while the rest of them began picking off the dozen or more neighborhood undead who were gathering in increasing numbers.

When the men came back outside, they must have confirmed that the house was empty. The little guy grabbed Angie by the shoulders, violently shook her, and then slapped her hard across the face. Becks could feel her finger tightening on the trigger, but she needed to see how this would play out. Maybe they would think it was all one of Angie's delusions and go away.

It looked as though that might happen, until she pointed at the wreckage of the two Humvees and spoke in a very animated way with a lot of hand waving, seemingly reenacting the story Becks had told her about the accident. The massive hole blown in the road and the charred pieces of Humvee provided pretty powerful evidence that Angie was telling the truth about the Army doctor with the weapons, and so many MREs that she could give them to dogs.

As both ends of the street were starting to get thick with zombies, four of the men appeared to get antsy, but the little bully was determined. He thrust a megaphone into Angie's hand and directed her to say something.

"Rebecca, dear, if you can hear me, please come out," Angie said, as her amplified voice attracted even more zombies like a homing beacon. "Mr. Reggie wants me to tell you that our group could really use a doctor and that you will be very well fed and taken care of."

Mr. Reggie! Becks thought, completely taken by surprise. *This is the godlike Mr. Reggie I've heard so much about? Angie is crazier than I thought!*

From Angie's glowing descriptions of the leader of The Rovers, one would have thought that the man was at least six and a half feet tall, had the physique of Adonis, and was as brilliant as Da Vinci. From what Becks could tell, he was just an angry little man with visions of post-apocalyptic grandeur.

He yelled something at Angie with growing rage, and she once again put the megaphone to her lips, but this time with trembling hands.

"Please, dear, you're upsetting Mr. Reggie. He's just trying to help. Please come on out so we can get you to safety."

Obviously, Becks had no intentions of going anywhere with these thugs. After waiting another minute—in which time the men shot at least twenty more zombies who had drawn within 100 feet—Mr. Reggie ripped

63

the megaphone out of the old lady's hand. He then pulled out a pistol and pressed it firmly against her forehead.

"Okay, we don't have time for this and we are done playing hide and seek," he shouted in more of a high-pitched squeal than a voice. "Come out now, or your new friend here will be zombie chow!"

Through the scope, Becks could see the shock and heartbreak in Angie's face. The old woman was devastated, not only because the man she had foolishly revered and trusted didn't give a damn about her, but also because she suddenly realized she had now jeopardized the safety of someone she cared about.

Thoughts raced through Becks' mind as she tried to figure out her next move. She assumed Mr. Reggie wouldn't have any qualms about carrying through on his threat, but even if he didn't shoot her, he would certainly make Angie's life miserable going forward. If she joined the group, maybe she could manage to get along, and help the people who were sick and injured. Maybe she could also convince them to *join her*, and they could all get back to the highway or the Picatinny Arsenal. It was a risk—a big one, but she had negotiating skills and some bargaining chips that just might make this all work out.

Becks prayed that she wasn't making a huge mistake as she eased her finger off the trigger and was about to announce herself by shouting out the window. However, before she could speak, Angie grabbed the pistol that was against her forehead, but not to try to save herself. Instead, she pushed hard on Mr. Reggie's index finger, causing the weapon to discharge a deadly round through the front of her skull and out the back.

Everyone—including Mr. Reggie—was momentarily frozen with shock, but Becks was the first to recover her senses. She knew exactly what Angie had done. Like Becks' parents, Angie had sacrificed herself to try to protect her. Maybe Becks could continue hiding and wouldn't be found by The Rovers, but she knew they didn't survive this long by giving up, especially if she had food, weapons, and knowledge that they needed. And Becks would be damned if she was going to let Angie's brave sacrifice be in vain.

The crosshairs of her hunting rifle settled just above Mr. Reggie's right ear, but pure hatred and anger drove her to reposition her target to his abdomen. She wanted him to have time to think about what was

64

happening. The gut-shot Mr. Reggie grabbed for his stomach with both hands and dropped to his knees, squealing like the proverbial stuck pig.

When the shot rang out, the four men scrambled for defensive positions behind the ATVs and a car. Not knowing where the shot came from, they had no idea which side of the vehicles to hide behind, which left two of them completely exposed to Becks' rapid second and third shots. Although less vindictive with her aiming, the shots would nonetheless prove equally fatal.

The two remaining men now knew Becks' position, and a flurry automatic fire peppered the side of her safe house. Ducking down, she was surprised when she heard more shots, but this time, none of them hit the house. What were they shooting at?

When Becks peered over the edge of the window sill, she saw that dozens of zombies were now within twenty feet of the two men behind the car. Some of the zombies stopped to begin munching on Angie's scattered brains, and the severely wounded, but still very conscious, Mr. Reggie. The ensuing screams were unlike anything Becks had ever heard, and god help her, but she felt no sympathy as the tyrant who had terrorized, abused, and no doubt murdered, many innocent people was being chewed into tiny pieces.

One of the men made a dash for his ATV with guns blazing, but before he could start the engine he was overwhelmed. He was yanked off the ATV to the pavement, and *his* screams bothered Becks for some reason—perhaps because they caused her to recall her own terrifying experience of lying on this road being bitten—and she covered her ears against his death shrieks. She might have taken a shot at his head or neck to try to end his suffering, but she decided to conserve her precious ammunition, so the bloody murder couldn't have bothered her *that* much.

The remaining man—more of a teen, really, was also quickly surrounded, but managed to fight his way out of the thick of the crowd. Injured, but still able to run, he scrambled into one of the backyards across the street with the horde of zombies in close pursuit. While she couldn't see what was happening, Becks heard more screaming, and assumed he had also met his fate beneath the filthy teeth of the undead.

There was nothing more she could do, at least with her rifle, so she went downstairs to start packing food and gear in duffle bags. It wouldn't be long—maybe only hours—before more Rovers would be back, looking for their missing leader and men. With any luck, Angie hadn't known the house number or name of the street, which might buy her a few more hours, possibly a day, if darkness fell quickly enough.

If only she could hop on one of the ATVs and take off right now, but she saw what had happened to the last person who tried that. And now that there were six dead humans and dozens of dead zombies to feast upon, the street would be filled with the undead, packed shoulder to shoulder, fighting for scraps of muscle and lumps of organs.

On the plus side, with so many zombies jamming into Sparrow Lane, she could probably slip quietly through the property of the house behind her safe house, into that street, make her way to the main road and attempt to go west again. First, she would have to retrieve more of the MREs she had hidden in the shed.

Cautiously opening the back door, she didn't see anyone in the yard. Staying low, she crept to the side of the RV, and then used it to block any view from the street as she rushed back to the shed. There was quite a lot of noise from the feeding frenzy on the street, but she still slid open the squeaky metal shed door ever so slowly. Once inside, she removed the lawn Santa and boxes of icicle lights from the tops of the cases of MREs. She obviously couldn't carry all of them with her, so she just chose her favorites; as many as she could stuff into a backpack.

Replacing the Christmas decorations as cover—in case she ever had to come back, god forbid—she hefted the backpack over her shoulder as she exited the shed and headed back toward the house, until the butt of a rifle against the back of her head made the world fade to black.

When Becks woke up on the cold, dirty concrete floor of the basement, she was clad only in her bra and panties, and her left wrist was handcuffed to a pipe. Her head was pounding in pain, and although the blow hadn't been to the area of the skull that had sustained the fracture, this second concussion brought back more vertigo and nausea. But that was the least of her problems.

"So this is the great doctor Angie told us about!" a young male voice said from the shadows of the basement, startling Becks. "You don't look like much of no doctor to me."

"Yeah, I get that a lot," Becks replied, in too much pain to let fear get the better of her, for the moment.

A figure emerged into the patch of fading sunlight filtering through the grimy basement window. He was average height, and had a rather scraggly beard on his otherwise fresh-looking 19-year-old face. He appeared to be well fed and healthy, except for the bloody rags that had been wrapped around his hands and arms. This was the boy who Becks had assumed had been killed behind the neighbor's house, and she was now paying for that hasty assumption.

Although sustaining multiple bite wounds, there didn't appear to be any life-threatening injuries, if they could get to some Eradazole, of course. The boy saw Becks focusing on his makeshift bandages.

"That's right, bitch, you've killed me," he said, pulling off a rag on his right forearm to expose an ugly bite wound. "And you killed Reggie, and all my friends. Wait until I get you back to Reggie's brothers. You'll *wish* you had been killed, too."

"I really *am* a doctor, and if you help me get to the highway, or to the Picatinny Arsenal, we have medicine that can save your life. We can help all of your people," Becks said, trying to project an air of confidence and authority.

"You can't help my friends out there who are being torn apart and eaten by those filthy bastards, *can you?*" the boy shouted, tears filling his eyes from both grief and rage.

"*Your* people killed Angie, how was I supposed to react?" Becks said bluffing, hoping that he hadn't seen that it was Angie who made Reggie pull the trigger. From the boy's reaction, it was clear she had scored points with that comment.

"Angie…she never hurt nobody. Reggie shouldn't have done that to her," he whispered, rubbing the sides of his head trying to figure it all out, while coping with the virtual death sentence he thought he had received with the zombie bites.

Becks saw her opening and told the boy all about West Point, the Arsenal, Eradazole, Trident, the strawberries and ice cream, and all of the things that could possibly persuade him to let her go. He was clearly wavering, and just as she thought she had won her case, an awful moaning sound arose from the street as a new pack of zombies arrived on the scene and started struggling with the ones already eating for whatever bits of flesh remained. It was a chilling and effective reminder that the boy's friends were the ones on the menu.

"No! You're lying! Reggie told us there was nothin' left of the army, and there was no cure. *You're a liar and a murderer!*" he shouted, wild-eyed. "When I bring you back they are going to make you suffer!"

"Please, calm down and listen to—"

Becks words were cut off as the boy rushed forward and grabbed her by the throat.

"*Shut up!* I won't listen to any more of your lies," he screamed into her face. But then his grip loosened and his expression changed to one that really made Becks' blood run cold. "Maybe there's some other ways you can convince me to let you go? Maybe you and me can have some fun?"

As his hands began to wander, there was a sudden banging noise coming from above.

"Shit!" the boy whispered, grabbing his pistol and running for the stairs.

When he dragged Becks into the house, had he locked the back door? As he quietly ascended the stairs to check it out, Becks sprang into action, or at least tried to. Tugging on the handcuffs until her wrist bled, she quickly realized the pipe was not budging. She then sprawled out face first on the floor, trying to grab something, anything, but nothing was within reach. For the first time, panic was beginning to set in with the realization she could not talk her way out of this, and she had no weapons.

"I can't very well kill someone with my underwear!" she said out loud, sobbing and laughing simultaneously.

But then she calmed down and also had a strange change of expression. Fumbling with the clasp of her bra, she yanked it off and hurriedly went to work.

Upstairs, the boy carefully moved from room to room, shaking with fear. He couldn't stand the horror of being bitten again, and if a pack of zombies had entered the house, before he could be surrounded, he would put a bullet in his own brain. Barely able to catch his breath, he silently went through every room in the house, but it was clear. Both the front and back doors were locked, and no zombies were on the doorsteps. So where had the noise come from?

Suddenly, the banging sound shook the house again, and it had definitely come from the back door. With wobbly pistol raised, he moved quickly down the back hall again, just as another gust of wind blew open the unlatched storm door, and promptly slammed it again.

"Son of a bitch!" the boy said laughing.

To shake off the jitters, he pulled a bottle of tequila from a cardboard box in the kitchen and took a few big gulps. He decided to linger over a few more hits of the bottle, just to put him more in the mood and give his helpless captive some time to think about what was going to happen to her. It was the least he could, so he thought, to pay her back for what she had done.

Twenty minutes later, full of liquid courage, he staggered down the basement stairs, fully prepared for the time of his life; or at least what was left of it. And with any luck, he would also infect her in the process so she would know the terror and pain of the zombie parasites spreading through her body and brain.

"You ready for me, bitch? Because here I—" the words caught in his throat as he saw Becks seductively leaning back against the wall—topless.

"You're right," she said in a deep, throaty voice. "We're both going to die, so why not have all the fun we can before we go?"

The tequila bottle slipped from his fingers and smashed on the concrete floor. Still fumbling with his belt buckle, he fell upon Becks like a starving vulture. But all the blood that had been rushing to his groin was suddenly spraying out of his neck. The doctor had specifically targeted his left common carotid artery with her thin, curved weapon, and had obviously punctured it with deadly accuracy.

Falling onto his back, the boy desperately clutched at his throat, as his life quickly spurted away in measured heartbeats. Becks grabbed for the boy's pistol from the holster on his thigh, then calmly reached into his pockets for the key to the handcuffs. Once freed, she started for the stairs, but something made her go back to the dying boy. Perhaps she felt the need to justify her actions to him, or prove to herself that she hadn't completely lost her soul.

"I'm sorry it had to come to this," she said, actually placing a comforting hand on his chest. "I really was telling the truth—I could have saved you."

A terrible sadness filled the boy's eyes, making him look like a lost and frightened child.

"N...Nick...my...name is...Nick..." he said between gasps, as his eyes suddenly went glassy and his hands dropped away from his throat.

Two weak spurts of blood later, and the heart Becks had felt beneath her hand stopped beating.

Only then did she let her weapon drop to the floor.

In her frantic scramble for any kind of defense, she pictured Angie fighting a pack of zombies with just a knitting needle, which had given her an idea. Years ago, she had a favorite pink satin bra that she liked so much, she wore it until the underwires in the cups poked through the fabric. Even then, she wore it until the little protective plastic caps at the ends fell off. Finally, when the tip of one of the hard, sharp, flat wires had poked a hole into her, she threw the bra away.

Using her teeth to tear through the fabric of her bra, she had pulled out one of the underwires, and scraped it on the concrete to remove the plastic tip and sharpen the end to a deadly point. Then it had just been a matter of distracting her attacker, which she knew would be all too easy.

Her quick thinking and handiwork had saved her life, but as she looked at the arterial spray dripping down the cinderblock walls, and the lifeless body of the boy—Nick—she didn't feel like congratulating herself, especially when she heard the distant roar of more ATVs.

The blow to her head had made her woozy enough that she had to sit down while putting on her clothes. There was no question about trying to make a run for it now—with this latest injury, and zombies *and* Rovers in the neighborhood, she would just have to hide and hope for the best. She would have liked to get Nick into the street to dispose of his remains, but now there was no way she was in any condition to carry a body up the stairs. She had enough trouble getting herself up the stairs.

Fighting back a few dizzy spells, she carried her weapons and supplies into the attic. The crowd of zombies was still so thick on Sparrow Lane that she doubted any rescue party would risk coming up the street, but she had to be prepared.

I'm not going to get caught with my pants down again, she thought, too focused on the task at hand to realize the irony of her choice of words.

From the attic window facing south toward the main road, a street or two away to the east she heard two or three ATVs, and maybe a motorcycle. From what Becks could tell, they appeared to be methodically searching, street by street. That was the best news, because if Angie had told them the Serviss house was 37 Sparrow Lane, they no doubt would have made a beeline to that address.

It took several minutes, but the group eventually turned off the main road onto Sparrow, where it came to an abrupt stop. Through the rifle scope, Becks could see two ATVs driven by short, chubby, bald men with glasses and red cheeks. These weren't just Mr. Reggie's brothers; they had to have been triplets! They were accompanied by a very big, brawny man on a motorcycle, who demonstrated his strength by picking up an elderly male zombie who had gotten too close, snapping the old zombie's back with his knee, and then tossing the body away like a ragdoll.

Note to self, Becks thought, *don't get within arm's reach of that gorilla!*

One the Reggie look-alikes reached for a megaphone, while the other scanned the street ahead with binoculars. Even with the dense pack of zombies, he could see glimpses of the missing ATVs. It was obvious that at least some of their friends must have been killed, but they held out hope that some had survived and had taken shelter in one of the houses.

"It's Mickey," the man's high-pitched voice echoed through the streets. "Can you hear me, Reggie? Can anyone hear me? Give us some sort of a sign."

The noise of their vehicles, and now the screeching voice over the megaphone, shifted the pack of zombies *en masse* toward their direction.

"Come on, Reggie, please give us some sign that you're alive," Mickey said with genuine emotion. "Chris! Nick! Jason! Morris! *Anyone!*"

The only response was the collective moan of hunger and desire for fresh flesh that arose from the pack. Unlike the stubborn Reggie, though, his brothers were not about to confront these overwhelming odds. Scrambling up and over a front lawn, they turned around and headed back down the main road at high speed. Once the sound of their vehicles had faded into the distance, Becks finally relaxed her finger from the trigger.

Only after night fell, did her body relax, and she curled up in the fetal position in front of the woodstove. Her mind still raced with thoughts, though, as so much had happened that day. An innocent woman Becks had befriended had died for her sake, she killed four people, and had been injured and barely escaped much worse.

While she looked upon shooting Reggie and the others as just another day at the office, initially, she felt very bad about the death of Nick, as it

71

was her first "up close and personal" kill with her own hands. But then a little voice in her head reminded her of what Nick was about to do to her, and she quickly erased all regrets. In fact, the more she thought about it, the more pleased she was by the clever and bloody manner in which she had vanquished her would-be assailant.

Her thoughts then turned to an unlikely subject—Buttons and Smidgey. They would miss Angie terribly, if they were still alive. Becks literally shuddered at the thought of the Rovers feasting on Shih Tzu Stew. She just had to hope that some of the other people in the community had adopted the two dogs, and would care for them even half as much as Angie. It was the only conclusion she would allow herself to make, as even with all of the human carnage of the day, the thought of any harm befalling the silly pampered pooches with the ribbons in their hair was the one thing she couldn't handle.

Sleep was not coming easily, but she didn't dare take any sleeping pills and risk not being fully aware, or awake, if the Rovers returned. Becks chose instead to think of Cam, and the long nights they spent in front of campfires, fireplaces, and woodstoves. Often they laughed, sometimes they sat silently just looking at the stars or the falling snow, and some very memorable evenings they made love on the grass, carpet, or bare wood floor next to the warmth of the fire.

Any combination of those memories warmed her now, heart and soul. Cam was another reason for her to persevere and get out of this suburban New Jersey hell. And if that meant killing every one of Reggie's ugly brothers, every Rover, and every zombie, she would do it if all she had were fly swatters and toothpicks for weapons.

With those lovely thoughts swirling through her drowsy brain, sleep finally came.

Chapter 6

A frigid, bleak dawn greeted Becks as she stretched and yawned. She thought about a real cup of coffee, crispy bacon, an omelet, and a thick slab of her mom's homemade bread, toasted and dripping with butter, and decided she just might literally kill for a meal like that. The pork sausage MRE she heated up didn't quite cut it, but at least it was a hot meal, and for that, she was very thankful. She was also thankful that the pain in her head had subsided to some degree, and she only felt dizzy if she leaned over or lifted anything heavy. That was still not good news, but it was better than having the entire room spin just by standing.

Becks had to assume that the Rovers would return, in force, to search for survivors or recover bodies—or what was left of them—knowing full well the latter was more likely. If nothing else, they would want to recover the weapons and those five ATVs, which was another reason she couldn't ride off into the sunset on one. If an ATV went missing, they would know the Army doctor was still alive. It didn't take a West Point tactician to realize that when outnumbered and alone in hostile territory, the best course of action was to make the enemy think you were dead or gone.

She was even gladder now that she hadn't taken out Reggie or the others with a headshot. Bullets through the skull were rather telling, especially after zombies scoured the flesh clean off the bones. With no obvious gunshot wounds, perhaps they would just think that the group had simply been overwhelmed. The fact that Angie's skull was shattered by a point blank shot was most likely not a problem, as a lot of people had probably wanted to shoot her.

Nick's body in the basement was a problem, though. If the Rovers searched the house and found him with a hole poked in his neck, they would know Becks was probably still alive. Unfortunately, while one can physically hide a body, it's very difficult to mask the telltale odor of decomp, but she hoped she had a solution for that.

Returning to the scene of her crime, so to speak, she managed to drag the boy's body into the back corner of the basement without feeling too dizzy. Covering it with a pile of old drapes and curtain rods, and anything else she could find that would have no value to the Rovers, she then took a deep breath and braced herself for the second part of her plan.

Prying back the lid of the large plastic bin in which she had placed the bodies of the two boy zombies she had dispatched when she first entered this house, the stench filled the room with the power of a solid object hitting her in the face. Becks was certainly not squeamish, and decomp was a prevalent odor since society had started to crumble, but this was a special kind of revolting. By wrapping the bodies in plastic and sealing them in a bin, she had created the foulest smelling, gelatinous mess that biology could devise. Feeling her pork sausage breakfast on the verge of becoming the ammunition for projectile vomiting, Becks retreated upstairs for a breather.

Donning a medical mask, she searched the kitchen cabinets and found some mint extract. Placing a few drops on the mask as an odor shield, she reluctantly returned to the basement. Unfortunately, nothing could shield her from the sight of the soupy stew of runny flesh and bones. Working as quickly as possible, she poured out some of the disgusting goo and remains of one of the boys near the base of the staircase, which should deter anyone from wanting to search the rest of the basement.

Dragging the bin with the remaining stinking guts upstairs, she dumped the contents on the lower steps leading to the attic. As Becks planned to hide in the attic if the Rovers returned, she hoped no one would want to step in that obscene muck, therefore assuring her safety.

The opportunity to test her strategy would come very soon, as a different type of engine sound suddenly caught her ear. This was no puny ATV. This was something big. Grabbing all of the gear, weapons, food, and water she could carry, she headed for the attic stairs.

"Oh crap! Why didn't I bring everything into the attic *before* I dumped the guts on the stairs!" Becks said out loud, astounded at her own stupidity.

She was able to step over the putrid remains, but the long stretch compromised her balance, so she had to make several trips with smaller bundles of her supplies and weapons. Once everything was hidden way back under the eaves behind boxes labeled "Photo Albums" and "Marching Band Uniforms"—and what was more worthless in a zombie apocalypse than that!?—Becks pondered the wisdom of leaving the attic hatch door open or closed. She decided that the psychology of an open door—coupled with the stinking guts on the stairs—might influence any searcher to think that the attic had nothing to hide. Perhaps she was overthinking the situation, but the slightest advantage could literally mean the difference between life and death.

By this time, the deep rumbling of a truck was very close. Crouching beneath the south-facing window, which Becks decided to keep closed against the cold air, in case she had to be up there for any length of time, she could see a large vehicle, like a semi-trailer truck, pulling some type of modified trailer. Not until the massive vehicle was about to turn onto Sparrow Lane could Becks make out all the details.

This wasn't any ordinary trailer truck; it was one of those massive, heavy-duty tow trucks designed to haul away broken down 18-wheelers and their contents. Huge steel plates had been welded on the front in a V-shape, like the zombie equivalent of a cowcatcher on train. A long cargo container was attached to a flatbed in tow, and it had gun ports cut into all the sides to allow 360 degrees of shooting flexibility. On top of the container was a crude but effective turret with a pivoting machine gun. The container was a weapon of war, and everyone on board was at battle stations.

Becks allowed herself a soft whistle in admiration, and she also felt more than a mild pang of jealousy as the powerful truck effortlessly pushed aside fallen tree limbs and knocked down and crushed every zombie in its path. As most of the meat on the street had already been consumed, the shoulder-to-shoulder crowd of zombies had thinned to about half its previous number, but that still left a couple of hundred targets for the deadly juggernaut.

The zombies not getting squashed in the path of the truck were suddenly flying to pieces as all of the weapons sticking out of the gun ports and the machine gun on the roof erupted at once. Despite the fact that Becks had undoubtedly become the mortal enemy of the Rovers, she couldn't help but silently cheer them on as row after row of the undead finally became the dead, once and for all.

As the truck rolled slowly down the street, Becks switched positions to the north window so she could see what would transpire by the row of ATVs. The hail of gunfire slowly died down to a sporadic shot here and there, to make sure that what went down stayed down. Even then, Reggie's two brothers waited another five or ten minutes to exit the cab of the tow truck. They were obviously much more cautious than their impetuous sibling. They had also thought to wear high rubber boots to wade through the bloodbath of fresh kills. Gingerly stepping over the new bodies, they used sticks to poke around all of the older chewed-up remains. Becks doubted that anyone, short of a team of seasoned homicide crime scene investigators, would be able to make any kind of identifications in the tangled masses of bones and shredded clothing, but these two men were determined.

As it was clearly going to take a while, one of the brothers barked some orders back to the cargo container. Immediately, a half dozen men in biohazard suits jumped out, with another half dozen heavily armed men and women right behind them to watch their backs. The men in the protective gear started carrying bodies to the side of the road to clear a path to get the ATVs on the truck.

When two of the men couldn't budge a particularly rotund male corpse, the big gorilla of a man Becks had seen on their last trip emerged from the container. Snapping on a big pair of yellow rubber gloves, he reached down, grabbed a couple of fistfuls of the fat zombie's clothing, and picked him up and tossed him like he was carry-on luggage. He then remained on the street, keeping a watchful eye on the two brothers.

As the third ATV was being loaded into the back of the cargo container, one of the brothers started shouting to the other. He was in the exact spot where Reggie had been shot down, and with the toe of his boot he was pushing some bones around. When the other brother joined him, he pointed to something on the ground and was very animated. Squatting down, he thrust one of his gloved hands into the muck. Becks used her rifle scope to get a closer look as the man rummaged around. He grasped something, but it slipped away twice before he was able to yank it free. Holding it high above his head, both brothers began sobbing, and everyone else stopped what they were doing.

A gore-encrusted, gold crucifix hung at the end of an even more blood-covered, heavy gold chain. The two brothers reached down under the tops of their coats and each pulled out identical crucifixes on identical chains, touching them together like some morbid toast to a fallen comrade. The ensuing wailing and beating of their chests was worthy of the most dramatic Irish wake, but other than the big gorilla, no one else appeared to be the least bit upset by Reggie's obviously gruesome demise. In fact, as their eyes darted back and forth between one another, the only emotion they displayed was fear. Becks imagined that they were all wondering how *they* would be made to suffer for the brothers' anger and grief.

Becks felt nothing but contempt. Perhaps the three brothers considered themselves to be very religious, and were very close and genuinely cared for one another, but they probably didn't give a damn about anyone else. They certainly didn't care about Angie, whose shattered skull and clumps of gray hair they roughly kicked aside as they began slowly picking up the remaining bones of their brother, placing them with great ceremony in a cardboard box.

"Hurry up already!" Becks whispered, as she hoped they would just take Reggie's remains and leave.

But she would not be so lucky.

Once they placed the box in the truck and draped a cloth over it, they both began barking orders and pointing up and down the street. The last two ATVs and all the weapons they could find were loaded in the cargo container, and then several groups of three people began house-to-house searches. Becks couldn't be sure if they were searching for her, supplies, or both, but she wrapped herself in an old, musty quilt and squeezed in next to her supplies behind the large marching band uniform box. She had overturned a few other boxes and pulled out their contents and scattered them, as if the attic had already been thoroughly searched.

With a pistol in each hand, she breathlessly listened as one person came in the front door—which Becks had left unlocked and slightly ajar, and two more came in the unlocked back door. She strained to hear what they were saying and could just make out someone instructing one person to check the basement and another to check upstairs.

The young woman tasked with searching the basement fearlessly opened the door with her pistol raised, only to stagger back a few steps when the decomp stench wafted up to greet her. Holding her breath, she descended the stairs, but rather than step into the muck at the bottom, she instead "searched" the basement by shining the flashlight back and forth. Seeing nothing but ordinary household items and a pile of drapes and curtain rods, she quickly retreated upstairs and reported that there wasn't anything useful in the basement. She then helped the man giving orders carry away all of the firewood in the house, and then started on the pile in the backyard.

The older man, who had been ordered upstairs, climbed the steps slowly, as his arthritis had been tormenting him since the cold weather set in. After pulling out dresser drawers and rifling through the bedroom closets, he filled the plastic garbage bag he was carrying with some warm sweaters, flannel shirts, socks, and underwear. On top of that, he emptied out what was left in the bathroom cabinets. All the while, the odor of the gelatinous decomp on the attic stairs had been assailing his nostrils, and he had no intention of stepping in that filth, or in taxing his already aching joints on those steep and narrow stairs. He did shine his flashlight up into the open hatch for a minute, but as long as no zombies looked down at him, he would report "all clear."

It probably wasn't much longer than ten minutes that the three people were in the house, but it felt like hours to Becks, who barely took a breath and didn't dare move an inch. When they exited, she let out a long sigh and took several slow, deep breaths. Her tense body slowly uncoiled, but her relaxation was short lived.

"We found her! We found her!" someone shouted in the street.

"*What the fuck?*" Becks swore as she sprang to her feet in a panic. "How the hell did they find me?"

Her mind raced as she tried to figure out how she had gone wrong and given away her position. Were there still hot embers in the woodstove? Had she left bloody footprints? Were all the bullet holes in the side of the house from Reggie and his men a dead giveaway? Were the staged gelatinous remains just *too* staged?

After half a minute of pure anguish, she realized it didn't matter how she had been discovered. The important thing now was how she was going to play this thing out. The brothers had no clue that she had shot Reggie. She could claim that she was out looking for supplies, and when she came back she found the ATVs and all the zombies feasting on bodies. Or, she could make a run for it out the back and into the next street, Bennett Lane, but the Rovers had a lot of people and a lot of firepower, and she wasn't physically one hundred percent. Surrender went against every fiber of her being, but the "living to fight another day" concept was making a lot of sense—assuming she was able to surrender and wouldn't be shot down on sight.

Holstering her weapons, she prepared for the second time to give herself up, this time to try to save her *own* hide. It didn't work so well with Angie the last time, but Becks would do her best to keep a bullet out of her own skull. As she was about to step down through the hatch onto the stairs, there was a huge commotion on the street and a woman was screaming.

Rushing to the north window, Becks saw a couple of the Rovers dragging a woman past the pieces of Humvee and the explosion crater. She was tall, emaciated, with large eyes and skin the color of someone who had spent a few months in the Caribbean. She was trying to struggle and break free, but only had the strength to scream. Even that effort

78

threatened to make her lose consciousness, as her screams were interspersed with violent coughing fits.

"It's not me!" Becks practically shouted, and then instinctively clamped a hand over her mouth.

Her relief in finding out that it wasn't her who had been discovered was short lived, however, as she watched this pitiful-looking woman being hauled before the two brothers. Becks dared to open the window a crack so she could hear what was being said.

"You that doctor?" one of the men shouted at the screaming woman.

He asked again, and then smacked her hard across the face to get her to quiet down. It worked, and the terrified woman stared blankly at the man who had just slapped her.

"What is your name?" the other brother shouted. "Where are your supplies?"

The interrogation was brief and fruitless, as the woman fainted. Her wrists were bound with a plastic zip tie, as if that was really necessary, and she was carried into the back of the cargo container. A few minutes later, after the other teams had returned with whatever they could scavenge from the houses, the truck began to slowly back down the street. It was unfortunate that an innocent woman had been taken by the Rovers, but Becks prayed that this would be the end of it, and she wouldn't see any of them again. She just needed a couple of days to fully recover from this latest blow to the head, and then she would start heading west.

The weak sunlight through the high overcast did nothing to warm up the temperature, so after several hours, when she was certain the Rovers weren't returning that day, Becks took the risk of breaking up some furniture and cardboard boxes to burn in the woodstove, since all the firewood had been confiscated. She knew full well she was breaking the rule about no fires in daylight, but her nerves had been so rattled these last few days that she had the shakes, and the cold wasn't helping. The fire would at least drive away the physical chill.

The warmth started making her drowsy, and just as she was drifting off to sleep, she heard a voice at the front door. Was she dreaming?

"Hey!" the voice said again, bringing Becks to her feet so quickly she was woozy. Steadying herself against the couch, she pulled out both pistols and held her breath.

"Please, I know you're in there," a deep male voice said. "I'm not one of them. I'm not one of the Rovers. They took Isabella today. They took my wife and I need your help!"

Becks cautiously moved to the front bay window and pulled back the curtain. On the front steps, there was a large man with long, black, curly hair, clad in military pants and a parka. He reminded her of one of those big Samoan football players. He had two overstuffed duffle bags beside him. She couldn't see any weapons, but the parka and bags could have held an arsenal.

"My wife and I have been watching you for weeks," he continued. "We live up the street. We heard that awful explosion the night of the storm. We've seen you running between houses. I wanted to contact you, but Izzy, my wife, she didn't trust anyone. Especially since our boy was killed by the Rovers. She hasn't been the same since. She kind of gave up, you know?

"Anyway, I can't go back to the house. Once they question her, they'll know about me. They'll know I have weapons. I know you are a fighter, and a good shot. I saw you shoot that bastard Reggie. I *need* to get Izzy back! She's all I have left."

This was one of those moments where Becks' conscience was slugging it out with her primitive fight-or-flight response. Her heart told her to open that door. Her amygdala told her to open that door and put a bullet in his brain. She settled on a course of action in the middle.

"How do I know you aren't with the Rovers?" she shouted, backing away from the bay window in case he opened fire.

"Look, I could have gone to the Rovers and told them all about you, and where to find you, in exchange for Izzy. But I didn't. I came to you. Honestly, I don't know you, and I don't give a rat's ass about you, but I won't trade a human life…not even to save my Izzy."

He was saying all the right things, and then some, but Becks had heard good stories before and then been stabbed in the back. But there was another element in play here—guilt. Becks knew damn well that none of this would have happened if the Humvee accident hadn't happened on this street. And the search parties were looking for *her*, not this man's wife. Of course, they could have found her eventually anyway while looking for supplies, but Becks felt responsible, and that was a feeling that had the veto power over all of her other feelings.

Becks pulled open the front door, and made sure that two pistols pointing at his head were the first things the man saw.

"We're cool. Everything is okay," he said, raising both hands.

She waved him inside, but he hesitated.

"I would love to come inside, but I really don't want to leave my bags out here," he said, gesturing with his head, as his hands were still raised.

"What's in them?" Becks asked with narrow-eyed suspicion.

"Some food, some water, a change of clothes...and a shitload of badass guns!" he said proudly, with a wide smile.

There was something disarming about that smile, even when he was talking about bags full of weapons. If this man was lying and trying to deceive Becks, he was one of the best.

"Okay, bring 'em in," she said in a friendly manner, unable to maintain her scowl, but not lowering her weapons.

After bringing in the bags, Becks gestured toward the woodstove where he promptly peeled off his parka and sat in front of the fire.

"Saw them taking your firewood," he said, rubbing his hands for warmth. "I buried all my firewood, and most of my supplies. If you don't want people finding you or your stuff, dig a hole!"

"Well, I didn't think of that," Becks replied. "Didn't think a lot of this would happen. So, what's your story...uh, what's your name?"

"Ed Tasi, but my friends call me Big Eddie," he said, extending his hand to shake, and then withdrawing it when Becks held firmly onto her pistols.

Eddie then launched into his life's story, or at least the last few years BZA, and then everything AZA. It turned out his parents were from Samoa, but no, he never played football—much to his high school coach's dismay. He joined the Army right out of high school, and served two tours in Iraq, and one in Afghanistan, while his wife raised Eddie Junior. When he returned home, he got a job with the county doing maintenance, and picking up overtime wherever he could get it—driving snow plows, cleaning storm drains; anything to help make ends meet.

"Not that I'm complaining," Eddie said, shaking his head. "Never was afraid of hard work, and I was just grateful that we were able to have a little home of our own and put food on the table. We made a good home for Eddie Junior, and you know, that's all that was important. You got kids?"

"No, I don't. But I do know what you mean," Becks replied, even though she wasn't sure she meant it.

"Then the neighborhood got kind of crazy when the infection began. Neighbors turning on neighbors, you know? Guess it was the same everywhere. Most of the people took off right after quarantine. Izzy thought we should go, but where was I going to take my family? I know my house, my street, my town, and I knew I could defend it. I didn't want to go driving off to God-knows-where into God-knows-what."

"Yeah, I stayed in my house, too," Becks interjected.

"And it turned out to be the right call, didn't it? My wife has a green thumb. She made a garden across a couple of backyards and grew a lot of food. We collected rain water. There were plenty of deer and rabbits in the neighborhood, and in the park a few blocks down. I'm not saying it was easy, but we were doing okay, you know? Had to kick some zombie ass now and then, but nothing I couldn't handle. Give me a zombie over a sneaky Taliban motherfucker any day!"

Becks couldn't help laughing, and ever so slightly lowering her pistols. But at that moment, Big Eddie stood up. Becks used her legs to push herself backwards across the floor to get out of arm's reach, while cocking the hammer of her Smith and Wesson.

"Whoa, whoa! Hang on their, killer," he said, raising his hands again. "The fire is going out. I'm just getting some more wood."

Slowly moving to an old rocking chair, he lifted it up and snapped it to pieces like it was made of toothpicks. He opened the glass door of the woodstove, thoughtfully placed the pieces of the chair to generate the best fire, and then sat back down at a respectful and nonthreatening distance.

"You do realize how many times I could have taken you out?" he said with more than a hint of exasperation at having two pistols trained on him. "Trust me, you *never* would have known what hit you."

"Is that supposed to reassure me?" Becks replied, although realizing it was the honest truth. She didn't even know Eddie and Izzy were living a block away, yet he knew her every move. "Oh hell, my arms are getting tired anyway."

Taking a leap of faith, or more accurately a calculated risk, she holstered her pistols. When Eddie didn't move a muscle and just continued on with his story, she breathed a little easier.

"Anyway, where was I? Oh yeah, so we were holding our own with the zombies and avoiding the Rovers. And we were together, as a family. That was the only thing that really mattered, you know?

"Then a few months ago, Eddie Junior—he was a really smart kid, not like me—he decides he wants some more books to read, because you know, there's not a whole lot to do in a zombie apocalypse. He says he wants to go to the library. Can you stand it!? There's zombies and Rovers everywhere, and this kid of mine wants to go to the library! What were we going to say? If it made him happy and took his mind off all this horrifying shit around us, then it was worth it.

"I told him I would go into town alone and get him some books, but he says, 'Dad, really, do you even have any idea where the physics and chemistry section of the library is?' So his mom and me decide he can go with me."

At this point, a flood of emotion swept across Eddie's face, and his voice broke. He had to pause for a minute before continuing.

"We get downtown without so much as a sniff of a zombie, and we don't see any Rovers. The library door is already busted open so we walk right in. Well, you should have seen Eddie Junior's face light up surrounded by all those books. I hadn't seen him smile like that since before all that zombie parasite shit began. He starts stuffing all these big books into our knapsacks, and I say, 'Hold on, Einstein, we need to be able to run if we have to,' so he reluctantly goes through them all again and just takes 'the essentials' he says.

"As we are leaving the library, a couple of zombies are coming across the street at us. They were the couple who ran the movie theater in town; a nice old couple. Sure hated to split their skulls with my machete, but what are you going to do?

"Eddie Junior's not so good with the killing stuff, and he gets kind of upset and stumbles as he starts running. One of the books falls out of his knapsack. I tell him to leave it, but he says it's the best one. He runs back to get it, and just then a Rover patrol is driving by from a side street. I duck into an alley and yell at Eddie Junior to hide—we're about fifty feet apart—but he just has to have that book.

"One of the Rovers thinks he's stealing some of their supplies, and…and…"

Tears welled up in Eddie's eyes, and Becks told him he didn't need to continue.

"No...no, other people need to know about my boy. I don't want Eddie Junior to be forgotten," he replied, wiping his eyes and somehow finding the strength to finish the story. "Eddie Junior picks up the book and starts running toward me. He's no more than fifteen feet away and they shoot him. The bastards *shoot my boy in the back because of a book!* He falls to the ground and looks right at me, and you know what he does? He puts his finger to his lips, and whispers for me to be quiet and save myself. Save myself so I can take care of his mom.

"I know gunshot wounds. I knew he wouldn't last more than a minute or two. And maybe God will damn my soul to hell, but I ran. I took off and left him there to die in the street alone. And not a day has gone by since then that I haven't wanted to track down every one of those Rover fuckers and slash their throats from ear to ear. And now they have Izzy. I thought she was safely hidden—I had made a false wall space for her in a closet—but she started coughing, you know, and I was in the attic and I saw there were just too many of them out there..."

The darkness that now filled every line of his agonized expression made Becks gasp. Such single-minded, hatred-driven revenge frightened her, but it also cemented the level of trust she was looking for. If he had wanted her dead, or to do her harm, she truly would have never seen it coming. This was a man who would tear apart someone with his bare hands to protect his family, and if he wanted Becks on his side, she couldn't ask for a better ally.

"I may live to regret this," Becks began, "but how can I help you get your wife back?"

Chapter 7

Isabella Tasi was too good for this world, and she had endured too much hardship and grief. The sleepless nights and anxiety attacks during her husband's three deployments were too much on her fragile system, but she somehow managed to hide her condition from Little Eddie, as she called her beautiful, curly-haired, baby boy from the day he was born.

When Big Eddie finally returned to them safe and sound, she allowed herself to believe that she would never spend another day living in fear.

BZA, she worked at the local elementary school as a teacher's aide, where she was affectionately known as Mama Izzy. She told everyone she took the job because they needed the money, which they did, but that wasn't the real reason. She worked at the school because it gave her the opportunity to see Little Eddie here and there throughout the day. Even a glimpse of her boy made her heart swell with love and pride.

"He's such a smart boy, not like me," she would tell anyone who would listen, "And I would scrub floors and work three jobs if I had to, to make sure he gets a great college education. Of course, my boy is *so* smart he will get all the scholarships he needs, but I will do whatever it takes for him to succeed."

When the infection began, the schools were one of the first places to be hit hard. Concentrations of children were always prime breeding grounds for the spread of viruses and bacteria, and the ZIPs were especially adept at jumping from child to child. Little Eddie hated the idea of the schools having to close "temporarily" until the health crisis could be resolved, but he begrudgingly had to admit "it was an epidemiologically sound strategy," as he told his fifth grade teacher.

Despite the gradual collapse of civilization and the mortal peril of the rise of the zombie population, the real blow for Little Eddie came the day the Internet went down for good. Up until that point, he had at least been able to continue his studies, and communicate with a few friends he had made across the globe, thanks to a gifted child website. He loved his mom and dad with all his heart, but they were hardly able to provide the mental stimulation he needed.

From the day the news broke about the seriousness of the spreading infection, Izzy spent every waking moment worrying about her son's safety. While she knew that Big Eddie was a veritable one-man army, and would move heaven and earth to protect them, the harsh reality of the world AZA was too much for anyone to ever reasonably expect to live another day. This realization pounded away at her, body and soul, until at times she actually believed that she might shatter into a thousand pieces like a plate glass window being struck with a sledgehammer.

Her sanity and physical health teetered back and forth over the edge, and just when she was certain that she would not be able to go on, Little

Eddie would kiss her cheek and tell her she shouldn't worry, because he had enough strength for the both of them. After such touching moments, she would rise again, mentally and physically, if for no other reason than to keep her boy safe, and make sure *he*, at least, *would* live another day. She would do well for a couple of weeks, or perhaps a month or two, but the relentless pounding eventually wore her down again and again, and every time the lows would get a little lower.

Then came the day that Big Eddie came home without Little Eddie. Life stopped at that moment as surely as if the bullet had struck *her* in the back. She still ate occasionally, slept a bit here and there, and spoke every now and then, but none of it seemed to be a conscious action. In her mind, she was already dead and buried. Only the ghost of Isabella Tasi still walked the earth, less alive than the zombies that occasionally shuffled over her son's shallow grave in the park across the street from the library.

Not that it would have been any consolation to Izzy or Big Eddie, but when the man who shot Little Eddie discovered he was just a kid taking books from the library, the man shot the commander of the patrol who had ordered him to fire, and then promptly turned the gun on himself.

In an odd and disturbing twist, Little Eddie, the man who shot him, the commander, and the zombie couple Big Eddie had killed, were all placed in that same hastily dug grave. Zombie apocalypses had a way of raising or lowering everyone to the same level, depending upon how you looked at it. In a way, it was the great equalizer, where everyone from all walks of life, and undeath, ultimately equaled zero.

The woman Becks had witnessed being dragged down the street was not only sick in her heart and mind, her body was obviously also ravaged by a severe respiratory illness. From Eddie's description of his wife's symptoms, it sounded like pneumonia, although in his state of denial he kept referring to it as simply "her nagging cold." Without the proper medications at Becks' disposal, she realized that even if they retrieved Isabella Tasi, they may just be rescuing a corpse.

Still, Becks had this thing about good people vs. bad people, and she couldn't live with the thought of bad people functioning with impunity, usually at the expense of good people. As much as she detested zombies, they couldn't help themselves. People had choices, and when they kept making the wrong choices that hurt other people, her blood boiled and she just had the strongest desire—no, the *need*—to kick some ass.

And considering that BZA she wouldn't hurt a fly, this newfound righteous indignation had turned her into quite a proficient killer, racking up an impressive body count. Between the people she had shot and intentionally infected, this former Angel of Mercy had grown quite a pair of black wings as the Angel of Death, and she was once again fired up and ready to rustle some feathers.

It would all have to be done wisely, however. Two people running into town with guns blazing wouldn't get the job done. And as Becks had no idea what the town was like—Ridgelawn Park, she finally found out—she would have to rely on Eddie for the layout of the streets, buildings, and lookout points. Of course, with hundreds of people in dozens of private homes, condos, and apartment buildings spread over about nine square blocks, there was no telling where Isabella was being held. However, as they would have to start somewhere, Eddie suspected she would be near The Capitol, as Reggie and his brothers called the fine, white house where they lived, and declared *their* laws.

It wasn't uncommon for small towns to have their best homes on their main street become funeral homes, and this late 19th century gem was no different. The family that owned it for generations could no longer pay the taxes and maintain it, so in the 1980s it became the Francis Smith Funeral Home and Cremation Services. When society began to break down, it didn't bother the brothers at all to commandeer the former funeral home and move in. Considering they had spent all their lives in a few dark rooms with poor ventilation over their family's deli, this was a palace. Who cared if they had to toss out a few dozen coffins and the place reeked of flowers? It beat the constant smell of corned beef.

Isabella was indeed being kept very close to The Capitol, in an unheated shed in the backyard. Her nerves and illness had put her in an incoherent state. That, coupled with the fact that the brothers suspected whatever she had might be contagious, they at least decided not to beat her into speaking, lest her germs spread to them. During a zombie apocalypse, everyone in their right mind becomes a germaphobe, but the brothers were especially paranoid. And no one was more afraid of germs than the big gorilla of a man who acted as a bodyguard to the brothers.

In any event, it didn't look as though they would be getting any useful information out of this woman any time soon, or so they thought. As evening started to fall, a member of the housekeeping staff at The Capitol, Jennifer, was told to bring Isabella some water and crackers. When Jennifer entered the shed, she immediately recognized "Mama Izzy," who had been a favorite of her two girls at the elementary school—before they had been killed at the local mall when the entire staff of Hot Dog Paradise switched at once and went on a rampage.

"Please, Mr. Riley," Jennifer almost whispered, sheepishly addressing one of the brothers, although which brother she could never tell. At least with Reggie gone, she had a 50-50 chance between Pat and Mickey, but she would never dare address any of them by their first names. "That's not the army doctor. That's the nice lady from the school. She's real sick, Mr. Riley, got a high fever, and coughing something awful. Could I please bring her to my place and try to get her warmed up and get some hot soup in her? She can share my rations, I won't ask for extras."

Whichever brother it was, didn't say a word and left the room for a minute to consult with the other brother. Then they both returned and grilled Jennifer for everything she knew about Isabella Tasi. They learned that her husband had been in the military, they had a son, and they lived somewhere in town, but she didn't know where.

After dismissing Jennifer and allowing her to take Isabella and her germs home, Pat or Mickey opened a drawer in the former funeral director's desk and took out two valuable post-apocalypse resources—a phone book and a map. In the early days of scavenging for supplies, they had made a list of the affluent customers at the deli, looked them up in the phone book, and raided their houses first.

If these people happened to still be at home and resisted the Rovers— who had been named after the brothers' bowling team—that was too bad for them. The timid ones gave up everything they had and joined the resurrected community of New Ridgelawn, with the three brothers each representing one of the Executive, Legislative, and Judicial branches of the regime. In truth, many of the people the Rovers "rescued" wouldn't have lasted long on their own, but there is that old saying that those who give up freedom for security deserve neither.

One of the brothers thumbed through the worn pages of the phone book until he found "Tasi, E., 53 Sparrow Lane," thereby confirming that the address was the same place as where the woman had been found. But where *was* E. Tasi and their son? Where were all the supplies they must have stockpiled? And was this army doctor dead or alive? If there was anything the two cautious brothers hated, it was loose ends. They were in conference late into the night to plan how to tie up those loose ends, or cut them clean out of New Ridgelawn once and for all.

Two other people were making their own plans that night. Becks and Big Eddie also worked long after dark, carefully formulating Plan A and Plan B. They also framed out Plan C, but they hoped it wouldn't come to that.

Right on schedule, Becks and Eddie heard the massive suburban assault vehicle rumbling toward Sparrow Lane shortly after dawn. However, this time they watched as it turned onto Bennett Lane to avoid the massive crater in the road caused by the exploding Humvee, and the charred pieces of the huge oak tree that had fallen on it. Easily pushing aside all the debris on Bennett, it turned the corner and came down Sparrow, stopping directly in front of the Tasi house—just as they had hoped.

Becks and Eddie had an excellent view of what was going on, because they were in the attic of a house on Squire Lane, the street *behind* the Tasi house. Since the mass exodus when quarantine ended, Eddie had used all that time wisely to clear and set up no less than eight different safe houses. Not only was it a prudent defensive strategy to have a number of fallback positions, it helped to break the apocalypse monotony when the family would take "vacations" to one of the other houses for a couple of days.

Becks was in the prone position on the floor of the attic with her eye to a high-powered scope, with the silencer end of the sniper rifle from Eddie's arsenal masked by a false vent he had installed the year before. While he had planned for many emergency scenarios, none had been quite like this. Still, Eddie's foresight gave them options other than defending against a full scale assault.

Eddie held no weapon. Instead, he had a walkie talkie in one hand, and with the other he held together the ends of a few thick blankets wrapped around his head just below his eyes to muffle his voice. It was a good plan they had devised and everything was ready—although what Becks didn't know, is that if the brothers brought Isabella and offered to release her if Eddie turned himself in and gave up all their provisions, he would abandon that plan in a heartbeat.

The brothers were too cautious to bring Isabella, though, and they left the majority of their fighting force back in town. They figured it would only be a matter of time before Eddie would come looking for his wife. But they still had about 30 shooters—if you could call the dozen or so scrawny and scared adolescents, and the disinterested women who weren't quite sure how to even hold their weapons, real shooters. Still, there were at least fifteen men and women who looked like they meant business. Overall, it was a sizable force against only two people.

Unfortunately, the brothers were also too cautious to exit the cab of their truck. Instead, one of them held a megaphone out the window.

"Eddie? Eddie Tasi?" the voice squealed. "Your wife is very sick. We are doing our best to take care of her, but she needs you, and she wants to see her son. Let us bring you both to her."

Becks didn't need to turn around to know that flames of hatred had turned Big Eddie's expression to one of a volcano about to erupt. On a positive note, the brothers were unaware that Little Eddie was already dead, so Isabella couldn't have given them much information, if any at all.

Seconds of tension ticked by as the shooters spread out. Then the silence was broken by a voice from *inside* the Tasi house.

"GO...FUCK...YOURSELVES!"

Eddie shouted those words into the walkie talkie, which were transmitted loud and clear to the other walkie talkie cranked up to full volume by an open window in his house. The trick fooled everyone into believing Eddie was inside. The next move was Becks'.

The big gorilla was out of her line of sight behind the truck, so she settled on the next biggest, meanest, badass motherfucker in the brothers' army—a satanic-looking version of Mr. Clean—and silently put a bullet through his skull. The pink mist sprayed the faces of two adolescents next to the slain man, and they promptly dropped their weapons and ran back into the cargo container, crying and screaming.

A few others ran, but the rest opened up on the Tasi house, spraying it with bullets from top to bottom, as they had no idea where the kill shot had come from. As fast as Becks could, she "culled the herd" of shooters, only rather than the weak, she concentrated on the strong. Eddie quickly joined her and took out a few of his own targets, until the Tasi house burst into flames. Then the two snipers stopped firing and just observed, so as not to give away their position on the next street.

The brothers yelled at their diminishing army to get into the house to grab supplies and weapons. No one moved at first, until the big gorilla emerged from behind the truck and "suggested" that three of the men get their asses into the house. Kicking in the front door, a lashing tongue of propane gas-fed flame shot out, singeing them from head to foot. An instant later, numerous propane tanks in the living room exploded with an awe-inspiring, spilt-second sucking sound, followed by a deafening *WHOOOSH*, as huge splinters of wood and flaming debris killed the three men, and severely wounded at least ten others.

In the midst of the chaos of the retreating army, dragging and carrying their wounded into the cargo container, Becks decided to take two more quick shots. While she didn't dare hit any people—thereby signaling that she and Big Eddie hadn't been killed in the Tasi house blast—she couldn't resist puncturing tires in the truck and in the flatbed trailer which carried the cargo container. Whichever brother was driving, he had a hell of a time backing up the street with two flats. But before the brothers could curse their ill-fated attack, or Big Eddie and Becks could rejoice in their victory, something happened that made everyone stop and look up in amazement.

It was a helicopter—an Army helicopter! It didn't fly directly overhead, but the smoke, flames, and explosion had clearly attracted its attention. It made one wide, arcing pass around Sparrow Lane, then headed off to the southwest. Becks knew that there were semi-regular flights between West Point and the Picatinny Arsenal, sometimes following particularly large convoys on Interstate 287, and she wished she had been outside to wave a big flag or send up a flare.

But obviously they had found another way to get the Army's attention in the form of the enormous bonfire that was once the Tasi residence—and the house next door, which had ignited when a flaming propane tank rocketed through the wall and exploded. But for now there were more pressing matters, and as the suburban assault vehicle rattled and squeaked away, grinding on its rims, and zombies drawn by the noise waited patiently for the hot flames to subside so they could chow down on the casualties, Becks and Eddie fine-tuned phase two of Plan A.

"What the fuck!?" one of the brothers shouted in their office back in The Capitol. "I mean, *what the fuck*!?"

"I know! How could we expect that crazy bastard was going to blow himself up?" the other brother lamented, looking over the list of the names of the eleven dead, and the four others not expected to live—not to mention the eight people who were severely burned and bloodied.

"He must have known that his wife was going to die anyway," the other brother said.

"But his child? His own son? How could he let his son die?" the other yelled to no one in particular, as he nervously scratched a spot on his bald head that he had already rubbed raw.

There was a moment of silence before the other brother responded.

"Do we even know if his son was alive?" he said thoughtfully, trying to make sense of it all, as best as the deli-manager-turned Commander-in-Chief could. "After all, Jennifer had no knowledge of the family since the schools closed. A lot has happened since then, brother."

"Yes, brother, you're right. The world has lost a lot of good souls since then," he replied, missing the irony of the fact that they were responsible for their share of departed souls.

"But the helicopter! Maybe the military has started their push this way?"

"Ssshhh!" the other brother cautioned. "Don't let anyone hear you. They haven't shown any other signs of movement, and it's doubtful they would start anything right before winter."

"You're right, brother. The helicopter must have just seen the explosion and smoke. We have nothing to worry about from the Army."

"And Ed Tasi is dead."

"Yes, Ed Tasi is dead."

"But what about that doctor?"

"Probably killed in the swarm that got Reggie—God rest his soul."

The brothers both paused to cross themselves.

"And if not, and she was with Eddie, she's dead."

"And if not, she's probably long gone, because she doesn't want to have anything to do with the mighty Rovers!"

As the brothers high-fived one another, two figures dressed head to foot in camo, bristling with weapons, began their slow and careful journey toward the heart of New Ridgelawn.

Chapter 8

BZA, the sound of ringing phones was as ubiquitous as traffic noise, the buzz of airplanes, and the incessant chatter of people everywhere. No one anticipated how quiet an apocalypse would really be, and for many people, they just couldn't adapt to the silence. Therefore, the ringing of a phone was now as jolting as an air raid siren.

Frederick Mackenzie, or Freddie Mac, as he was commonly known at the compound, was at his post in the central watch tower early one morning when the satellite phone rang and he almost jumped out of his skin. It could have been anything from a routine status check from West Point, to a warning of a massive zombie herd coming their way. Or, it could be that a friend or relative of someone in the compound had made their way to a military survivor camp somewhere and was calling to let their loved one know they were alive.

Those were usually the best calls, but not always, as Freddie Mac knew from experience. He had been certain that his wife, Emily, had been killed when they were trying to flee to Canada after the quarantine. Their car had broken down, they were overrun by a ravenous pack of zombies, they ran for their lives, got separated, etc.—the same story that had literally played out millions of times around the world, AZA—and he had heard her terrified screams off in the distance. What he thought were her death cries haunted him every night in his dreams.

However, during his waking hours, he had slowly overcome his grief and found solace in the arms of Rachel, a pretty, young widow at the compound. They had recently been married by The Monk, and were expecting a child. Then a few weeks ago, the sat phone rang and there was a voice from the grave—Emily was calling from the Air Force survivor camp at the airport in Plattsburgh, New York. She told him all about her horrific journey and many near-death adventures, and how she only made it through by thinking of him and praying they would one day be reunited. Then, when she saw his name on the Official LOL (List of the Living), she knew all her struggles to survive had been worth it.

Of course, he was thrilled to find out that Emily was alive and well. Unfortunately, he doubted that Rachel would be as pleased by the news.

But he couldn't be sure, as he hadn't found the nerve to tell her yet. He also failed to tell Emily about Rachel.

Emily was scheduled to come to West Point in a convoy in just a couple of days, so Freddie Mac almost hoped the phone call was to inform him of a rampaging horde of zombies descending on Saugerties. It would be far less painful than the impending "Two Wives Apocalypse." Unfortunately for Freddie Mac, he was to have no such luck. The call was actually from Phil at West Point, who wanted to speak with Cam about some "curious news."

"Hey, buddy, what's up?" Cam asked, after Freddie Mac had jogged over to Cam's cabin with the phone.

"Now don't get your hopes up," Phil began cautiously, but couldn't continue as Cam immediately jumped to conclusions.

"They found signs that she's alive? Where is she?" Cam practically shouted into the phone as he sprang to his feet and began pacing nervously.

"Let's try this again," Phil said laughing. "Now don't get your hopes up, but an Army recon helicopter photographed something curious."

With Cam constantly interjecting that Phil should hurry up—which, of course, only slowed down his story—Phil finally managed to tell him all about the burning houses that just happened to be on the same street where Becks' convoy had the accident. When the high-res photo was analyzed, they also found fresh bodies in the street and a large vehicle driving away.

"This means that she *is* alive!" Cam concluded with absolute certainty.

"No, Cam, please don't set yourself up for more heartbreak like this," he cautioned his friend, even though Phil had jumped to the same conclusion when he heard the news from the Picatinny Arsenal. "All it means is that *someone* is alive in that neighborhood. It could have been survivors fighting zombies, rival groups fighting one another over supplies; it could have been anything."

"And it could have been our girl stirring up a hornet's nest of trouble," Cam said in a more subdued tone, while wiping away an errant tear.

"Yes, this does have Becks written all over it, doesn't it?" Phil admitted, his own emotion rising in his throat.

94

Once again, Cam was ready to gear up and bring his men down to New Jersey, but Phil could not stress strongly enough how dangerous that would be. Recon photos also showed the streets choked with zombies for miles around. The Army was planning to begin an offensive in early spring, but there was no way in hell they would participate in, or even allow, any rescue efforts until they could begin thinning the herds.

If that activity on the ground did indeed indicate that Dr. Rebecca Truesdale was still alive, she would have to find a way to survive on her own through the winter.

Chapter 9

Becks was amazed at how silently and almost gracefully Eddie moved, for a big man. She wasn't exactly a bull in a china shop, but no one would ever mistake her for a ninja, either. Of course, with not one, but two head injuries, she was just lucky she could stand up and move at all. If she only had another day or two to rest—but the clock was ticking with Izzy's fragile condition.

In the dark, the eyesight of the undead was even worse than their living counterparts, given the general tissue degradation from the ZIP network management of the body. The parasites seemed to allow for the minimum requirement to keep a corpse upright, mobile—and most importantly—feeding. Other than that, everything else was nonessential. In other words, there was an acceptable level of decomp.

Still, while living humans had the upper hand at night, it all became a moot point if you turned the corner and went face-first into a couple of dozen zombies, regardless of their poor vision. So, moving with extreme caution was still the best way to approach night maneuvers—that, and the helmet-mounted, night vision goggles that Eddie had bought for himself and his son. He had hoped the extravagant purchase would encourage Little Eddie to go out hunting and camping with him, but the boy had been much happier sitting inside, examining the unit's optics.

AZA, the goggles had saved Eddie's life at least a dozen times, and were particularly helpful when searching dark basements for supplies. It just creeped him out how these damn zombies would "nest" in basements by huddling together in corners or under staircases. Of course, flashlights helped, but they also acted like beacons to help the zombies see *you*, too. The night vision googles kept the zombies in the dark and gave the wearer a lethal advantage.

Becks had used similar goggles before, but just for the Midnight Paintball parties that Cam and his men had at the compound. They used some special paint that fluoresced, and any time someone was hit they looked like a 100 watt bulb running through the woods, which only made them a bigger target. It was all great fun, but it was also a great learning experience, driving home the point Cam endlessly stressed—the most dangerous enemy is the one you can't see.

Remaining invisible was what Becks had been striving to do from the day she was stranded in this suburban New Jersey hell hole. Of course, she had no idea she was failing miserably, because Eddie had been watching her every move. At least she was able to take some pride in the fact that the Rovers never found her, even after she gut-shot Mr. Reggie.

The game was changing now, though, as they would be walking right into the Rovers' stronghold. But in their favor were the facts that Eddie had carefully studied New Ridgelawn's defenses, they had night vision goggles, Pat and Mickey Riley were idiots, and everyone thought that Becks and Eddie were dead, so they weren't expecting company. If Plan A continued to go as they hoped, they would get in, get Izzy, and get out before anyone realized that Eddie, at least, had not died in the propane explosion ruse.

As they slowly and carefully ducked in and out between cars, and behind backyard sheds and shrubbery, part of Becks was telling her she was crazy. A voice was telling her she should have grabbed a sack full of MREs and run like hell to the west, toward Interstate 287—until a louder and more persuasive voice spoke.

"Izzy is the only reason I have left to live," the big man said, as they crouched behind the shell of an old Mustang that no one would ever restore. They waited for a pair of adolescent zombies to shamble on by, and then Eddie continued, "If I lose her, I lose myself."

"We *will* find her," Becks whispered, choosing her words carefully. Finding her was one thing. Finding her and keeping the dangerously ill woman alive was another.

Normally, exterior perimeter patrols around New Ridgelawn would take place every half hour, day and night, by foot and by car. However, as

96

the effective fighting force had been seriously diminished, there were no patrols beyond the barricades and fences that night. There were still lookouts in the plywood and two-by-four towers spaced about a block apart, but without searchlights, they could do little more than listen for clumsy zombies to shuffle their way to within shooting range.

Of course, even though the threat—namely Eddie Tasi—had supposedly been neutralized, everyone in town was on edge. This was the biggest thing to happen in over a year, and the first raid to go catastrophically wrong. Many who lost loved ones were inconsolable in their grief, but many more were silently rejoicing that the Rovers had their asses kicked and lost several of their worst thugs.

For the majority of their journey towards town, Becks and Eddie went out of their way to avoid packs of zombies, stopping only occasionally for Eddie to whack a lone straggler over the head with a powerful blow from his machete. However, when they were within a few blocks of the main gate, they started looking specifically *for* packs of zombies—but not too big, and not too small. Something around 25 or 30 would be just right. They found what they were looking for at a gas station, which still had its tattered, makeshift banner, spray painted on an old bed sheet hanging over the pumps:

NO GAS LEFT
RUN FOR YOUR LIVES

In a surreal scene, about two dozen zombies were standing together under the banner, apparently attracted by the flapping strips of fabric, but looking for all the world like they were waiting for a tanker truck to deliver more gas. For whatever reason, some of the undead were far more susceptible to the lure of things like wind chimes, loose shutters banging in the wind, or plastic soda bottles blowing down the street. Some actually tried to eat the bottles or wind chimes, but for the most part, they were content to just follow the sounds, and then stand and stare at the source of the sound for days, weeks, or even months.

Since the earliest days of infection, when zombie attacks were big news and videos blanketed the Internet, Becks had studied their behaviors and eccentricities. She did so because she had a natural scientific curiosity, but primarily because she looked for any vulnerabilities, which she could then use against them. Having once observed several zombies follow a beach ball for at least a mile down a stretch of highway, she came up with a plan for creating a diversion. Fortunately, Eddie was able to supply the necessary hardware to make it happen.

While Becks stood guard behind a minivan across the street from the gas station, Eddie removed something from his backpack and fiddled with some sort of controls. Then he pulled out something else and placed it in the road.

"You ready?" he whispered.

"Let's do it," Becks replied, raising her faithful hockey stick with the knives that had proven to be a very quiet and effective zombie killing weapon.

Pushing a few buttons, the object on the ground lit up and began to move. It was a radio-controlled "22nd Century Lunar Explorer" that Little Eddie had built, with tank-like treads and a clear plastic dome, surrounded by a host of flashing LED lights and polished chrome. Big Eddie skillfully maneuvered the vehicle toward the zombies at the gas pumps, and it didn't take long before their fascination turned from the tattered fabric to the bright, shiny object buzzing around their ankles.

Like a school of fish, they all turned toward the Lunar Explorer and began following it as Eddie guided it toward New Ridgelawn. The trick for Becks and Eddie was to stay hidden to avoid drawing attention, while staying close enough for the limited range of the radio-controlled vehicle. It was a bit awkward at first trying to keep a steady pace, but in the span of the first block, Eddie figured out that if he moved the vehicle in quick, short bursts, the pack of zombies would lurch forward in response, and in those moments he and Becks had time to dash to a new position of cover and then prepare for the next move forward.

Things were going smoothly down the second block, until a very decomposed male stumbled out of the shadows. Becks was momentarily startled, as she was also a little too fascinated by the twinkling lights of the Lunar Explorer, but her reflexes kicked in and she swung her hockey stick around in a vicious arc that came up under the zombie's bearded jaw. The decay was so severe that his entire jaw came off, tongue and all, and stuck to the blade of the knife taped to the curved end of the stick; yet still the zombie moved toward them.

Not wanting to blow their cover, and the entire mission, by firing a shot, Becks spun her hockey stick around to the straight end, which had a narrower blade. Holding her breath for a moment to steady her aim, she lunged forward and thrust upward, driving the blade through the zombie's left eye socket, and momentarily getting the sharp tip stuck to the inside of the skull. Raising her right boot, she placed it in the zombie's abdomen and gave him a shove backward, dislodging the knife point. Then with the same boot, she stepped on the bloody jaw and tongue, pressing it firmly to the road so she could pull out the blade.

"You got it?" Eddie whispered, trying to keep his eyes on the pack to make sure no one was noticing Becks' handiwork.

"Got your back, Jack," she replied calmly, scraping the gore off her boot on the edge of the curb.

Despite their perilous situation, she couldn't help but poke the zombie here and there to test its tissue integrity, and found that it was so rotted that skin and muscle were sloughing off in sheets. Clearly, these ZIPs were not managing their host properly. Becks silently wished the parasites were all that inefficient, which would swiftly put an end to mankind's troubles. Unfortunately, the two dozen healthy and vigorous zombies eagerly following the Lunar Explorer down the street illustrated that mankind wouldn't get away that easily.

Refocusing on the mission, Becks continued to follow Eddie and watch his back, as he played Zombie Pied Piper. It was a slow process, probably taking 20 minutes to go a few blocks, but it was necessary if they were going to create a diversion that didn't look like anyone was creating a diversion. Unfortunately, an essential part of achieving that goal necessitated turning off the Lunar Explorer before its lights came into view of the guard in the tower by the gate. And once the radio-controlled vehicle's lights went out and it stopped moving, the pack stopped, too.

Where the job of the high-tech remote ended, however, was where the empty vegetable cans came in. Becks tossed the first one about twenty feet in front of the pack. The sound wasn't as attractive as the Lunar Explorer, and at first the pack didn't react, but then one of the younger zombies must have decided a bouncing tin can was better than nothing, and started moving again. Not knowing why they were following the young zombie, the others dutifully started moving again, as well.

Eddie moved ahead in the shadows and tossed the next can, and then Becks moved ahead of him and tossed the third, and so on, until they were all in sight of the dim lantern light in the watch tower. Eddie made sure with his final toss that it was close enough to the front gate to get the guard's attention, as well as lure the pack dangerously close to the town's line of defense. As if on cue, the guard, who was just a boy of no more than sixteen, switched on his halogen flashlight and was horrified to see the beam reflected in dozens of zombie eyeballs.

Frantically ringing an old school bell which used to be on display at the local historical society, he shouted for reinforcements, which only drew the zombies closer. A few seconds later, he started firing wildly toward the crowd, with one shot going so far afield that it struck a tree just two feet from Eddie's head. Silently signaling to Becks to hightail it out of there, the two ran back a block, and then cut west a few blocks, before heading south again to a cemetery on the edge of the town's perimeter.

After easily running through all the rows of headstones, thanks to the night vision goggles, they came to New Ridgelawn's western line of defense, which was nothing more than rows of parked cars running six-deep and stretching end-to-end across the street to the buildings on either side. The blockade was impenetrable to an uncoordinated zombie, but a piece of cake for a human.

Waiting for the guard in the nearest tower to descend and run toward the main gate to repel the zombie pack, Becks and Eddie began climbing over hoods and bumpers. Becks had a slight dizzy spell jumping from a blue Ford Taurus to a green Chevy Cavalier, but it only lasted a moment and they were quickly on the ground in enemy territory. Now the real work would begin.

For some reason, Becks expected New Ridgelawn to be a clean and tidy little town where picket fences were still painted white to boost morale and remind everyone of the good life, BZA. Instead, stinking piles of garbage lined the streets, rats scurried everywhere, and every lawn was overgrown with shoulder-high weeds. It looked far worse than the abandoned sections of town. An occasional flicker of candlelight behind a grimy window was the only sign that there was any human life in these houses.

Fortunately, unless one was on guard duty, there was a strict curfew after dark, so no one was out and about. To be fair, this was not a rule born of the three brothers' totalitarian desires, but a practical, self-preservation measure. In the early months of the makeshift community, more residents were shot at night by nervous guards mistaking them for zombies, than were actually being killed by zombies.

Still, even though no one was out, Eddie and Becks stuck to the shadows and moved as quietly as possible. Their objective was 238 Maple Street, the home of Gabriela Alvaro and her son, Donnie. Eddie had been good friends with Jose Alvaro, Gabriela's husband, as they had worked together for years. Jose had been one of the first to get infected when he helped break up a fight in the local hardware store. As it turned out, a customer had switched right there in the store and attacked a stock boy. Jose saved the boy, but was bitten in the process.

Eddie and Izzy had done whatever they could to help Gabriela and her son when they took Jose away to a containment facility, but once the real chaos descended and the brothers took control of the town, they lost touch. Eddie had pleaded with Gabriela to come and stay with his family where he could protect them all, but she stubbornly—and foolishly—clung to her home and the belief that life would be good in New Ridgelawn.

As they approached the Alvaro house, it was obvious what a mistake it had been to stay. The little piece of property Jose had been so proud to keep in *Better Homes and Gardens* condition was now a suburban jungle of thick stalks of dead weeds, littered with cans, bottles, and various empty cardboard and plastic food containers. A dead raccoon was splayed out across the walkway leading to the front door. Its advanced state of decomposition showed it had been there for months, but no one had bothered to take a minute to shovel it off into the weeds, choosing instead to just walk over it. A black plastic leaf bag was taped over some broken panes of the living room bay window, where a tree had fallen and shattered the glass. One limb was still sticking into the house, but another plastic bag was taped around it, rather than simply cutting the limb and sealing the window properly.

Eddie signaled for Becks to follow him around to the rear of the house, which was more easily said than done, given the dense overgrowth that surrounded the back porch. The neglected boards of the porch squeaked beneath Eddie's weight, and they momentarily froze and held their breath to see it the sounds drew any attention. When there didn't appear to be any reaction, they slowly continued to the back door.

It was locked, so Eddie tapped gently on the dirty glass. They waited a minute, and then he tapped a little louder, and then as loud as he dared.

Finally, a flashlight beam illuminated an upstairs window. They watched as the bright light descended the stairs and headed for the back door, and they had to flip up their night vision goggles to avoid being blinded.

They could see a frail, nervous, hollow-eyed, 9-year-old who just stood at the door staring, but didn't say a word.

"It's Eddie, Eddie Tasi, your dad's friend. Is that you, Donnie? You've gotten big!"

Moments passed and the tension rose, as Donnie still did not speak, but instead started backing up slowly.

"I thought this kid looked up to you like a father?" Becks whispered sharply.

"He did. At least, he used to, but it's been a while and—"

Eddie didn't get to finish his sentence as the boy began screaming and ran for the front door.

"Kick it in! I'll go to the front," Becks shouted as she raced down the porch stairs three at a time and leapt over the weeds to try to get to the front door before the boy could escape and alert the entire town. But before she turned the corner of the house, the boy was silent. With one powerful kick, Eddie had shattered the back door. A few big strides got him to the screaming boy and then one massive hand clamped down over the boy's mouth to muffle his cries for help.

Becks waited a few moments to see if the neighborhood was stirred by the sounds, but the gunfire and shouting back at the main gate must have masked the boy's screams. When she entered the remains of the back door, Becks saw the flashlight on the floor of the hallway, and Eddie seated next to it, holding Donnie between his arms and legs like a giant anaconda so that he could neither move nor speak. Eddie was trying to reassure him in soothing tones, but it was clear the boy was both terrified and enraged, like a caged animal.

"Please Donnie, relax. Relax, son, we just want to talk to you," Eddie said as he slowly loosened his grip. However, the instant his mouth was clear he began shouting again, and flailing his arms and legs, until the giant anaconda grip was renewed.

"Great! Now what?" Becks whispered angrily, realizing that if Donnie didn't cooperate, Plan A was doomed.

"I don't know! He was such a polite and quiet kid," Eddie replied at a complete loss.

"And where's his mother?" Becks asked, picking up the flashlight and scanning the living room and kitchen, piled high with garbage and dirty laundry. "Let me check upstairs."

The three bedrooms were just as bad, if not worse, as buckets of urine and feces were everywhere. Rodents of all varieties had also added copious amounts of their filth to the mix. There was no sign of Gabriela, or any other supervising adult, and there was every sign that Donnie had been alone for a long time and living like an animal.

"Any luck?" Eddie asked, as Becks descended the stairs, holding her nose.

"You *do not* want to go up there," she replied, trying to repress the gag reflex. "I don't think anyone else lives here. This kid has been on his own for quite a while."

"Oh, poor Donnie," Eddie said softly. "What happened to your mom?"

He started to pull away his hand again in hopes of a reply, but the boy once again just tried to scream. Becks wished she had her medkit with her, with its collection of mood altering and knockout drugs. But as this was a household in the good old U.S. of A.—the pharmaceutical capital of the world—she hoped the medicine cabinets would have what she needed to subdue the boy. Unfortunately, after a quick search, Becks came up empty. Obviously, the Rovers had confiscated all drugs and medical supplies. But there was more than one way to drug a child.

"What did Jose like to drink?" she asked Eddie, who seemingly wasn't tiring of keeping the boy immobilized and silent.

"Oh lord, he liked some sickening blue liqueur he would drink straight. Tasted like bitter oranges. Yuck!" Eddie replied, sticking his tongue out to emphasize his point. "Gabriela didn't like him drinking, but he always kept a couple of bottles in the basement, under his workbench."

Sure enough, Becks found two dust-covered bottles of blue Curaçao liqueur behind boxes of drill bits and nails. Opening a bottle and taking a whiff, it didn't smell too bad, but after taking just a small sip she spit it out. In a mixed drink it may add a pleasant flavor, but straight it was just vile.

"Okay, this isn't going to be easy, but the faster we get him to drink this the better," Becks said, transferring a hefty portion of the 60 proof blue liqueur into a plastic sports bottle with a spout, so she could squeeze the alcohol down the boy's throat.

Eddie pulled back his hand, and just as Donnie started screaming, Becks jammed the bottle in his mouth and squeezed, but the boy had just enough fight in him to spit it all out onto both of them. The second attempt wasn't much better, but they finally devised the best delivery system.

Eddie just spread his fingers wide enough for Becks to stick the spout through, but kept the boy's mouth closed so he couldn't spit it out. It took quite a while, as occasionally some of the blue liquid ran out of Donnie's nose as he fought and gagged on the foul-tasting liqueur, but slowly, enough of the potent alcohol actually reached his stomach that it began to have an effect on the malnourished little boy. Becks couldn't help wondering how many years in prison they would have gotten for this BZA, and she had to keep reminding herself that it was ultimately for a good purpose. To be honest with herself, she also had to admit that if they couldn't do something to keep the boy quiet for a few hours, she would probably have to kill him.

"I think he's pretty looped already," Eddie said as he pushed back the half-empty bottle from the boy's lips as Becks was about to administer another dose.

Releasing his grip, the boy barely moved, except for his head lolling to one side. Eddie gently lifted him and carried him into the living room, where Becks pulled heaps of smelly laundry from an overstuffed recliner so that Eddie could lower the boy into the chair. Kneeling down and stroking the boy's hand, Eddie tried again to get him to speak.

"Hey, Donnie, how are you doing, son? It's me, Little Eddie's dad. Remember how much fun you and Little Eddie had together at the playground, and that day at the beach? It was such a perfect summer day, and you two ate hot dogs and built sand castles."

Eddie kept talking about happy times and after a few minutes a look came over the boy that finally showed some spark of recognition. There was a glimmer of light in his eyes, which suddenly clouded with tears.

"My...mm-mom died last year," the boy said in a tone that almost wrenched their hearts in two.

"I'm so sorry, Donnie," Eddie said softly, gently pushing back the long, tangled strands of hair from the boy's face. "Your mom was a wonderful person."

Giving the boy a moment to linger in his grief, Eddie then asked if he remembered Little Eddie's mother.

"Mama Izzy gave me a chocolate bunny for Easter last Sunday," Donnie said with slurred speech, clearly just a little *too* intoxicated to think clearly.

Eddie shot a furrowed-brow look at Becks, who raised her arms and shrugged her shoulders, as she said, "Sorry. I'm not up on the latest recommendation from the American Medical Association on how much blue Curaçao to pour down a kid's throat!"

"Yes, yes that's right," Eddie continued smiling. "Mama Izzy gave you a chocolate bunny for Easter. Have you seen her since then?"

"She's real sick, like my mom was," the boy replied, drooling ever so slightly.

Becks and Eddie exchanged wide-eyed looks and nods before he continued.

"Yes, Mama Izzy is sick and needs our help. Donnie, where can we find her?"

"The nice lady is helping her," he replied just before he yawned and closed his eyes.

"No, Donnie, please stay awake," Eddie said, gently shaking the boy until his eyes opened again, although Becks could tell they were most likely focusing on double images as the liqueur really started to kick in. "What's the nice lady's name, and where does she live?"

"She's a nice lady. Nice, nice, nice, nice," he replied, and then started giggling at something he found funny.

"Yes, she's a very, very nice lady, and I want to go see her," Eddie said, shaking the boy a bit more forcefully. "Let's go see her, and maybe Mama Izzy will have another chocolate bunny for you."

"No, the brothers would take it. They would see her give it to me and take it away."

"Why would the brothers see?" Becks chimed in. "Does the nice lady live near The Capitol?"

"She has to!" Donnie said with some alarm. "She has to keep everything clean so she lives right across the street…right there across that street so she can clean, clean, clean, clean, clean."

The boy paused only so he could blow spit bubbles, which by his drunken expression were the most fascinating things he ever saw in his life.

"Donnie, how do you know Mama Izzy is with the nice lady who cleans The Capitol?" Eddie asked, trying to make sure they didn't head out on a wild goose chase on the words of a highly inebriated 9-year-old.

The boy had obviously grown weary of the all the questions and wanted to get back to his spit bubbles, so he concentrated all of his limited attention on one final statement.

"When I went to get my rations I saw the nice lady helping Mama Izzy out of the shed and across the street to the nice lady's house. It's yellow. The nice lady has a yellow house, like the color of the ribbon around the neck of the chocolate bunny!"

"I know that place," Eddie said, standing up, his hands instinctively gripping the pistols on each hip. "It was the Saltzer's house. They used to run the dry cleaners next door."

"So what are we waiting for? Let's go!" Becks said, anxious to complete Plan A and get the hell out of this stinking town.

As she turned to go, Eddie grabbed her arm to stop her.

"Wait, we can't leave Donnie!" he said, incredulous. "We can't leave this poor boy alone in this rat nest!"

Becks felt a twinge of guilt that she hadn't experienced any guilt at the thought of leaving an innocent, defenseless child in these circumstances.

"We *can't* take him," Becks replied with that measured and firm tone she had to use when she worked in the emergency room at Nyack Hospital when people were being unreasonable—which was most of the time. "How are we going to rescue your wife with a drunken kid who could start screaming at any second?"

Becks recognized that Eddie Tasi's heart was so big he wanted to save the whole world, but sometimes you had to make terrible choices. The conflicted look in his large, expressive eyes showed that he knew it had to be Donnie or Izzy, not both. Becks felt bad for him, but time was wasting. The gunfire at the front gate had already stopped, so their diversion had lost most of its usefulness. Not to mention they would be going right to the heart of the security zone around The Capitol.

"But, but we can't leave him here all alone. He'll die," Eddie said with tears in his eyes, the scene of his own boy's death obviously playing over and over in his head.

"Look, how about we get your wife, and tell the nice lady to look after Donnie?" Becks offered, somewhat disingenuously. Everyone in town must have known about Donnie being alone, and if the nice lady had wanted to help, she would have by now. Becks suspected the boy's emotional problems made him too much of a handful for people who were hanging by a thread to their own sanity.

"Yeah..." Eddie said thoughtfully. "Yeah, that could work. And once we get Izzy out of here and she bets better, I can come back for Donnie."

Becks just smiled and agreed. It was clear that Donnie wasn't the only one who didn't have a grasp on reality.

Eddie shook the mouse droppings out of a couple of blankets and covered Donnie, who was already fast asleep in the chair. He also placed a bottle of water and a couple of granola bars in the boy's lap. He suggested cleaning up the place a little, and putting some boards over the broken windows, but Becks would have none of it.

"We need to go rescue your wife. *She needs you, now*," Becks emphasized, trying to get Eddie's head back in the game.

"Yeah, okay, okay," he replied, putting a fatherly hand on the boy's shoulder, and leaning down to whisper in his ear. "We will be back for you, Donnie. Izzy and I will take care of you like you are our own son."

Eddie at least insisted on wedging the splintered pieces of the back door together enough to keep out the cold, and then they left through the front door. As bad as all the rotting garbage in the street smelled, it was like a breath of fresh air after the fetid stench inside the house. Becks forgot about the raccoon on the walkway, which made an unpleasant crunching sound beneath her boot as they made their way to the street. Lowering their night vision goggles over their eyes, they began their roundabout journey to the yellow house where the nice lady lived.

As the house was just across the street from The Capitol, where torches burned all night and four guards were posted at all times, Eddie decided to give that location a wide berth and approach the house from the street behind it. As they drew closer, they could clearly hear the commotion at the front gate, which was just a block and a half from The

Capitol. They were already loading bodies on a truck, and firing the occasional head shot to make sure the undead stayed dead this time.

They had to scramble once to hide beneath a pile of leaves and brush as a patrol car took to the streets to search for any stragglers or breaches in their defense line, but other than for that tense moment, the coast was clear. A small, eight-unit apartment building was on the property behind the yellow house, and as they crept past several bedroom windows on the ground floor, they couldn't help but peek inside. One of the small bedrooms had at least six people huddled together on the floor in sleeping bags, with a single, pale candle for lighting. They weren't sure what was going on in there—were these people all forced to share a single room, or did they feel there was safety in numbers? The next bedroom they passed had no light, but from the distinctive sounds of the man and woman inside, they had no doubt as to exactly what was going on in there!

Momentarily distracted by the noisy encounter, Eddie and Becks refocused and looked for a way to quietly and easily get over the tall chain link fence at the back of the property. There were no holes in the fence, so Eddie grabbed one of the support posts and slowly but surely bent it down almost to the ground. Becks just shook her head and smiled as she accepted Eddie's hand to assist her climbing over the now prone section of fence.

Surprisingly, the nice lady's backyard was neat and trimmed. An Adirondack chair sat next to a semi-circular flower bed and birdbath, and on a warm, summer day it must have been a serene haven from the crazy post-apocalyptic chaos of the world. Frost had long ago killed all the flowers, but Eddie stooped over to pick a few dried marigolds.

"What the hell are you doing?" Becks whispered, not believing her own eyes.

"Izzy loves marigolds," he said as casually as if he was picking out a bouquet at a flower shop. "She will like these."

Becks had no reply as they spilt up to look in the two windows at the back of the house. Eddie saw that the kitchen was dark, but Becks could see through the dining room to the living room, where a few candles illuminated a figure on a couch. She couldn't see anyone else, but a brief movement of a shadow suggested there was another person in that living room.

The original plan was to break in through a door or window, find Izzy and take her, or, if they encountered the nice lady, explain who they were and hope she wouldn't start screaming. The latter plan may have worked out on Maple Street, but across the street from The Capitol, where several guards had gathered on the sidewalk to have a smoke, even the briefest scream would attract unwanted attention. Instead, Becks came up with Plan A-2.

Waiting for the guards to finish their cigarettes and get back to their posts, Becks then cautiously went around to the front of the house—leaving her goggles, hockey stick, and leather jacket covered in silverware with Eddie. She knocked on the door and attempted to look as casual as possible. She also tried not to notice the front curtain being pulled back so whoever was inside could get a good look at her. The curtain fell back into place, and the shuffling of ill-fitting slippers followed, leading up to the door. Several locks were clicked, and the door opened a crack.

"What do you want?" a female voice said in the shadows.

"Hi, we haven't met yet. I'm Samantha, and I'm kind of new here," Becks began in as friendly and non-threatening a manner as she could muster. "I was just on patrol with some of the guys and they mentioned you're taking care of a woman who is really sick. I used to be a nurse's aide—ages ago—but I thought I would use my break to see if I could help in any way."

"Oh, uh…yeah, I guess so. I'm Jennifer. And I guess it's okay for you to at least take a look at her. But I couldn't let you do anything without the consent of the three—I mean two, brothers."

"Of course not! Just want to see if I can help," Becks said, not hesitating to literally get her foot in the door.

When she stepped inside, she saw a 40-something woman who probably looked at least ten years older than she was. She had short, blond hair, rather thin and limp, but clean. Stress and poor nutrition had engraved deep, dark circles under her eyes, and she walked with a slight Quasimodo hunch and sway. It had possibly been the result of an injury, but Beck's suspected some sort of congenital malformation. In the dim light, she also detected some bruising on the woman's left cheek. Knowing what she did about the brothers' proclivity for smacking people around, she suspected the marks were the penalty for some minor transgression.

109

"Here, this way," the woman said timidly, avoiding eye contact. "Isabella is in here. I couldn't get her upstairs, she was too weak. I'm trying to keep her warm, but I don't have much kerosene left for the heater."

Even as Becks approached the woman on the couch, she could plainly hear the rasping and rattling of lungs stricken with pneumonia. Placing a hand on Isabella's forehead, which was wet with sweat, Becks estimated that her fever was about 104 degrees. She was dehydrated, her pulse was rapid, and her lips were slightly blue from lack of oxygen. If the pneumonia was bacterial, and Becks had immediate access to potent antibiotics, IV fluids, and an oxygen tank, she might have some chance of saving her. As it was, Isabella Tasi had a day, maybe less, before she would be joining Little Eddie.

"Jennifer, listen to me very carefully. Isabella is in critical condition. Do you have any kind of medical facilities here? Any supplies, or nearby hospitals or physicians' offices where I could get supplies? Any erythromycin, doxycycline, vancomycin, *anything*?" Becks asked, dropping the phony nurse act and sounding very much like a doctor on a mission.

"Uh, we, uh, have a clinic, but you need special permission from the brothers for any medications. There's no doctor in town, but Sally, the girl who used to work at the drugstore after school, might be able to help. She's the closest thing we have to a doctor," Jennifer replied, getting a bit frazzled. "But you will have to ask the brothers in the morning."

"I'm afraid we can't wait that long," Becks said as she walked toward the kitchen.

"Wait, where are you going? What's going on?" Jennifer asked, as she shuffled after Becks in her oversized, fuzzy slippers.

Before Jennifer could reach her, Becks had unlocked the back door, and Eddie quickly came inside. Jennifer looked as if she about to scream, or faint, but a sudden look of recognition spread over her face.

"You're Isabella's husband!" Jennifer gasped, as if a spirit from the grave had just materialized next to her stove. "But, but, you're supposed to be dead!"

"Eddie, this is Jennifer," Becks said quickly, hoping the woman's shock wouldn't turn to screaming. "She's the nice lady who is caring for your wife."

Eddie extended one of his massive hands and Jennifer blinked several times and accepted the friendly handshake, although it was clear she was in sensory overload and didn't know what to do. Harboring an enemy of the state would get her more than a slap across the face, but she couldn't turn away a man who was willing to risk his life to rescue his wife, either.

"Where's Izzy?" Eddie asked, already hurrying down the hallway.

Becks had wanted to tell him the situation and prepare him for the worst, but she might as well have tried talking to a passing freight train.

Eddie gently cradled Izzy in his arms, kissed her hair, placed the dried marigolds in her hand, and spoke words of love and comfort. However, when there was no response, his eyes became wild with fear and he turned to Becks.

"What's wrong? What have they done to her? She'll be okay, won't she? You're a doctor, *do something!*"

Jennifer also turned to look at Becks as it finally dawned on her that this was the infamous doctor who she had heard had done so many terrible things. It was obvious that the brothers had been lying, but harboring two enemies of the state would mean banishment, or worse.

"You're supposed to be dead, too!" Jennifer exclaimed, as her voice reached another octave higher. "Oh, what am I going to do!"

Becks ignored the nearly hysterical woman and spoke plainly and directly to Eddie.

"It's pneumonia and it's bad. Very bad. Even if I could get her to a hospital right away, there would be only a slim chance of saving her. I'm sorry, but with no medical supplies I can't do anything."

The grief and rage that played across Eddie's features was both heartbreaking and frightening. At that moment he became a ticking time bomb, and the only question was when he would go off.

"Eddie! Eddie, listen to me," Becks pleaded with the big man as she grabbed him by the shoulders. "I know what you're going through, but don't do anything stupid. Let's be smart about this. Let's talk about this."

"Done talking. Time to start shooting. This is all the brothers' fault. They've taken everything from me. They have to die."

Despite Becks' tight grip on the shoulders of his jacket, Eddie only needed one hand to push her away. She stumbled backward over a foot stool and fell hard to the floor, and the loud sound brought Isabella out of her stupor.

"Ed… Eddie…baby, is…that you?" Isabella whispered, barely able to say two words without having to struggle to take a breath.

Eddie's rage suddenly melted as he rushed to his wife's side and took her hand. Becks picked herself up from the floor, rubbed her sore hip, and moved close enough to hear what the dying woman was saying.

"It's me, Izzy! It's Eddie! I came for you, baby. I'm going to take you home and you're going to get all better," he said, wiping away tears that were now flowing freely.

"Oh…Eddie…we never…lied to…one…another before. Don't…lie to me…now…sweetie."

A violent coughing spell ensued that looked as though it would tear the fragile woman apart.

"Can't you do *something*!?" Eddie shouted, grabbing Becks' arm so tightly it hurt.

"I'm so sorry. There's nothing I can do," Becks replied, wincing from the pain of the desperate grip, but not backing away from it.

Fortunately, he let her arm go to hold both of his wife's hands. When her coughing finally subsided, Isabella was so weak she only had enough strength for a few more words.

"Love…you always…baby. Bury…me…with…Little Eddie."

With that her eyes rolled back and closed, and her breaths became slow and shallow. Becks felt her pulse and put an ear to her chest. Then she looked Eddie right in the eyes and just shook her head twice. It would be any time now.

Chapter 10

For as many times as Becks watched someone die, it never got any easier—unless it was someone she was *trying* to kill, of course.

Isabella Tasi inexorably sank deeper and deeper into that black void that for her, would finally bring peace after years of torment. For Eddie, it would plunge him, heart and soul, into complete darkness. He spent every minute by her side, alternately speaking words of love and then falling silent, at a total loss for words. Becks and Jennifer sat at a respectful distance, not saying a word, and occasionally dozing off for a few minutes at a time.

It was during one of these naps a few hours before dawn that Eddie shook Becks awake. She instinctively reached for her pistol, but one of Eddie's big hands clamped down, preventing her from pulling it from her holster. He gave her a moment to recover her senses.

"She's gone. It's over," he said from a million miles away. "She looked so peaceful at the end. I know Little Eddie was there to meet her."

Jennifer woke up to hear the news, and both women expressed their heartfelt condolences.

"Jennifer, please promise me that if I don't return, you will honor my wife's dying wish and have her buried in the park with our son. Do you know where that is, Jennifer?"

"Uh, yes, I know the spot. I, uh, yes, I promise," Jennifer replied, more fearful at that moment of Eddie's complete lack of outward emotion than any of the brothers' frequent tantrums. His face was like the deceptively cool, bland exterior of a nuclear weapon.

Becks knew the actions of the next few hours were inevitable, so she didn't bother arguing. But as her life would also be on the line, she would do her damnedest to not go about it half-cocked and rage-driven.

"No one needs to know we were ever here, Jennifer, so don't worry. And if things go well and you want to leave with us, then that's okay with me," Becks added, actually getting the woman to make eye contact for a moment and smile. She then addressed Eddie. "We go in quietly. No shooting unless we have to. We kill the two brothers and get out. We take Jennifer and Donnie, and we run."

Eddie remained silent, but Jennifer spoke up.

"It's very nice of you to offer, but I just couldn't go with you," she said, eyes downcast. "I'm not treated well here, I think you know that, but I just don't have the courage to go *out there* with all those horrible creatures. I'm a coward, and I'm not ashamed to say it."

Becks often forgot that not everyone had the intestinal fortitude to look a zombie in the eye and then drive a knife through it. To people like Jennifer, the tyranny of New Ridgelawn was heaven compared to the alternative of fending for yourself and fighting for your life. The New Hampshire motto of "Live free or die," was just not everyone's cup of tea. Becks wasn't about to waste her breath or her time trying to convince Jennifer of the benefits of risking her life for freedom, because it was either a desire you had, or you didn't.

113

"What's the best way in and out of The Capitol? Where do the brothers sleep?" Eddie asked in a steely tone that indicated he wanted all the information, and he wanted it now. Or else.

Jennifer's voice trembled as she divulged the necessary information about the doors, room layout, and placement of guards. To her way of thinking, this was a no-win situation. If the plan failed and the brothers discovered her role in the plot, she would be fed to the zombies.

If the plan succeeded and the brothers were killed, the community might fall apart and she would be on or own, or someone else even more despotic and deranged might take charge. The possibility that someone benevolent might form a true, democratic society, actually making life better, never entered her mind. She was someone born into disappointment and never failed to sink below the level of any challenge.

At least Jennifer wasn't so cowardly that she would actually turn in Becks and Eddie to score some major brownie points with the brothers. Even she had her limits. She also didn't want to see any of the good people in town get hurt, so she found the courage to speak up and ask that they limit their killing to the brothers and their personal guards, who were truly the only genuinely cruel and ruthless people in town. But then she went too far with her next suggestion.

"You know, the brothers don't know you're alive, so you could just leave now and everything would be okay."

This ruptured the first crack in Eddie's stone-faced exterior, but before he went ballistic on the woman, Becks took her by the arm and hurried her to the kitchen. She explained all about Little Eddie's murder, Isabella's kidnapping, and the raid on Eddie's house. Becks even told her about Angie's death, although she left out the part about shooting Reggie. Jennifer held a hand over her heart as Becks spoke, and said, "Oh my," several times, but couldn't think of anything else to say. When they went back into the living room, Jennifer apologized to Eddie and "quite agreed the brothers should be punished."

Jennifer then got the cleanest and least tattered sheet she had to place over Isabella's body, and Eddie placed the dried marigolds on top of the sheet. He whispered a few words, stood up, and blew a kiss toward the body of his wife. Then he began a systematic check of all the weapons he was carrying.

"I'm going to be the one to actually kill those two bastards," Eddie stated in an end-of-discussion manner.

"I have no problem with that," Becks said as she conducted her own weapons check. "Just so long as it's quiet and fast."

They both thanked Jennifer before slipping out the back door. Adjusting their night vision goggles, the two hopeful assassins began retracing their path through the yard and onto the apartment house property. As they passed the bedroom window where the amorous couple had been making such a racket, the same loud moans and groans could plainly be heard. They were either still at it, or at it again—either way, it was impressive.

The town was still and quiet, except for the constant rustling of garbage from all the rats. Even though the brothers had initiated an aggressive rat trapping campaign—which coincidentally saw a simultaneous increase in the availability of meat stew rations—the rodent population continued to grow in leaps and bounds. Rat bites were now more frequent that zombie bites, and while not nearly as fatal, they did spread their share of disease in the community.

Cleaning up all the garbage should have been the obvious first step in eliminating the infected rodent problem, and god knows what other diseases that were lurking in the wide variety of filth mixed with human waste that lined the streets. But other than the well-fed brothers and their personal guards, the rest of the population of New Ridgelawn appeared to be seriously malnourished, depressed, and apathetic. They were alive, but they certainly weren't living. Other than going on patrol or carrying out their work assignments, their days consisted of nothing more than eating, sleeping, and huddling in their cold, dirty homes in a sort of zombie-like state. And apart from that "marathon couple" at the apartment building, no one had any desire or energy for anything else.

Becks thought of the contrast between this town and Cam's compound up in Saugerties, NY. Cam knew the value of keeping everyone engaged physically, mentally, and emotionally. They had all certainly faced many dark days, but through his leadership, the people all managed to rise back up and persevere. Becks would have given anything at that moment to be back at the compound with Cam, and she couldn't help the unpleasant twinge of wondering if she would ever see him again. Presently, however, she did not have the luxury of entertaining any

115

memories of the past or hopes for the future. She had to focus solely on the mission goals—kill and escape.

One at a time, they raced across the intersection that was just two houses away from The Capitol. No one seemed to notice their movement, so they continued to creep behind trees, piles of trash, and long-dormant cars caked in thick layers of dirt and leaves. Their planned route was to once again approach from the rear. There were a few small houses on the street behind The Capitol, and these places were occupied by members of the personal guard and were in much better condition. Obviously, it was someone's job to keep the ruling class' yards and homes in good order.

As they were about to go between two of the houses, Eddie spotted a large doghouse in the backyard to their right.

I wonder, he thought, but before he could voice his concern a huge Doberman launched out of the doghouse to the end of his 8-foot chain like a tethered rocket. And his ferocious barking seemed just as loud as a rocket launch. Eddie withdrew his machete and started running toward the dog, but Becks was two steps ahead of him.

She was reaching for something else—her "emergency" chocolate bar she always kept with her for those days when she just had to have a bite. This particular candy had been part of the old Halloween stash of Dylan and his brothers in the first house she had broken into after the accident. She had eaten all the other stale mini Snickers and Mounds, and this was her last one—partially crushed and half-melted Twix bars that nonetheless would have made her feel like she had died and gone to heaven. But now it was needed to keep her from literally dying.

Rushing toward an angry Doberman wasn't the safest thing, but Becks had a way with agitated dogs—much more so than people—and she prayed her "dog whisperer" skills would not fail her now. The dog was clearly surprised that his fierce barking had not made the people run away, and had instead caused them to run *toward* him, and he actually fell silent for a moment and stepped back as Becks raced over to him and slid down onto her knees, while thrusting the candy bar package under his nose.

"Who's a good boy? Oh, what a sweetie pie you are," Becks cooed softly as she dared to rub the mighty watch dog behind his ear, while keeping the candy bar under his nose. Eddie could have silenced the dog with one swift blow, but Becks was such a sucker for animals, especially dogs—so much so, she was willing to risk her neck, and even sacrifice her last chocolate bar.

The brute of an animal immediately started drooling and his demeanor instantly transformed to one of I'm-a-good-boy-who-deserves-a-treat, as the little stump of his tail wagged wildly. Eddie stopped short, machete raised, and just watched in wonder as Becks unwrapped the Twix bars and actually got the dog to sit and give her his paw before she fed him his treat. She then got several appreciative licks in the face, before she unfastened his collar and let him go running happily off into the night to chase rats.

However, before they could move on, they heard other animal sounds from the oversized doghouse. This was more pathetic than threatening, and the whimpering sounded oddly familiar. Becks leaned over to look, and there were Buttons and Smidgey, huddled together and trembling in a back corner of the doghouse. Their hair was dirty and matted, and the brightly-colored bows were gone, but at least they were still alive, and had made a big, powerful friend.

It took a little coaxing, but Becks was able to get the frightened animals to come out. It was a moment or two before they recognized her, but when they did it was like a little explosion of nervous energy which resulted in frantic licking of Becks' face. Twice, she had to wipe dog licks off her night vision goggles.

"Do you have any more energy bars?" Becks whispered to Eddie.

"You want me to waste them on these dogs?" he replied, incredulous.

"Just think of it as bribery to buy their silence."

Eddie reluctantly pulled another energy bar from his pack, and broke it in half. Smidgey and Buttons practically took off his fingers grabbing their shares, and then ran back into the doghouse with their feast.

Fortunately, the commotion with the dogs didn't rouse anyone from their beds, so Becks and Eddie continued their approach to the back of The Capitol, where they trusted no more noisy surprises awaited them. There was one guard sitting on a stool by the back door. The barking had momentarily awakened him, but after a few minutes he dozed off again.

"You want to give him a box of candy and rub his ears, or can I take care of him?" Eddie whispered.

Becks looked at the greasy-haired, middle-aged man whose tattooed belly was hanging out from under his jacket and spilling over the top of his jeans, and she quickly gave Eddie the go ahead to do his thing. That thing happened to be silently creeping up on the man and cleaving his skull in two, right down to his neck. Eddie then calmly wiped off the blade of his machete on the man's pants. Becks' only thought as she watched this was that she wished she possessed that kind of strength.

The door was unlocked, but it creaked and groaned just a bit as it opened. They entered the former kitchen of the house, which had been turned into an office for the funeral home. It was now used as a storage room for boxes of food and supplies—only a small fraction of which would ever be distributed to the community. Becks caught sight of a cardboard box labeled M&Ms, but she resisted temptation and followed Eddie to a back staircase that Jennifer said led up to a hallway between the brothers' bedrooms.

Mr. Reggie's had been the first bedroom on the right, with the other two brothers having their bedrooms on the left. What Jennifer forgot to tell them was that the Big Gorilla—inappropriately named Ned, of all things—had moved from his sleeping quarters in the embalming room in the basement into Reggie's room to be closer to the other brothers in case of an emergency. But if all went according to plan, that oversight wouldn't matter.

They paused in front of the first door on the left, and Becks pressed her ear against the cool, white, glossy paint. Someone inside was snoring, and she gave Eddie the thumbs up. Turning the doorknob ever so slowly, there was a sharp *click*, but the snoring didn't change its rhythm. Becks stayed by the door as lookout while Eddie silently tiptoed across the thickly carpeted floor toward the bed. As he approached, he raised his machete and thought, *This one is for you, Little Eddie. And the next one will be for Izzy.*

Beck expected the distinctive *crunch-slurp* sound of metal slashing through bone and brain, but seconds ticked by. Glancing in the room, she saw Eddie standing beside the bed, machete at the ready, but not moving. And even with his eyes covered by the goggles, Becks could see his expression was one of that volcano about to erupt.

Oh, no, no, please, NO! Becks thought as she wasn't sure what she should do, but that decision was instantly taken out of her hands.

"You SICK SON OF A BITCH!" Eddie roared, as if he wanted all of northern New Jersey to hear him.

Plans A, B, and C went right out the window when Eddie discovered that this brother was not alone in bed. There was also a girl—maybe 10 years old. She could have been a classmate of Little Eddie, and now was a plaything for this vile man. That just broke everything loose inside of Eddie, who had lost his son just a few months earlier because of the brothers, and his wife, less than an hour ago.

Becks pulled out both pistols and faced down the hall to the second bedroom on the left, expecting the other brother to come out of his room. What she didn't expect was Ned, the Big Gorilla, to come hurtling out of the door behind her, like a freight train hitting a box of crystal glasses. Both guns flew out of her hands, and as she hit the floor, with the beast on top of her, all the wind was knocked out of her lungs. The incredible impact actually made her ears ring, and her head imploded with pain and dizziness. She didn't quite black out, but she was so dazed and out of it she couldn't function past a few involuntary twitches.

By the time Ned got up off of Becks, rushed into the first brother's bedroom, and switched on the light, he saw a sight that shocked even him. With his left hand, Eddie had the brother by his fat, sweaty neck, pressed against the wall about three feet above the floor. With his right hand—the hand that gripped the machete—he was just completing a sternum-to-pelvis gutting, which resulted in a rush of sliced intestines and organs spilling onto the floor in a sickening *plop, plop.*

The young girl shrieked and then fainted. Eddie let the brother drop to the floor, onto the pile of his own guts, where he made a couple of gurgling sounds until his breathing stopped forever. Whether savoring his kill, or stunned by his own brutality, Eddie paused long enough to give Ned the opportunity to plow into him from behind. Eddie was a big man, but Ned had several inches in height and at least 60 pounds more weight, and the massive collision brought both men down hard onto the bloody and gooey remains of the brother.

Eddie's right arm bent at an awkward angle, thrusting the tip of the machete into his left thigh. It barely missed severing an artery, which quickly would have been fatal, but it still bled profusely as the two giants grappled with one another. Furniture splintered, glass shattered, and iron fists connected with stone jaws as this clash of the titans seemingly threatened to turn the entire house to rubble. Despite being the smaller man—in relative terms, of course—Eddie was the better fighter, and was slowly but surely pummeling the bigger man into submission.

Becks could only surmise what was going on, and her eyes flickered open just long enough to see a pair of chubby bare feet, with dirty, yellowed toenails that desperately needed clipping, come rushing out of the second bedroom on the left, hesitate, and then none-too-gently step over her prone body. Then a gunshot rang out, which made her ears and head pound even more, and her eyes closed once again as she sank back into a twilight state.

The bullet from the only remaining brother's gun had passed just inches from Ned's and Eddie's heads. Ned dropped to the floor, and before the brother could pull the trigger again on his now unobstructed target, Eddie launched himself Superman-style toward the lace curtain-covered window, his bulk easily smashing the strips of wood that held the six, large panes of glass. The roof of the side porch broke his fall and held his plummeting weight, and as the brother stuck his pistol out the window and started emptying the clip, Eddie rolled off the roof and dropped to the ground, quickly disappearing into the darkness.

Guards came running from every direction, and were dumbfounded and appalled when they came upon the barely conscious stranger in the hallway, the battered and bloodied Ned whimpering on the floor nursing his wounds, an unconscious pre-adolescent girl in the bed, and one brother crying hysterically over the gutted corpse of the other brother.

Minutes passed before the sobbing brother was able to blurt out, "Eddie Tasi did this! Find him and kill him! Kill him, kill, him, kill him!"

"Uh, what…what about the girl…and that woman in the hall?" one of the guards sheepishly asked, having no clue about what had transpired.

"Never mind the girl, and bring that woman to my office!" the brother shouted, and then walked over to Ned and gave him a swift kick. "Get up, you big baby! We need answers."

The glass of cold water thrown in Becks' face didn't quite bring her back to full consciousness, but the potent ampule of smelling salts—something funeral homes had in abundance—finally did. She was sitting in a chair, surprisingly not tied up, and as the scene came into focus she saw the Big Gorilla, both eyes blackened, nose broken, and two or three teeth knocked out, and one of the brothers, clad just in his boxer shorts and covered from bald head to ugly toes in his brother's blood. The brother

120

was obviously half out of his mind with grief and rage, and the gun pointed at Becks' head shook like a leaf in his trembling hand.

"Who are you?" the brother demanded. "Are you that Army doctor?"

Becks weighed her options—which were precious few—but before she could respond, the latest blow to her nervous system caused a few involuntary twitches in her eye, face, and hands. Both the brother and Ned audibly gasped and took a step backward. At that moment, Becks recalled something Jennifer had told her—the brothers and Ned were deathly afraid of the zombie infection, to the point where she not only had to clean the entire house every day, she had to *disinfect* it with bleach, top to bottom.

A plan, or at least the start of a plan, crystallized in Becks' abused brain and she actually chose not to speak. Instead, she spit. Twice.

Dr. Rebecca Truesdale gathered up all the saliva she could muster and spit half of it on the brother, and the other half on Ned. She then peeled off her leather jacket, pushed back her sleeves, and displayed her multiple bite scars, which still clearly showed the unmistakable outlines of human teeth.

"I was infected the day I got here!" she said, somehow finding the strength to stand and take a step forward, which prompted the two terrified men to take another step back. She then faked some more twitching before she continued. "I'm in the terminal stages, and I could switch any moment. And yes, I am Dr. Rebecca Truesdale, so I can tell you in no uncertain terms that my saliva, and my very breath, contain millions of ZIP eggs that are now finding their way into your sinuses, that scrape on your face, your mouth, your eyes, that cut on your foot."

"Stay back, or...or I'll shoot!" the brother said with a quivering voice, much too frightened to be convincing.

"And risk spraying my infected blood with all those mature parasites all over you? I don't think so. Now *you* listen to *me!* I can cure you, but we have to get to my labs at the Picatinny Arsenal or West Point. And the sooner the better. Your choice. Do you want to kill your only chance at survival, or are we going to work together and save ourselves?"

Of course, the Eradazole which Becks had been carrying with her the day of the accident, even though it had been compromised, was still viable enough to prevent infection from her zombie bite wounds. But between the bite scars, a few more well-timed twitches, and the men's extreme paranoia, she was banking on her bluff at least keeping her from being shot immediately, and possibly buying her some time.

"Parasites!" Ned yelled in an unnaturally high-pitched voice for a man his size. "What are we going to do?"

"Bleach!" the brother screamed. "Where's the fucking bleach?"

Both men exited the room in a panic, but did not neglect to lock the door behind them. Becks ran to the one window, but unfortunately found security bars across it that wouldn't budge. As she tossed the contents of the cabinets and desk drawers looking for some kind of weapon, she heard the door being unlocked again.

So much for buying time, she thought.

To her astonishment, however, it was Eddie who limped in.

"I thought you were dead!' Becks whispered, heading for the door.

"Not completely," Eddie replied, managing a grin on his bruised and bloodied face. "Come on, let's go down to the basement. There are too many guards outside. Oh, and here, you may need these."

Eddie handed Becks a box containing her pistols, knives, and night vision goggles, which he had liberated from the hands of a guard whose neck he had just snapped in two. Becks wasn't thrilled with the idea of remaining in the house, but it was probably the last place they would think of looking for them. Eddie had thought the same thing, which was why the second he hit the ground he ran right back into the house and down into the basement.

He had overheard the brother yelling about bleach and the infected woman in his office, heard the front door slam, and then watched through a basement window as the brother and Ned stood on the front lawn and poured bottles of bleach on themselves, and gargled with copious quantities of mouthwash—even pouring it in their noses until they choked. He assumed Becks was still alive and had somehow put the fear of god— or at least zombies—into them.

With everyone, save a single guard, outside running around looking for him, Eddie simply walked upstairs, dispatched the guard, and liberated Becks. They had bought themselves some time, but whether it would be enough time to get away remained to be seen.

"Your leg is bleeding way too much," Becks said, using her flashlight to examine the deep gash. "I need to stitch you up or you're going to be too weak to do anything."

"Yeah, that would be nice, but I think I left my sewing kit in my other pants," Eddie replied sarcastically, and then winced as Becks poked and prodded the gaping machete wound.

"Are you kidding me?" Becks said, spreading her arms wide. "This is the embalming room of a funeral home! Do you have any idea of the variety of needles and miles of sutures funeral homes use every year to prepare bodies?"

"No, I don't have any idea," he said, not comfortable with the glint in Becks' eyes or her knowledge of embalming. "How come you know that? Just what kind of a doctor are you?"

"The kind who had so much tuition debt that she had to take a part time job in a funeral home one summer."

Becks rose to her feet—a little too fast—and Eddie had to grab her arm to steady her. She explained that she was dizzy due to being tackled by the Big Gorilla, on top of her two previous head injuries.

"Yeah, about that…" Eddie began awkwardly, "I'm sorry I lost it and almost got us killed."

"Hey, you just lost your wife. I never should have agreed to doing this tonight in the state you were in. We could have just left like Jennifer said, and come back another time if you still wanted to."

Becks was trying to be gracious under the circumstances, when she really wanted to slug him for going postal, but she had no idea what had really flipped Eddie's switch until he explained.

"Oh god, a little girl?" Becks said, feeling sick to her stomach. "I probably would have lost it, too."

They discussed possible courses of action while Becks rummaged around, assembling a nice collection of all manner of scary-looking needles, a box of sutures, and some isopropyl alcohol. Her vision was a little blurry, and her hands weren't exactly steady, but she had to close the wound and stop the bleeding, so she had no choice. She handed Eddie a towel and told him to roll it up and bite down on it.

"This is going to hurt like a mother," she warned a moment before she poured some alcohol into the jagged slice in his thigh.

Eddie's body tensed like a coiled spring, but amazingly he didn't cry out. He even managed to hold the flashlight steady, despite her having to thrust the long, curved needle in pretty deeply several times. Since he was doing so well, she went right ahead and stitched up a gash on his cheek from the glass of the window he went through, and a couple of cuts on his hands he sustained in the fight with Ned. Becks' eyes had streamed like faucets when she had to suture her own scalp, but Eddie remained stoic and his eyes stayed dry.

"You are a better man than I am, Eddie Tasi," Becks declared, as she tied off the last knot and began applying some makeshift bandages.

"Oh, I don't know," he said thoughtfully, with a smile. "Pound for pound, you may be more of an ass-kicking machine. And you can sew better than most girls, too."

He knew that last crack would get a rise out of her, but they didn't have time to continue the banter as shots suddenly rang out very close to the house. They both hit the floor and reached for their pistols.

"Stop shooting, asshole!" a voice cried out, not far from the house. "It's us, stupid!"

Profuse apologies followed, as the guards who had been shooting at other guards ceased their friendly fire. Then there was an even bigger commotion inside the house, when it was discovered that a guard had been killed and Becks was gone, too.

As neither Becks nor Eddie was in fighting or running shape, and it was starting to get light, they decided to hunker down in a dark storage room in the basement, and pray that the brother didn't order a complete house search. A tense hour later, when they heard some of the ATVs and motorcycles heading toward the front gate, they were more relaxed. Obviously, the remaining brother assumed the fugitives were running for their lives.

It was hard to hear what was going on in the house from behind all the boxes in the store room, but they did hear someone shouting orders to Jennifer to "double-bleach everything." They also heard two men being ordered to go out to one of the storage sheds to get a coffin for the dead brother. Becks didn't need any light to know that Eddie was steaming over the thought that the evil, perverted brother would get a decent burial, while his angelic wife would be thrown in a shallow hole covered only in a tattered bed sheet. Still, he took some comfort in knowing *he* had put that brother in his grave.

Fatigue soon got the best of both of them, and while they each tried to keep watch while the other slept, they were both soon fast asleep. It was late afternoon before they were awakened by the sound of footsteps coming down the basement stairs. It was remarkable how quickly two people curled up on the floor in a deep sleep could be standing with guns and machete drawn. They waited breathlessly, hoping the person would go only as far as the embalming room, but no such luck. The footsteps came right into the storage room, and the beam of a flashlight started weaving back and forth across the stacks of boxes.

Becks and Eddie crouched down, which was no easy thing for a woman with a head injury and a man with stitches in his thigh, but they held their position, ready to spring, and waited to see if they would be discovered. Becks had made Eddie swear on his wife and child that he would stick to the stealth approach from now on, no matter what.

Fortunately, the person seemed to be searching for something other than them, and as he or she was reaching for something on the other side of the storage room, he or she inadvertently knocked several boxes to the floor.

"Oh my! Well, oh my heavens!" came the stern oaths from the cleaning woman who had been looking for more bleach.

Becks considered remaining hidden, but they needed information. She motioned for Eddie to stay down, as she stood up.

"Jennifer?" Becks whispered softly.

"Oh my!" the startled woman gasped, bringing both hands to her chest. "Who is it? Who's there?"

"It's me, Becks," she replied, stepping out from behind the boxes with her hands raised, but turning her head as the flashlight beam caught her squarely in the eyes.

"Oh good gracious! What are you doing down here?" Jennifer said as she swayed back and forth as if about to faint. "The entire town is out looking for you two. Where's Eddie?"

"He was badly wounded and jumped out the window," Becks replied smoothly, not exactly lying, but not telling the whole truth, either. "They took me prisoner and were going to kill me, but I escaped and hid down here. Jennifer, could you please let me know what's happening?"

The timid woman hesitated, but she knew she was already in too deep for it to get any worse for her.

"Well, of course I heard all that shooting last night. Then this morning they had me start cleaning and disinfecting the house again—and oh, the blood in the brother's room! Oh my, it was a horrible scene. I didn't see the body, but it must have been a terrible fight.

"And I've never seen Mr. Riley in such an awful state, and not just because Eddie killed his brother. He keeps rambling on about being infected, and having to 'find that Army doctor'…uh, b-word, he said, to save him. He has everyone out searching the streets in all directions. You're to be brought back alive, but Eddie is to be shot on sight."

Becks just knew that Eddie was busting to know one other thing, so before he revealed himself, she posed the question.

"What about Isabella's body?"

"Oh, yes, the poor dear. I was able to get some neighbors to bury her where Eddie asked me to. They took care of it first thing this morning, God rest her soul."

"Thank you so much for that, and for all you've done," Becks said, placing a hand on the woman's trembling shoulder. "And don't worry, no matter what happens to me, no one will ever know you had any contact with us."

"I should get back upstairs with the bleach now," Jennifer said, desperate to just get back to her work and to stay out of trouble.

"Of course, of course, but before you go, is there anything else you can tell me that might help me escape? The sooner I'm gone, the sooner you can stop worrying."

"Well, they are having the wake for Mr. Riley tomorrow morning at 10 o'clock at the community center," she said, now genuinely trying to be helpful if it meant getting rid of Becks. "Everyone is expected to go, at some point. And the burial will be tomorrow afternoon at the cemetery on the east side of town. Does that help?"

"I don't know, maybe," Becks replied, not really sure how that information could be used, as they couldn't possibly risk leaving in daylight. "Does that mean everyone will be out of the house tomorrow?"

"Why yes, I guess so. At least until after the funeral. But I really have to go now. Good luck, I really hope you do get away safely and get back to your people."

With that, Jennifer took her two bottles of bleach and hurried upstairs.

"What are you thinking?" Eddie asked, once Jennifer was gone.

"I'm thinking we could both use another day to rest and recuperate. Tomorrow morning we get more food and water from upstairs when everyone is gone. Then tomorrow night—when everyone should be good and drunk if this will be a real Irish wake—we get the hell out of New Ridgelawn. What are you thinking?" she was almost afraid to ask.

"The same thing, but with one addition. Anything in that embalming room that's flammable?" he asked with a devilish look in his eyes.

"Hell yes!" she replied, liking the direction of his thoughts, as they could use a diversion to escape. "Embalming fluid is mostly composed of formaldehyde and methanol, and I saw enough bottles in there to bring a tear to any arsonist's eye."

Over a meal of their few remaining energy bars and a couple of bottles of water from the storage room, they began constructing the new Plan A.

Chapter 11

As darkness fell, an icy mixture of rain, sleet, and even some snowflakes made it miserable for the teams of people out searching for the fugitive murderer, Eddie Tasi, who had so ruthlessly and brutally butchered one of their leaders in cold blood. In truth, the majority of the population was ecstatic, and wished they had been the ones to do the deed. But if they wanted to be fed, they had to pretend to be outraged and heartbroken, and keep combing the streets within a few mile radius, or as far as the packs of zombies allowed.

As for the Army doctor, they were told, she was obviously a deluded, innocent pawn of the evil Tasi, who had somehow tricked or threatened her into following the madman into his scheme of revenge. When she realized his awful plan to murder the brothers, she tried to stop him, but Eddie beat her unconscious and left her for dead. She was now out there somewhere, dazed and confused, and needed to be rescued and brought to safety. *Under no circumstances*, the search teams were warned, should the doctor be harmed in any way.

As the cold, wet, hungry, and exhausted teams of searchers finally returned for the night, Becks and Eddie were quite warm and comfortable in the little "nest" they had built behind the boxes with some blankets and pillows they found in the storeroom. The pillows were actually coffin pillows, and their blankets were quilted coffin liners, but they tried not to think about it as they snuggled into their little nest to sleep, which they both did for many hours.

It was full daylight by the time they woke up, and the scurrying and shuffling of footsteps above them was an indication of the preparations for after the funeral, when just a select group of the inner circle would be invited back to the house. Only the best booze and food would be served then. The cheap stuff would be for the public at the wake.

Several times Becks and Eddie went on high alert as people came down into the basement, but each time they went to a different storeroom—the one that held the real essentials of beer, whiskey, canned peanuts, and bags of pretzels and chips. Once they overheard the men talking about all the food in the other room, Eddie tested his leg and found it felt good enough to make a quick dash to grab some Fritos, Wise potato chips, and two cans of Planter's honey roasted peanuts. And what a wonderful breakfast resulted!

After they gorged themselves on all the decadent, high-fat, junk foods, they went over their plans one more time. Then it was just a matter of waiting for everyone to leave the house for the wake. Half an hour after the last footsteps and door slamming, they cautiously made their way to the first floor. Becks was quite relieved to find she was steady on her feet and only had a slight headache, and Eddie, though quite sore all over, wasn't bleeding from any of his wounds.

They found the front parlor set up with a bar of the finest brands of alcohol, and empty serving trays and sterno that would be filled with fresh, hot dishes just as the guests arrived. Becks certainly had no interest in sampling any of the liquor, and Eddie was smart enough to refrain, as well, to keep his head clear.

Instead, their objective was the former kitchen turned storeroom, with its cases of pasta, cereal and granola, energy bars, and candy—all light-weight food easily carried, providing good doses of carbs and calories to keep them going. Becks even found a case of Flintstones multiple vitamins, which not only brought back fond childhood memories, but reassured her that they would at least not become too deficient in anything anytime soon. Even after their packs and pockets were stuffed, Becks somehow found enough room for not one, but two, pound-sized bags of M&Ms.

"Woman does not live on Flintstone vitamins alone," she said in her defense, as Eddie rolled his eyes. "And don't think I didn't see you stuff those packages of Little Debbie brownies in your pants!"

Cautiously looking out the windows to the front and the back, they actually considered making a run for it right then and there, but a passing patrol car ended that thought. Better to be patient and wait until dark. Plus, "PyroEddie" had more chaos to spread.

Becks was amazed at the sheer quantity of dangerous and toxic chemicals stored in the embalming room. The place must have done a booming business over the years, or they might have just ordered extra amounts when people first started dropping like flies. Funeral homes actually became one of the most dangerous places to work in the early days of infection, as more than one embalmer was surprised and killed when the corpse got up off the table and attacked. In fact, it happened with such frightening frequency during the first few months, that the majority of funeral homes closed their doors and refused to accept bodies at any price.

This had prompted most towns to establish "cremation service centers," which more often than not, were just hastily dug pits where bodies would be dumped on top of piles of scrap wood, sprayed with gasoline, and ignited. Even then, someone had to keep an eye open—and a rifle handy—for any flaming corpses trying to climb their way out. For people who died and switched right away, the course of action was clear and swift. But those who took hours to turn zombie fooled a lot of people into a false sense of security. Many fatal mistakes were made before the true nature of the infection, the ultimate death of the body, and switching to zombie mode was fully understood.

In any event, this particular funeral home was packed to the gills with formaldehyde, methanol, and many other hazardous and highly flammable solvents and chemicals. Becks happily switched into laboratory mode, and working quickly and efficiently together, they made Molotov cocktails of sorts; only these were not made to be thrown. Utilizing the packing material that was stuffed into cadaver orifices to prevent seepage, they made combinations of wicks and corks for the bottles of flammable liquids they placed throughout the house in closets under clothing, in the backs of cabinets, and dresser drawers, but primarily around the perimeter of the basement, up into the walls and on the wooden supports of the old house.

They needed the flammable fumes to be concentrated enough to be susceptible to ignition, but not so strong as to illicit suspicion and prompt a search. Their job was made easier by the intense smell of bleach everywhere, which they enhanced by pouring even more bleach in areas where they were concealing their incendiary devices. With only bucket brigades and fire extinguishers at their disposal, the designated firefighters of New Ridgelawn wouldn't have a prayer of stopping this fire if they didn't react immediately and in all the right places.

Their last act before retreating to their nest, was to put some sturdy wooden crates near a basement window that led to the backyard, to use as a stepping stool. They also removed the nails that had kept the window shut. And finally, they made damn sure that Eddie could fit through that window!

Around 3:30pm, the women of the town who had been assigned to do the cooking and serving began to arrive at the house. They lit all the sterno cans under the serving dishes—which was the reason why Becks and Eddie didn't place any incendiary devices anywhere near the parlor—and began heating all the food they had spent the entire day preparing.

In the past year, there was only one other time the women had all seen so much food in one place—for the recent funeral of Mr. Reggie. Everyone knew the brothers had storehouses of food stashed all over town, and kept the most and best for themselves—how else do you manage to stay so fat in the middle of a zombie apocalypse?—but as long as the residents kept getting their meager handouts, they weren't going to make a peep. Jennifer's attitude of acceptable levels of abuse and degradation in exchange for rations was most definitely not the exception in town; it was the rule.

Of course, not everyone was so docile and accepting of the tyrannical leadership, but they were also not so brave and bold as to sneak away in the night and go it alone.

"Oh hell no, are those meatballs I smell?" Eddie moaned, starting to salivate like one of Pavlov's dogs, or at least like a Doberman with a Twix bar.

Becks had just also caught a whiff of what smelled *almost* as good as her mother's meatballs.

"Yeah, afraid so," Becks replied, wondering just how many people she would be willing to kill to have a good home cooked meal. Eddie must have been thinking the same thing.

"We could run upstairs, shoot everyone, grab the meatballs, and run," he said in a tone that made Becks wonder if he was really kidding or not.

"Yes, but consider this: what's the most abundant source of meat in town?" Becks asked, making herself queasy by her own intimation.

"Ugh! You mean they're probably ratballs?" Eddie said, grimacing.

"Well, how many herds of cattle have you seen in northern New Jersey lately?"

"I draw the line at rats!" he exclaimed. "I will eat just about everything else, but I'll be damned if I'll eat a filthy rodent!"

"Amen to that! You're preaching to the choir, brother," Becks said, confident that she would never be so hungry that she would ever have to stoop that low.

The funeral party arrived already rip-roaring drunk, if the over-the-top wailing and crying were any indications. It all sounded so phony and staged that it became extremely irritating after just a few minutes, and it went on for a couple of hours, when finally there was a genuine and lovely moment. Someone with an exquisite tenor voice did a stirring and heartfelt rendition of *Danny Boy*. Becks actually dared to leave their nest and creep to the basement stairs to better the lovely singing.

Unfortunately, the drunks with their awful voices then started giving their pathetic renditions of *Danny Boy;* so many times, in fact, that Becks wanted to scream. She had to press a coffin pillow over each ear to muffle the terrible caterwauling. But hour by hour, voice by voice, the singing and talking subsided, until finally the house was blissfully silent. It was at that moment that Becks and Eddie started the final countdown.

Exactly one hour later, they left their nest, opened the basement window, and got out their disposable lighters. There was an awkward moment in the darkness that probably called for someone to give a heartfelt speech, but instead, Eddie just gave Becks an affectionate bear hug, and they both wished each other good luck.

They started in the storeroom which held all the liquor. Eddie felt it was something of a crime against humanity, but they opened a few dozen bottles of some of the most expensive alcohol money can buy, and poured out the contents all over the other cases of booze. He couldn't resist a few sips here and there, and Becks pretended not to notice. After all, this could be their final moments on this earth.

As Eddie lit the first wad of packing material in their homemade incendiary device, they realized the alcohol was nothing compared to the potent power of the embalming chemical cocktail Becks had mixed up. Just seconds after lighting the bottle, which was wedged up between the walls, there was a frightening *whooosshh...BANG,* and the dried wood structure of the old house seemed almost anxious to succumb to the intense flames.

"I think we have to do this really fast!" Becks whispered, somewhat shocked by the ferocity of her own device.

"You think?" Eddie said, smiling by the fire light, clearly delighted. "Let's spilt up and really get this party started."

In the less than 60 seconds it took them to race around and light the majority of the bottled cocktails in the basement, there was already a thick layer of choking, black smoke roiling along the ceiling.

"That's enough. Let's get the hell out of here!" Becks said, in between coughs.

She scrambled out of the window first, and then Eddie handed out all of the packs and gear. With all the food in his pockets, he just barely squeezed through, and not a minute too soon as tongues of flames were already darting out the window. They had so much pent up nervous energy from being trapped in the basement for so long, they wanted to take off running immediately, but there were still patrols on the streets, and they needed to make sure everyone's attention was drawn to The Capitol.

They went around to the back of the house, where Becks was delighted to see her bladed hockey stick still leaning against the tree where she had left it. Making their way to the yards in the back, where the Doberman was once again tied to his doghouse, this time they came in prepared with packaged snack cakes and a bag of pork rinds. Buttons and Smidgey got their fair share, as well, and none of them made a peep.

Crouching behind the huge doghouse for cover, Becks and Eddie waited impatiently for someone to come running out of the house and sound the alarm, but perhaps they had done their jobs too well. Flames had already spread to the first floor, and even at this distance they could hear the little explosions as each successive cocktail ignited. Apparently, though, everyone inside was so drunk they had no clue they were about to be roasted alive.

Minutes passed, and the roaring flames quickly chewed gaping holes in the walls, which in turn, added oxygen to fuel the fire's relentless path of destruction. To Becks, it almost seemed like the fire was a living thing, spreading through the structure along the veins and arteries of its support beams and rafters. Like Eddie, she became mesmerized by the sight—until she heard the pitiful cries for help from those who were finally regaining consciousness, and awakening to face the fiery pit of hell that surrounded them.

"Fire, fire!" an old man on patrol a block away yelled, as he hobbled toward the burning building, alternately shouting and blowing his whistle.

Some residents in the area looked out their windows to make sure it wasn't their house on fire, and then went back to bed. Others, when they realized it was The Capitol, hurriedly got dressed, so they could enjoy the show. A few, fearing the loss of rations, actually ran to try to help. Soon, all of the patrols were converging on the conflagration, but the structure was already so fully engulfed by the time they arrived, they just stood there with their buckets of water and fire extinguishers in their hands.

Many turned away and went home when they heard the screams of the victims choking and burning inside. A few people in flames jumped out of windows, but the smoke was so deadly it quickly overwhelmed most of the funeral party, who had passed out on the parlor floor and sofas. The big question was whether Mr. Riley and the Big Gorilla got out, but in the mass confusion, no one knew.

Hurrying toward the front gate with the aid of their night vision goggles, Becks and Eddie did not see anyone, and hoped that they, themselves, had not been seen. They chose to go this way, instead of over the rows of cars at the west end of town, because they knew the ATVs and motorcycles were often kept here, and they wanted to get as far away as they could, and as fast as they could. The only obstacle was a lone female guard standing in the plywood and two-by-four watch tower at the gate. Shooting her would attract unwanted attention, and it would be difficult to sneak up the tower and climb the ladder without being seen.

After a brief discussion, Becks removed her goggles and leather jacket covered in silverware. She then ran out of the darkness toward the tower yelling at the top of her lungs.

"Fire! They need everyone's help. Hurry!"

The terrified woman in the tower was probably a slightly overweight soccer mom driving an SUV and hosting a monthly book club at her house with tea and finger foods BZA, and was now a haggard-looking shell of a human with patches of hair missing from anxiety and malnutrition, and eyes so dark and sunken they almost weren't human.

"But...b-but my post...they'll p-punish me..." she stammered, breathing heavily for the exertion of just speaking.

"The Capitol is on fire! They need everyone's help. NOW!" Becks shouted, looking as frantic and worried as she could manage.

"The Capitol!" the woman cried, picturing all that wonderful food inside burning to a crisp, but not giving a thought to the potential loss of what was left of the governing body.

On wobbly legs, and with great difficulty, the woman descended the ladder. Becks stood by to help in case she fell, and actually put her hands on the woman's back and shoulder to steady her the last few rungs. The woman was wearing a thin, threadbare wool coat, under which Becks could easily feel her protruding bones. Becks thought that there were zombies who were in better shape than this poor creature.

Becks wanted desperately to give this women some energy bars and a bottle of the Flintstone vitamins, but that would surely give her away. She was also tempted to have Eddie just throw this sack of bones over his shoulder and take her with them, but if she was anything like Jennifer, she would rather stay in this virtual concentration camp and wither away than fight for her life.

"Hurry," Becks said, giving the woman a little push down the street toward The Capitol. "I have to get everyone else."

As the woman ran as best she could—looking very much like a skeleton marionette operated by a spastic puppeteer—Becks pretended to run east along the fence, until the woman was out of sight. Then she hurried back to the gate, where Eddie had already undone the latch and swung it open. Becks jumped on the closest ATV, but Eddie had his sights set on a big, old Harley. Revving their engines, they lurched forward through the gate and stopped. They had to close the gate behind them, because they didn't want to have zombies overrun the town and kill any more innocent people.

Becks felt a great sense of relief as they zoomed down the street. They were home free, and with any luck, they might even be able to make their way to Interstate 287 that very night. If there was an early morning Army patrol, they could be having bacon and eggs at the Picatinny Arsenal for breakfast, right after they took a long, hot shower. Her wonderful fantasy got derailed, however, just a few blocks down, when Eddie veered to the left and stopped by the curb.

Becks followed, and saw that he was looking at the pile of freshly dug dirt that covered the grave of his wife, next to the grave of his son. She decided to say nothing and give him a few moments to say goodbye, and tell them they could rest in peace now that his revenge on the brothers was most likely complete. When these few moments stretched to a full minute, and then almost two, she couldn't remain silent.

"Eddie, we *really* have to go," she said nervously, scanning the street for patrols, or zombies drawn by the noise.

"I can't go," he replied, as though he was a million miles away.

"I'm sorry, *what*?" Becks asked, not believing her ears.

"I can't leave them."

"Oh, Eddie, I know this is hard. But they're gone. And the best way to keep their memory alive is for you to keep alive," she said, placing a sympathetic hand on his arm.

"No, no, that's not what I meant," Eddie said, much to Becks' relief, which unfortunately was short-lived. "This is *my* town, and I can't leave all those people. Donnie, Jennifer, that pathetic woman in the tower, they all need me. And how do we know that the last Riley and his henchman are all dead? I need to stay to make sure this is really finished, and I need to stay to help these people!"

"Eddie, *I need* your help!" Becks insisted. "And you can best help these people by getting back to one of the Army bases and letting them know what's going on. They are planning an offensive in the spring, and can air drop supplies in the meantime, with food and medicine and-"

"No, my place is here," he stated unequivocally. "You can make it on your own, I know you can. And when you get back, you can send help."

"Eddie, don't do this!" Becks pleaded, as he turned his motorcycle around. She was naturally concerned for his safety, but admittedly, she was more concerned about being alone again, and yes, even afraid.

Eddie took off his pack and put it in his lap, and rummaged deep down into it. It took some effort, but he pulled something out and handed it to Becks. It was a bloodstained chemistry book.

"If I don't make it, don't let the world forget about Little Eddie," he said, pressing the book into her hands.

This was the library book for which Little Eddie had been shot and killed. Becks knew at that moment that there wasn't any force on the planet that could change Eddie's mind about staying, and for all she knew, he was making the right decision. There were no guarantees they would make it to 287, or that the Army would even be able to send help before most of these people perished.

"Eddie...I..." Becks voice trailed off, at a loss for words as so many emotions competed for supremacy.

"Just be as brave as Little Eddie was, and you'll be fine," he said, gripping her hand tightly for a moment, before speeding back toward New Ridgelawn.

Becks put the book inside her jacket, hit the throttle, and headed away from New Ridgelawn. She had only known Eddie for a short time, but it seemed like a lifetime. She felt as though she was saying goodbye to her big brother; a brother she might never see again. For a second or two, she thought she should turn around and go back with him, but she still believed her best way to help the people of this town, and all the towns still standing, was to get back to civilization and work on better ways to eradicate the ZIPS once and for all.

Chapter 12

The bitter night air stung Becks' face as she sped away, leaving Eddie and New Ridgelawn behind, but it felt good. It felt like freedom.

The cold had driven most of the zombies from the streets, and the few that remained were easily avoided by taking the ATV up and over lawns, debris, and even the occasional dried up corpse. Becks headed straight back to Sparrow Lane—not to stay, because that was too risky if the brother or any of his minions had survived and came looking for her—to get to her stash of precious MREs.

As she stuffed as many as she could fit into a long duffle bag and strapped it to the back of the ATV, a light snow began to fall. Becks couldn't suppress a shudder as the raw, damp air started to seep into her bones. She would have loved to just go in the house and start a toasty fire in the woodstove, but this street was no longer safe, and she had her sights set on getting as far west as possible.

Heading back down Sparrow, she turned right on the main road and went west—the direction she started to go before she had heard Angie's cries for help. That seemed so long ago, and so much had happened since then—and none of it good. But it could all be forgotten with that first bite of bacon in the morning…

The road went up a short hill, then down steep, winding curves along a wooded stretch and over a stream, before opening up onto a relatively straight section of block after block of typical, nondescript, suburban New Jersey houses. After about two miles, the snowflakes became larger and thicker, making it almost impossible to see more than about thirty feet ahead with the night vision goggles, so Becks had to slow way down. She began cursing Mother Nature and her bad luck, until she went into a blind curve and almost drove right into a solid wall of zombies.

They looked almost as surprised as she did, but they hesitated only a few seconds before the huge mass of undead flesh moved as one—shuffling straight for her. Gunning the engine, Becks spun in a tight turn, speeding back up the curving road. The precipitation had obviously started as sleet or freezing rain here, and the ATV slipped and slid several times before gaining enough traction to stay ahead of the hungry horde of pursuers.

Turning right at the first cross street, she didn't get more than a few hundred feet before she almost went into a wall of another sort—a wall of furniture, overturned cars, fencing, and anything else the neighborhood residents could find to make a barricade. It had been a common practice after quarantine to barricade streets and neighborhoods to "remain safe from infection." Of course, what nobody realized was that most of the people were already infected, and when they started switching to zombies, the penned-in victims were easy prey.

The spray painted sign nailed to the front of a dresser in the middle of the pile still spoke volumes:

"STAY OUT! We don't trust anyone and will shoot you on sight."

Becks drove from end to end of the old barricade, and while some sections had collapsed, the wall was still way too high to drive over. Turning around and heading back slowly, as visibility had been even further diminished, she could just see a line of figures stretched across the intersection. Maybe she could have plowed through them, and maybe she would run right into the center of the herd; she just couldn't see well enough to know what would happen.

Ahead of her were zombies, behind her was the barricade. To her right, she could probably go through some yards to return to the road further down, but that would take her back the way she came, and Becks never liked giving up ground. Even as a little kid, her parents often remarked how stubborn she was; she would rather scrape her knees climbing over an obstacle than go around it. So habit and obstinate genes left her no choice than go left into a wooded area.

Branches clawed at her as she bounced over fallen tree limbs and down a rough embankment. She was splashed, head to foot, with icy water and cold clumps of mud as she crossed a half-frozen stream. But the ATV forged ahead, and she wasn't about to give up and turn around. She finally came out to a storm drain surrounded by a gravel slope. Opening up the engine to full throttle, she sped up the slope—perhaps just a little *too* quickly—as she went airborne off the high curb and hit the road with a bone-jarring *thud*.

The heavy snow now made the night vision goggles useless, so she flipped them back and turned on the headlights of the ATV. Just across the street was a large building; one of those post-WWII post offices that lacked everything but functionality. It wouldn't have been her first choice in accommodations, but *any port in a storm*, she thought, as she pulled into the parking lot and around to the back. A row of mail trucks sat in mute testament to the fact that the post office motto did not read, *Neither snow nor rain nor heat nor gloom of night, nor zombies, stays these couriers from the swift completion of their appointed rounds.*

Actually, the position of mail carrier became an extremely high-risk job in the early days of infection. They not only came into contact with a lot of people on their routes, increasing their risk of infection, they were also obvious targets as they had to walk everywhere, up to every house and into every apartment building, and a zombie could crop up anywhere, and usually did.

All Becks had on her mind at this point, however, was how fast she could get inside, and how quickly and safely she could clear the building. One of the upsides of an apocalypse is that people rarely bothered to lock doors as they were running for their lives from their homes and businesses. This was something looters quickly took advantage of, grabbing televisions and smartphones, until the power went out for good, and they realized the only things worth stealing were food, guns, and anything to help them survive.

Becks kept her fingers crossed that even the intrepid postal workers didn't give a rat's ass about Uncle Sam's letters and packages as they abandoned their posts and headed for wherever they thought they would be safe. Sure enough, the back door opened effortlessly, despite its security bars and brightly-colored stickers warning of alarms and surveillance video.

Before stepping inside, she flipped her goggles back down over her eyes and took a deep breath. As many times as she had cleared a building, it never got any easier. However, she had learned a few tricks. For instance, let the zombies come to you. After carefully making her way through a storeroom filled with mountains of mail sacks and packages, she entered a huge sorting room. Pausing in the doorway, she whistled, yelled, and banged on a long, metal table.

"Come out, come out, wherever you are!" she yelled in a singsong voice, and then waited silently for any sounds or motion.

As she waited, she read a large sign on the wall calling upon everyone's patriotic spirit to pull together, work long hours, and get that mail delivered. In the waning days of government, the president had promised that the mail system would continue no matter what, as it was "the cohesive force that bound American to American—the Rockies to the Keys, the Heartland with Hollywood, and the seats of government with its citizens." Two weeks later, everything collapsed, and special emergency distribution centers like this post office were abandoned with undelivered letters and packages stacked to their rafters.

Minutes passed, but there was no indication that anyone, living or undead, was in the building. Slowly making her way through the sorting room, she came upon another long room jammed floor to ceiling with walls of packages, before emerging behind the front counter where the postal workers dealt with customers. Hopping over the counter into the lobby, she was momentarily surprised when she landed on something crunchy, and discovered the desiccated remains of a man. Upon closer inspection, it was a postal worker who looked as though he had gone "postal" on himself, and put a bullet through his brain.

Becks didn't waste time wondering what had transpired and driven this man to shoot himself. Instead, she picked up his revolver, checked that it still had five rounds left, stuck it in the waist of her pants, and moved on to the front doors. They were also unlocked, and a ring of keys was hanging from one of the locks. She decided to lock the front doors, as well as lower the security gate. No sense taking any chances of unwanted strangers, of any kind.

Searching the rest of the main floor, she found a maintenance closet and a small break room with a refrigerator full of mold, but cabinets full of coffee, tea, and individually wrapped biscotti. Behind the break room was a tiny room, or more like a double closet, with a cot and some blankets. Someone apparently didn't mind sleeping on the job.

There were two sets of bathrooms, each with a shower, which only taunted her as, of course, there wasn't any water. The post master's office had a few bottles of soda, and a drawer with not one, but two boxes of Girl Scouts' thin mint cookies!

"Come to mamma!" Becks purred as she tore into a sleeve of the cookies, eating half of them before she forced herself to stop, reminding herself to ration everything.

With the first floor secure, she opened the door to the basement and was about to make noise to rile up any zombies, but decided that she was too tired and strung out to face any more surprises. Instead, she shut the door and found the key to lock it. Then she went outside to get her pack and bag of MREs, and covered the ATV with a tattered tarp she found. In the short time she had been inside, at least an inch of snow had fallen, and it looked as though the storm was only getting stronger.

Shaking the snow off of herself, she then locked the back door, the doors to the storeroom and sorting room, and then locked herself into the break room. Peeling off her wet and dirty clothes, she layered on all the other clothes and socks she had with her, and curled up on the cot under all the blankets. It was a cold, musty room in the middle of a post office, but compared with the circumstances of where she had woken up earlier that day, it was about 25 square feet of paradise.

Still, as she drifted off to sleep, her every thought was about Eddie. Was he dead or alive? Was he hurt? Was he being beaten and tortured? Or, had the last of the New Ridgelawn tyrants perished in the fire, giving Eddie the opportunity to create a new community and help the people? It was terrible not knowing, but she would have to deal with the fact that she would probably never know.

Becks awoke from a fiery nightmare, yelling and kicking. She had dreamt that after she and Eddie had lit the embalming fluid cocktails, they tried to escape, but the window started shrinking and they couldn't squeeze through. The flames were searing her flesh, and the acrid smoke was suffocating her.

In reality, she awoke to find that she had somehow managed to wrap the fuzzy plaid blanket around her head, so it was actually polyester fleece, not burning embalming fluid smoke, that was blocking her air supply. It took a few moments for her to get her bearings and recall the details of how she had gotten there, but the fire, the snow, and the zombies all came back into focus.

Keeping her fingers crossed, she got up, wrapped the fuzzy blanket around her shoulders, and shuffled into the break room, which had a tall, barred window. Using her breath and the corner of the blanket, she rubbed a clean spot to peer out, and couldn't quite comprehend what she was seeing. She thought there had been a few cars in the side parking lot, but now there were only rounded bumps in the snow. Grabbing the ring of keys, she hurried to the front lobby.

"*No!* No, no no…" she shouted, running from the doors to windows and back to the doors, horrified by the two feet of snow that had swallowed everything. Drifts had pushed that depth to over a yard at the front doors. Sinking to the cold marble floor, she put her head in her hands and said dejectedly, "No bacon and eggs for you today, Becks."

She was able to get out the back door and down the steps, because of a ten-by-ten awning, but that was as far as she could go. To add insult to the snow total injury, at least a quarter of an inch of ice had formed a crust on top. Trying to take a few steps, Becks first slid to her right, then to her left, and then fell on her butt, breaking through the ice and plunging into the deep, powdery snow. Even the ATV, which was a small rounded bump

141

in the snow, couldn't get through this. Without a snowmobile, or a tank, she was going to be stuck for a while.

After a breakfast of a hot MRE, biscotti, and only one thin mint cookie, Becks' morale had improved. She decided that if she was going to be here for days, or even weeks, she needed to know what—or more importantly *who*—was in the basement. Gearing up with a mask, her leather jacket and pants covered in silverware, and all her pistols, she switched on her night vision goggles and unlocked the door.

Banging on the walls and shouting for several minutes, she waited another full ten minutes. Zombies nesting in basements, in a full twilight state, sometimes took quite a while to regain their version of consciousness and become mobile again. When all remained silent, she carefully began to descend the stairs. Spider webs looked particularly creepy in night vision, their bright filaments floating by like phantoms as she tried to bat them out of her way. Clearly, no one had been down these stairs in a very long time, which was a good sign.

The basement was expansive, and windowless. It was filled with old stamp vending machines—worth their weight in gold on eBay, BZA—cases of outdated uniforms, hats, and coats, priority mail boxes, change of address forms, and even long banks of post office boxes, which by their various styles, had obviously been torn out and replaced at least three times over the decades. Of course, every tower of boxes could be hiding a potential threat, so Becks had to move slowly and methodically. Her heart leapt into her throat when her boot kicked a couple of 50-year-old Schlitz beer cans in a back corner, but fortunately, after almost an hour of searching, that was the only surprise.

Other than the coats and old uniforms for spare clothing, and the cardboard boxes and papers she could burn for warmth once she made some sort of fireplace, there didn't appear to be anything of much value in the basement. However, there was one locked metal door under the stairs she had yet to open. From its rusty hinges, Becks thought it looked as though it hadn't been opened since the Eisenhower administration, which actually wasn't a bad guess. After trying several keys, she found one that fit, and it had a piece of white tape on it with the faded letters "FOS."

The key reluctantly turned, after some coaxing, but the door was more stubborn. The hinges groaned in protest as Becks leaned back and put all her weight into it. Finally, she braced her right boot up on the door frame and groaned even louder than the hinges. Before she could regain her balance, the door swung open and she backpedalled several feet before falling over some cases of airmail envelopes.

"*Son of a bitch!* This better be worth it!"

Wiping off the dust and dirt, she slowly approached the open door, a pistol in each hand. To her surprise, there was a short staircase leading down to another metal door, and this one was much larger and stronger.

"What the hell?" she asked out loud, going down the stairs and gripping the heavy arm-type latch, feeling as though she was on a submarine.

The door slid sideways, like on a walk-in freezer, and a blast of ancient air, as though from a tomb, assailed her nostrils. The concrete-walled room was about twenty-by-twenty feet, and triple-high bunk beds lined the walls. In the left back corner was a shower curtain hanging next to a small sink and some kind of pump toilet. To the right, was a large stack of something covered by a tarp. Holstering her weapons, she used both hands to pull down the tarp and was stunned by what was underneath.

After whistling in amazement, she spread her arms and announced, "Welcome to the Cold War!"

There before her was barrel after barrel of Civil Defense food and supplies.

"Of course, FOS—Fall…Out…Shelter!"

It was common for government buildings in the 1950s and 60s to have fallout shelters in the event of a nuclear attack. Some were simple basement rooms large enough to hold entire neighborhoods, and some—like this one—were much more sophisticated and designed to just house local government employees and their immediate families.

Officials would argue that it was important to keep the government intact, but in truth, they often abused their positions of power simply to safeguard their own asses. The same thing happened generations later when the real apocalypse began and our elected officials retreated to their tax payer-funded, private, luxury bunkers, while their constituents got chewed to pieces.

Becks was somewhat familiar with these barrels and their contents, as her parents had bought and sold many Civil Defense items in their antique shop in Nyack. When she was about five or six, she got in trouble because she had opened one of the tins of survival crackers and was happily munching away on the decades-old food. But it wasn't so much that her parents were upset that she had ruined the value of the item. They were more concerned that she would get sick from eating something several times older than she was.

As it turned out, little Becks suffered no ill effects. And now, even more decades later, she would eat these crackers again if she became desperate. As she recalled, these barrels also contained tins of hard candies. Those she would start eating without being desperate.

The medical supplies might come in handy, for everything that hadn't expired during the Reagan administration, and there were probably some other things in these barrels she could utilize. Short of a snowmobile or a satellite phone, this was a great find, and it at least meant that starvation wouldn't be an issue for quite a while.

Becks had been so mystified, and then intrigued, by the room, she hadn't yet stopped to think about the lighting, ventilation, and heat. There was another tarp she had missed in the right front corner, and sure enough, underneath was an old generator. There were several pipes to vent the generator exhaust, and she found other pipes that connected to another pump that circulated and filtered outside air. She was no ventilation expert, but the stenciled label reading, "Ventilation Pump," was her first clue.

Scanning the ceiling, she saw rows of light fixtures, and two electric heaters. They were a sight for sore eyes, and chilled bones. Even if she couldn't get this antique generator running, she could remove one of these heaters and then scavenge the neighborhood to find a working generator— once the snow melted. There was most likely a good amount of gas in all the mail trucks, and some post offices even had storage tanks of gas on the premises for their fleet of vehicles.

But she was getting ahead of herself. First, she would have to see if she could get this prehistoric beast up and running. If only Cam were here, he would have it disassembled, cleaned, lubricated, put back together, and running by lunch. Even though she had helped him work on his endless stream of "automotive reclamation projects," as Cam called them—Becks called them junk cars—she would be thrilled if it only took her a few days to get it to work.

There was a basic toolkit on a shelf above the generator, along with an operating manual and a couple of cans of oil, so she assumed all she would need to work on it would be right there. However, working with the night vision goggles at close distances was very difficult as they were super bright, so before she began her generator reclamation project, she went upstairs to get some flashlights.

When she got upstairs, she found that the sun had finally broken through the clouds and light was streaming into the lobby through the tall windows. Grabbing a blanket, she settled down in a warm patch of sunlight and soaked up every blessed photon. Following the patch of warmth for the next two hours—getting up only once to slide the dead postal worker's body out of sight behind some trash cans—she actually felt better than she had in a long time. However, a bank of dark clouds and some scattered flurries broke the mood, and she decided to get to work.

On her way through the storeroom behind the counter, a box caught her eye with "Yankee Candle" printed along the sides. Realizing a few scented candles could work wonders in the musty fallout shelter, she took the box, hopped on top of the counter, crossed her legs and imagined it was Christmas. And it smelled like Christmas as her hunting knife sliced through the tape and the wonderful scents of bayberry and cinnamon wafted out. There were four large pillar candles, and a plastic tray of twenty-four votive candles of various aromas.

"Thank you, Mrs. Margaret Fleming of 130 Church Street," Becks said, reading the invoice in the box.

After taking a deep breath of bayberry and thinking how fortunate she was to have found the candles, she had an "Aha!" moment. Or perhaps, a "Duh!" moment was more like it. Rather than cursing her luck at getting stuck inside of a post office, she should have thanked her lucky stars that she was now in the midst of packages from every major online retailer who had been in existence BZA. Even eliminating the countless boxes of tanzanite rings and designer handbags from QVC, that still left hundreds, if not thousands, of items that could make her life more comfortable and help her survive.

Running back into the storeroom like a kid on Christmas morning, Becks searched for packages from L.L. Bean, Eddie Bauer, Eastern Mountain Sports, REI, and anything that sounded like a food company. An hour later, she was clad in various sizes and colors of silk long johns, premium cotton turtlenecks, down vests and jackets, and Gore-Tex pants. Not to mention the three cashmere caps that were now caressing her head

145

in soft, cozy warmth, as she feasted on cashews, jams and jellies, flavored pretzels, gourmet popcorn, jerky, and yes, the Holy Grail of mail order foods—assorted dark chocolates from some of the finest chocolatiers. Stale, hard, chocolate was still better than nothing.

Even after tearing into dozens and dozens of packages, Becks had barely scratched the surface of this massive cardboard monument to consumer gluttony. But she had spent enough time sunning herself and pretending it was Christmas. It was time to roll up those silk and cotton sleeves and tackle the generator—after one more stick of Cajun jerky.

Constantly referring to the manual, hour-by-hour and piece-by-piece, Becks began disassembling the generator and soaking the gummed up parts in coffee mugs filled with gasoline, as she was fresh out of carburetor cleaner. She didn't have a syphon, so she slipped and fell her way to the closest mail truck, and used a screwdriver and hammer to put a hole in the gas tank and drain the contents into two buckets from the maintenance closet.

Once everything she could remove was soaking in gas, she decided to leave them overnight. However, before she went upstairs, she took a look at the odd pump toilet. As long as she had buckets and access to the outside it wasn't really an issue, but still, it would be nice to have a little creature comfort.

Pumping the handle slowly up and down a few times, nothing happened. Then she saw a sign on the wall behind the toilet that read, "Pump Vigorously Until Desired Result is Achieved," which elicited an uncharacteristic giggle. Nonetheless, she followed the instructions and pumped away as if she was on a sinking ship. As she was about to give up, she heard a strange sound from deep within the bowels of the earth, as it were. Something was stirring in the pipes below the fallout shelter.

Continuing her rapid pumping, there was a sudden spurt of brown, smelly water into the bowl, but several pumps later, the water began to clear and flow evenly. She had a working toilet!

Could this day get any better? she thought, as she clutched the handle for the pump on the sink.

On the third pump, the handle snapped off at the base. It would have been nice to have running water, too, but with an endless supply of frozen water just outside the door, she wasn't too upset. Of course, the water being pumped into the toilet must be coming from the same well, but she just couldn't bring herself to drink out of a toilet. Even in an apocalypse a lady had her limits.

The next day was spent carefully cleaning and reassembling all the parts of the generator. It was slow and time consuming, but she wanted to get it all right the first time. She needed heat, and light would be an added bonus. Finally, she was ready and confident the generator would start, and if it didn't, it wouldn't be because of a lack of effort or attention to detail.

"Lights, heater, action!" she shouted, as she ceremoniously gave the pull cord a mighty tug.

The dry-rotted cord snapped in half and the generator remained silent. However, Becks did not, as she ranted, raved, swore, and kicked things. But not for long, as she immediately had to switch gears to find a Plan B to generate heat, as the plastic hummingbird thermometer outside the break room window was currently reading eight degrees. Granted, the basement was probably a relatively toasty 45 degrees, but her increasingly scrawny skin and bones body needed real warmth.

As her big toe throbbed from kicking one of the metal barrels, an idea started to form. She could just empty a barrel, take it outside, and make a classic redneck fireplace, but she didn't relish the idea of having to stand outside next to a barrel in windy, eight-degree weather, no matter how big of a fire she made. Examining the exhaust pipes attached to the generator, she realized she might be able to cut a hole in the lid of the barrel and insert the pipes. Then she would cut a hole in the front to stoke the fire and let the glorious heat spill out.

However, before she wasted any more time on hopeless projects, she would test it to see if heated smoke would travel up the pipe. For all she knew, it had been sealed off 30 years ago, or 50 years-worth of birds and squirrels had fallen down the pipe and clogged it. Detaching the metal pipe was a simple task, and on an overturned barrel she made a small pile of crumpled up Change of Address cards. Angling the large diameter pipe directly over the pile, she lit it.

At first, the smoke went everywhere, but as the heat intensified, the smoke was clearly drafting upward through the pipe. Becks kept the fire going for about 15 minutes just to be sure it wasn't going to back up into the room, and just because it felt *so good*.

Once her experiment was successfully concluded, she rummaged around the maintenance closet and found a small hacksaw and a pair of tin snips. The metal of the barrel was tougher than it looked, but by bedtime her custom redneck fireplace was cranking out heat, thanks to all the boxes, papers, and the wood from the banks of post office boxes. In fact, it got so hot, she had to take off several layers of clothes before bedding down on the middle bunk of the closest set of beds.

The following day, she shoveled snow into buckets and heated them on her barrel to wash her grimy hair and offensively filthy body. Becks put together a nice set of clean clothes—thanks to several ladies in town who most likely died or turned zombie right after placing their orders—which completed her "makeover" from scummy survivor to civilized human being again. She also couldn't resist opening some of those QVC boxes and soon had a tanzanite ring on every finger, as well as earrings, several necklaces, and bunches of bracelets. She couldn't remember the last time she actually wore jewelry, and it was a fun and frivolous diversion to play "dress up."

As it was another relentlessly cold morning with dangerous wind chills, she opted to spend the rest of the day in her bunk with a stack of mail to read for entertainment, by the light of honeysuckle-scented candles. She was surprised at how many people had written letters in the final days before the complete collapse of society's infrastructure. Granted, cell phones and Internet service had become increasingly unreliable over the course of several months, but Becks felt it was something more than that. In times of crisis, people like the comfort and security of something they can hold in their hands, something that will last without electricity and will travel anywhere they went.

Her theory seemed to be supported by the nature of the letters, as well. Estranged family members reached out to either beg or grant forgiveness for past transgressions that now seemed so petty in the face of the looming crisis. Dog-eared photos of children, honeymoons, and grandma's house crisscrossed the country, accompanied by heartfelt messages of love and remembrance. Some letters made Becks laugh, but most made her cry, as the themes of "Everyone I love is dying" and "I'm afraid I'll never see you again," played out on page after page.

"This probably wasn't the best idea," she said, wiping her eyes as she approached her barrel fireplace and was about to chuck a fistful of letters and photos into the flames.

148

But she couldn't do it. She couldn't obliterate the last traces of these people whose lives had been reduced to the contents of a business envelope bearing a first class stamp. The dreamer in Becks imagined groups of historians years from now, in a zombie-free world, collecting letters such as these to document the darkest age of human history. And what right did she have to destroy these letters and prevent the future publication of the best-selling series of books, *Letters from the Apocalypse*.

Which reminded her, she hadn't kept up her own diary—for obvious reasons—that she began in Dylan's notebook soon after the accident. How long ago was that? What day was it? Hell, what month was it? She didn't know. All that mattered was how long this winter weather would last, and when she could start the final push home.

After writing in her diary for about an hour, she found that it was even more depressing than reading other people's letters. Instead, she opened some more packages, looking for something to keep her occupied. There were a lot of boxes from Amazon, but few that actually contained books, and fewer still that had any appeal to Becks.

There were loads of eBay collectible flotsam and jetsam, 99% of which she categorized as complete crap—until she tore open a small box and came face to face with the cutest vintage sock monkey. Naming her Ginger, and giving her a tanzanite bracelet for a collar, Becks at least had someone to talk to now. Sure, it was crazy, but even pretending to talk to a stuffed toy lowered her anxiety level—which became even more necessary as the days stretched to weeks of bitter cold, snow, and even more snow.

Needing to conserve some MREs for when she hit the road again, she sustained herself only on what she could find in the packages, and a couple of the old Civil Defense survival crackers and biscuits every day. The Cold War-era food didn't taste good, but it didn't taste moldy or compromised in any way, either, so she wasn't about to look a gift horse in the mouth. And when she found a package of Aunt Edna's homemade, Maine blueberry jam—which never made it to her nephew, Randolph Hastings, of 225 Second Avenue—the crackers took on a whole new life.

By the end of the third week, cabin fever threatened to make her go postal. She had tried to remain in some shape by jogging around the sorting room and up and down the cellar stairs, but she wanted to get outside. She *needed* to get outside. She had found plenty of clothes and jackets to keep her warm, but her combat boots were no match for deep snow. There was a pair of well-worn rubber snow boots in the basement, from some long-gone mail carrier, but they were a men's size twelve. However, by stuffing a couple of children's Scottish cashmere sweater vests—meant for the young MacTavish residents of 16 Parkside Circle—down into the toes of the boots, she not only made them fit better, but added some much-needed insulation.

If she thought the 17-degree temperature was a shock to her exposed skin—which after rewrapping two scarves consisted only of her nose and a small patch of each cheek—then the 20-30 mile-per-hour gusts made it downright painful, and dangerous. A few flirtations with above-freezing temperatures, followed by long periods of single-digit deep freezes, over the past few weeks had left a dense, hard snowpack that held her weight, but made every step a challenge on the slick surface.

Balancing herself using a pair of makeshift walking sticks, crafted from broom handles to which she had duct taped some tacky commemorative Native American knives from the Home Shopping Network—ordered by Stan Wysneski, Terrace Gardens, Apt 2B—she made her way into the street and was able to see the neighborhood for the first time. A block to the south was a strip of small businesses, although she couldn't see what they were. Further down looked to be more open space like a park, or maybe a school.

More importantly was what lay to the north, which led to the road she hoped to take westward to Interstate 287. She had asked Eddie to draw a map of the best way back, but as he knew "the way like the back of my hand," and he was supposed to go with her, he never bothered to make that map. There were some maps in the post office, but they only covered the local mail routes. The road that had been choked with a zombie herd did seem to run due west, and if that was impassable she would have to travel through side streets and yards until she found a clear section.

Today would be a preliminary reconnaissance mission to determine the size of the herd, and how many might still be alive. Any living or undead creature out in this extreme cold for this long should have frozen solid and be permanently dead by now, which could create its own problems. A few hundred, or god forbid, thousands of corpses frozen together in the road would be as impenetrable as a castle wall.

150

She may not be able to make a definitive assessment with all this snow, but at least she was outside, the sun was shining, and there didn't appear to be any imminent danger.

Until the earth began to move.

Chapter 13

Becks could have made her way back through the woods she had crossed on the ATV, but she didn't want to tangle with all the branches and thorns again, not to mention the steep embankments where she would be unable to get any kind of decent footing. The road was clear and straight, although the snow drifts had formed a strange sort of rolling contour—something like a mild version of the moguls skiing course she had seen on the Winter Olympics.

Very cautiously approaching the intersection, she was quite surprised that there wasn't a huge herd, frozen where they had stood that almost fateful night. Carefully maneuvering the slick, bumpy terrain, she made it to the center of the intersection and looked to her right where she had encountered the blind curve, although she had approached it coming from the other direction. This side of the blind curve appeared clear, so perhaps it hadn't been such a large herd after all, and it had moved to the east, and away from the direction she wanted to go. Looking to her left, the strange bumpy terrain continued down the road as far as she could see, but no herds were in sight.

"Well, I sure lucked out!" she declared, feeling very good about her situation, until she felt something odd.

It was like the planet suddenly shuddered—an unnerving tremor that almost made her lose her balance.

"What the hell? Is it an earthquake?" she asked, looking down at her feet, and then turning 360 degrees to view the entire landscape for some clue as to what might be happening. And that's when a sick feeling hit the pit of her stomach.

The road sign poles were much too short. Even accounting for the couple of feet of snow, they were still a few feet too short, as if there was *something big under the snow...*

"Fuck...me..."

The ground shook again, this time more violently. The sound of cracking ice echoed around her, and all of the bumps and moguls seemed to come alive and start writhing, like frosty cocoons ready to burst open. But these weren't butterflies under her feet—this *was* the massive herd of zombies!

When Becks had spent the previous winter at Cam's compound in Saugerties, New York, she had seen small numbers of zombies caught out in the cold. They froze to death like grisly popsicles, often standing up together in clumps. However, she had never witnessed the winter behavior of the huge packs that existed in New Jersey.

She had no idea that when it snowed heavily, zombies lie down on top of one another in mounds and let the snow act as a blanket, while they "slept" in deep twilight states. Between the insulating layer of snow and their combined body heat, at least half their number could survive even for weeks with these brutally frigid temperatures. It would be a lesson that would be burned into her memory—if she managed to get out alive.

Just twenty feet in front of her, a mound broke open, and several sluggish zombies started clawing their way out. A few seconds later, two mounds to her right split apart as hands and heads pushed to the surface. As far as the eye could see to the east and west, the bumps in the road erupted like swarms of maggots bursting out of a corpse.

Moving was almost impossible as the sheets of snow and ice beneath her feet heaved upward and grasping hands thrust out. If the pack below her had enough layers of zombies, she could be swallowed up in the middle of the ravenous horde! One chubby hand got a hold of her ankle, and using her walking stick as a spear, she repeatedly stabbed at the hand, cutting off three fingers before she could break free. But more hands quickly appeared around her, like a macabre garden of limbs. Heads with snapping teeth were emerging, as well.

Several zombies right under her were trying to stand up, and she actually went a couple of feet in the air on the back of one of them, before she fell and slid into another mound about to erupt. The mounds were smaller and more scattered on the sides of the road, so Becks stumbled and crawled her way between the thrashing arms and gnashing teeth to a relatively safe spot. From there, she hoped to make a mad dash the half block back to the post office, until a large crack appeared ahead in the snow, like a fissure opening up in the earth—only instead of lava, rows of starving zombies flowed out and began to spread in all directions.

Another shift in the snowpack knocked her backwards to the ground again, where a strong pair of arms locked around her waist. Struggling to get free only helped to loosen the young, male zombie from his icy confinement. His mouth moved toward the back of her neck, and she braced herself for the pain of teeth sinking into her flesh. But this zombie had begun his version of hibernation with his mouth open, and a frozen ball of snow prevented his jaws from clamping down.

Becks couldn't waste any more time, as hundreds of zombies were becoming mobile, so she covered her right ear with her left hand, stuck her pistol behind her head and pulled the trigger. The gripping arms relaxed, and she scrambled to her feet to find the bullet had entered the zombie's cheek, and exited through his head, along with the top of his skull.

The streets were now alive with the undead, so her only chance of escape was to head into the woods. She tripped once over a head and shoulders that popped up in front of her. It was a female zombie in a fur coat, and she was still wearing expensive, rhinestone-studded sunglasses. As much danger as Becks was in, she found the sight to be so ridiculous as to be funny—but not so funny that she didn't immediately thrust one of the commemorative Native American knives through a dark plastic lens, into the zombie's eye, and deep into its brain.

Dozens of zombies were now within thirty feet of her, so Becks crawled the few yards to the edge of the storm drain embankment and ended up doing a headfirst slide down the steep slope. Flipping over twice, she landed hard against a big oak tree, knocking the wind out of her. Her left leg was also caught at a bad angle, and her knee painfully flexed backward. But as soon as she caught her breath, she dragged and crawled her way back up the slope a few feet to take refuge inside the large concrete drain pipe. She just prayed that nothing was already in there, as she slid deeper into the pipe to get out of sight.

A few seconds later, a couple of male zombies, wearing identical power company jackets, fell down the embankment and slid into the same oak tree. The first one hit head on with a sickening cracking sound, killing him instantly, but the other one managed to get to his feet. At least twenty or thirty others followed, as best as Becks could see, but fortunately, none seemed to see her.

153

Between her pair of makeshift spears, pistols, and two pockets full of ammunition, she would have been able to dispatch these zombies in the woods, but there was no way she could climb up the embankment again, especially with a knee that was already swelling. And even if she did reach the road, could she run and shoot her way back to the post office? No, she would have to sit and wait for the zombies to disperse, go back into a twilight state, or freeze to death—hopefully, before *she* froze.

The good news was that by late afternoon the temperature rose to around 40 degrees, making her feel much more comfortable. The bad news was that water started flowing through the drain, making her much more uncomfortable. The other good news was that the warmer temperature made the zombies in the woods more energetic and most of them had wandered off. The other bad news was that *all* the zombies in the area were now more energetic and continued to spread farther down the streets in search of food, which other than the dead zombies, consisted of her.

As the sun was getting low in the sky, Becks crawled out of the drain pipe to get a better view and test her knee. Running was out of the question, but with the aid of her sticks she would be able to walk, albeit with considerable pain. If she went south in the woods a few hundred feet, it looked as though the embankment leveled out. If she could exit there, she would be very close to the post office. The few zombies left in the woods—if they even noticed her—would be easy to pick off. However, as she turned to look up the embankment to the street, she realized that wasn't her greatest concern.

At least 50 snow-caked zombies stood on the edge of the road above the drain pipe, and *they* definitely saw *her*. With no understanding of the steep, icy slope being impossible to descend while upright, the hungry mob surged forward. Like a tipped over basket of apples, they came rolling and tumbling downward, as Becks dove back into the pipe. Undead bodies slid in all directions, some hitting trees, some getting entangled in thorn bushes or wedged into snowdrifts, and several coming straight down and smacking into the top of the concrete pipe, snapping a variety of limbs and vertebrae.

Their broken bodies rained down in front of the pipe, and then one by one they dragged themselves toward Becks' hiding place. At first, she used her spears to fight them off and kill a few, but when a clump of them

154

started pushing their way into the opening of the pipe, she had no choice but to open fire. The deafening roar of her pistols inside the pipe threatened to rupture her eardrums, but better that than ruptured blood vessels and torn flesh from getting eaten alive.

To avoid contaminated blood spatter, she moved back deeper into the pipe, onto a slimy, foul-smelling pile of god-knows-what. Her eight direct headshots made quite a pile of goo in front of her as well, as bits of brain, bone, and burst eyeballs rimmed the pipe. Over the pile of fresh corpses, other zombies tried to squeeze their way in, but Becks quickly shot them, as well, until there were so many bodies they plugged up the hole.

Sitting back in the darkness of the pipe, breathless, there was just enough light at the entrance to reveal the wall of shattered skulls and faces. Clearing an opening to escape would be a strenuous, bloody job, but with so many other zombies still out there, she couldn't worry about that now. She had no choice but to stay put and spend the night.

Switching on her flashlight and pointing it into the depths of the pipe, she found a couple of dirty plastic bags and several plastic soda bottles. Crushing the bottles flat, and spacing them around her swollen knee, she tied the plastic bags around the bottles to make a splint to try to immobilize the damaged joint. Then she found that if she stretched out lengthwise and angled herself just right on the curve of the pipe, she was actually able to stay out of the stream of water. In this position, and with no more attempted zombie incursions into the pipe, she eventually drifted off to sleep.

She dreamt that she was crawling through the woods, and branches kept scratching her face. In her dream she swatted at the branches, and as her hands moved in unison with the nightmare, they came into contact with something real, solid, and furry. From deep sleep, to sitting bolt upright and screaming in a heartbeat, she grabbed her flashlight and found that a column of rats had been scurrying over her on their way to the pile of corpses. Dozens and dozens of rats swarmed over the mass of flesh, plunging their pointed snouts and sharp teeth into eye sockets, nostrils, and mouths. Some were soaked in blood as they perched inside of skulls, slurping down juicy bits of brain. Others gnawed deeply into throats, fingers, and any other piece of exposed flesh they could find in their midnight feast.

155

If Becks had anything in her stomach she would have lost it. She yelled some more and banged the sticks against the wall, but barely a single beady eye bothered to even glance her way. This was the best meal they had in months, and Becks could yell all she wanted—these rats had no intention of leaving until their bellies were stuffed to bursting with zombie flesh.

Needless to say, Becks slept no more that night. Just the collective sound of all those rats munching and tearing and scurrying around drove her crazy, but at least with the flashlight off she couldn't see the ghastly buffet.

Inside the pipe, with the entrance blocked, it didn't get terribly cold, but she could tell the temperature had dropped below freezing again as the water stopped flowing. However, that didn't deter the steady flow of rats that continued hour after hour.

It had to have been one of the longest nights of her life. Finally, after what seemed to be two days, the faint light of dawn started filtering through the gaps between the corpses—gaps made significantly larger by the flesh excavating conducted by the army of rats. As repulsed as she was, Becks had to give credit to this horde of scavengers who had managed to clear large chunks of skin and muscle down to the bare white bones. Some of the corpses were already picked clean, right down to the rib cages.

Despite the disgusting scene, Becks' own stomach was growling for attention. She drank half her bottle of water and ate one of the two energy bars she brought. She usually carried a lot more food and water with her, but this was supposed to be just a short walk down the street. And the thought of killing and eating a raw rat was just too much, especially a rat who had just gorged itself on a zombie.

As she was banishing that thought from her mind, one of the rats started squealing bloody murder. She assumed two rats were fighting over a tasty morsel of lung or kidney, but when she looked, she saw that a zombie hand had reached in through the wall of bones and grabbed a big, fat, rat, which was furiously biting the hand that grasped him, to no avail. Tightly clutching the squirming rodent, the male zombie pulled it up to his face and sunk his teeth into its belly. Even with its little spaghetti-like intestines dangling down, the rat continued to fight, until the zombie bit through its neck and started crunching on its skull.

Within seconds, more hands reached in trying to grab a fresh rat breakfast, but the rats all panicked, turned and ran—right over the top of Becks, like a filthy, hairy, wave sweeping over her. Covering her face and curling up against the wall, it took all of her power to keep from screaming as hundreds of little feet clawed their way across her body. Finally, the last stinking rat raced off into the darkness, but the real excitement was just beginning.

One by one, the corpses were pulled away by zombies fighting over the remaining flesh. The strongest ones were able to drag their prizes away to feast, while the weaker ones frantically sucked up any tidbits left behind, and fought over slippery organs that had fallen out of the bodies. During the conflict, Becks quietly inched her way even further down the pipe, and just prayed that once the last corpse was removed, no one felt inclined to search deeper inside.

Obviously, her hopes of escaping that morning were dashed. As the hours passed, the water didn't start flowing again, indicating there would be no warm-up that day. Dark gray clouds lowered and thickened, and even inside the pipe it started to become bitterly cold. By early afternoon it was snowing and the wind was howling, sounding like a demonic tuba as it raced past the drain pipe opening. Becks shivered, but tried to remain positive. Perhaps this latest storm would be a blessing, if it drove the zombies to hibernate in clumps again.

Becks ate half of her remaining energy bar and drank most of her water. She could deal with the hunger, but was feeling dehydrated. As the storm raged, she dared to move to the end of the drain pipe. Every last piece of flesh from her kills had been consumed or dragged off, and any remaining pools of blood had frozen, so at least there was no risk of infection. As it turned out, there was little risk of being seen, either, as visibility was so low it was practically a whiteout.

There didn't appear to be anyone close by, so she quickly reached out, snatched a fistful of fresh snow, crawled back into the pipe, and slowly ate the snow. She hated putting anything cold in her mouth, but she needed fluids. She grabbed a few more handfuls over the next couple of hours, which became increasingly easier as a layer of several inches had formed right on the rim. If her knee wasn't so painful—and she could determine whether the zombies were scattered or becoming inactive—she would have tried to use the cover of the falling snow to crawl through the woods,

157

but as much as she recoiled at the thought of spending another night in this freezing rat hole, it seemed to be the wisest choice.

By the time the sun set, every inch of her body either ached or was numb from the cold. There was no longer any way to get comfortable on the hard concrete, and she just yearned for something soft to sit on, or to be able to stand up and stretch. Becks was determined to get out of that pipe one way or another in the morning, but first, she had to make it through this terrible night.

It was noticeably warmer farther in, and the wind couldn't reach her, so she went back about 40 feet, before ingrown roots and debris blocked her way. It smelled like mushrooms and feces, but it was worth the tradeoff for the increased temperature. Where she was sitting, there were squishy patches of unfrozen muck, so it was actually above freezing, which was a life or death difference from the sub-zero wind chills out in the storm.

Exhausted, freaked out, and miserable, she alternately napped, cried, laughed nervously at the absurdity of her situation, and talked to herself in a series of profanity-riddled pep talks. She also berated herself for being so stupid and careless as to climb to the summit of a snow-capped zombie mountain, but then forgave herself, because how could she possibly know that the suburbs of New Jersey *had* snow-capped zombie mountains?

Awakening from one of her short naps, she was grateful to see the night had passed, by the small circle of light at the end of the pipe. Wasting no time, she started to crawl toward the front, which was rather awkward and difficult, being unable to bend or put pressure on her injured knee. As she slowly made her way, she thought the opening looked odd, like some strange yin yang symbol of blue and white. Twenty feet away, Becks realized a curved snowdrift was blocking half of the opening, meaning the storm had to have dumped another one or two feet.

That was bad news for the hungry zombies who were hopefully driven back to their snowy cocoons, but it wasn't great news for Becks, either, especially if there was an icy coating over the snow. But there was only one way to find out. With a pistol in one hand and a spear in the other, she used her feet to push through the drift. It was hard to judge the depth until she dropped down out of the pipe and sank over her knees. But before she even tried to take a step, she slowly scanned the woods around her and the road above.

There were no zombies visible on the edge of the road, which of course, didn't mean that a thousand of them hadn't lain down on top of one another, forming a little mountain range she would have to climb over again. At first glance, she thought the woods were clear, but then she realized those strange tree stumps scattered about were really individual zombies frozen in a variety of grotesque poses, like some perverse sculpture display. There were several medium-to-large hillocks in the snow; one or two of which had hair and hands sticking out, so she knew that was where some groups of zombies had huddled together and were now dormant. At least she hoped they were dormant!

That was the good news. The bad news was that without snowshoes and with a bum knee, trying to walk in snow this deep would get her nowhere fast. But with only half an energy bar left, and being chilled to the bone, she had to get back to the post office even if it took her all day. There was no guarantee the bright sunshine wouldn't start melting the new-fallen snow, once again releasing the swarms of zombies.

Having no other choice, she holstered her pistol, strapped the spear to her back, and threw herself face down into the snow. By using her arms and right leg, she managed a type of crab crawl, which was awfully slow, but kept her moving.

Ha, look at me! Becks thought, trying to bring some levity to the situation. *I'm a snow crab!*

After twenty minutes, Becks was sweating profusely and completely winded from the exertion. Half her energy was being expended just by lifting her body up out of the snow, in order to push herself forward another foot or so. She would promptly sink back down and have to repeat the push-up/push-forward motion over and over, like a hellish punishment of boot camp calisthenics. Weak from hunger, lack of sleep, and stress, she had to take frequent breaks to catch her breath.

On one of her breaks, she rolled over on her back and was stunned to see a zombie draped over a branch about ten feet up in the air right above her! It looked to be in a twilight state, or had very recently died (for good). As to how it got up there, Becks had no idea, but she had no intentions of lingering to try to figure it out. She had already seen some suspicious, dark shapes under the snow beneath her several times, and while they could have been fallen tree limbs, they could also be zombie limbs.

After a grueling hour and a half of crawling, Becks finally reached a section of the woods that was past the embankment, and had a gentle slope up to the road. Her right leg was getting rubbery from fatigue, but she couldn't stop now. In fact, she was actually able to pick up the pace a little, as there were a lot of pines trees that had caught the snow, so it wasn't as deep on the ground. She was even able to stand and walk ten or twelve feet at a time in some spots.

Finally, she made it up to the edge of the road. The post office was about the length of a football field away on the other side of the street. Not far, but unfortunately there were a lot of heads and torsos sticking up out of the snow. Were they frozen to death, or in a twilight state?

Quietly crawling over to the torso of a pathetic, emaciated old man with white stubble on his gaunt cheeks, and wearing a red and black flannel coat and Elmer Fudd-type hat, Becks gently poked him with one of her spears. There was no reaction at first, but a less gentle poke drove part of the knife tip into his shoulder, and his eyes popped open. He could only manage a weak groan or two, and his arms flailed around for a few seconds, but he was clearly on his last legs, so to speak. Even though he would most likely die that day, Becks recalled the words of Cam:

"Every zombie you kill today, is one less that could bite you tomorrow."

Pulling the blade out of his shoulder, she then thrust it into his eye and deep into his brain. Greenish goo oozed out, signaling that the ZIPs network was breaking down and dying. She hoped that was the case with most of the other zombies trapped in the snow, but again, she wasn't going to wait around to find out.

However, even though the post office and its warmth, food, and safety were in sight, Becks paused long enough to reach around inside the man's flannel jacket and find his wallet. For some reason—maybe because in some ways he reminded her of her dad—she wanted to know who he had been.

His driver's license identified him as Burt Olson, 82 years old, and living at 75 Meadow Street. His wallet also contained his Veteran's ID card, a picture of his wife, kids, and grandkids, a couple of fishing licenses that expired in the 1980s, one credit card, a supermarket discount card, and fourteen dollars.

This was strictly against Becks' usual policy of not wanting to know a zombie's name, or any details that might humanize the inhuman creatures, but there was just something so sad and poignant about this man. However, when she noticed some long strands of black hair and specks of dried flesh stuck between his yellowed teeth, the sympathetic moment was shattered. He may have been a sweet old man in life, but he had nonetheless turned into a murdering geriatric zombie. Still, Becks pocketed his wallet before she began her final push for "home."

Several modest-sized mounds dotted the road before her, as the huge, compact herd that had literally stuck together in the first big snowfall, had spread out after Becks had awakened them. With this latest storm, smaller groups had huddled together and were then blanketed by the thick layer of snow. Becks hoped that smaller groups meant less total body heat, which meant a lower survival rate. However, she also wondered if this many were caught outside, how many were safely nesting in the countless houses, apartments, schools, and businesses around her?

Just as long as none of them got the urge to mail a letter, Becks thought, as she knew her first order of business upon returning to the post office was to conduct another full sweep for zombies—and scavengers.

Crawling and dragging herself as quickly and quietly as possible between the mounds, she was still forced to spear three zombies partially sticking out of the snow who had been awakened by her movements. One already had an eyeball hanging out of its socket, rolling back and forth across its cheek, which made it even easier for her to get the blade into its brain.

More than two hours after emerging from the drain pipe, Becks finally made it back to the post office parking lot, which was blessedly mound-free. She was also even further relieved to see that there weren't any tracks in the snow, which didn't mean someone hadn't entered the unlocked back door before the storm. As exhausted as she was, she picked up the pace the last 50 feet, and was thrilled to roll off the snow bank and onto the clear pavement under the awning by the stairs.

Standing up wasn't all she hoped it would be, however, as every muscle ached, and her head throbbed. Hanging onto both handrails, she methodically swung her stiff, swollen, left leg up a stair, put all her weight on her weary arms, and then stepped up with her right leg. The staircase

161

seemed twice as long as it was when she left, but finally, mercifully, she reached the door and got inside.

Too wired and tired for games, she immediately aimed a pistol at the ceiling and fired twice, and then started howling like a banshee. She figured if there were any zombies, that racket would have damn sure woken them up. If any scavengers had entered, they would probably be pissing in their pants right about now. Fortunately, after a full sweep, she found that no one else had breached her sanctuary.

Making sure everything was locked up tight, Becks went down into the fallout shelter and made a roaring fire. Stripping off her filthy clothes, she put on multiple layers of L.L. Bean fleece jackets and pants meant for Mrs. Jackie Greer of 44 Dobbin Court. Mrs. Greer's "wicked good" sheepskin slippers also felt like heaven to her half-frozen toes as she slipped them on.

The next order of business was food, and lots of it.

Like a rat on a corpse, she thought as she pushed food into her mouth at a completely uncivilized rate.

Then sleep.

A sleep so deep that not even images of rats crawling over her or zombies crawling into drain pipes could disturb her. She woke up briefly after eight hours, then again two hours later. Each time her only thought was that she wouldn't leave the post office again until spring. After fourteen hours of sleep, she decided to get up, but only to build another fire and eat more food. And even once fully awake, she swore that if she had enough food and water, she would not leave her sanctuary until every snowflake had melted, and every frozen zombie had rotted to mush.

Chapter 14

Was it January? February? Did it even matter? The dark, cold days of snow and ice stretched into weeks; maybe months. Every day was like the next, only the food reserves dwindled a little more, and anything that remotely tasted good was long gone. At least there was plenty of fresh water to be had by melting the seemingly unending snow.

Becks had completely lost track of time in her fallout shelter. Her only trips outdoors were limited to the post office parking lot for snow and gasoline. She had been able to get the generator going by replacing the rotted pull cord with the string from a massive, 4X pair of sweatpants, ordered in both black and starlight blue by Mr. Jeffrey Donnard of 42 Paxton Avenue. The electric heaters kept her sanctuary toasty warm, while the ventilation pump brought in much needed fresh air. The fluorescent lights were wonderful—even though they had that annoying buzz—and she spent days on end opening packages, reading books, and going through some of the huge sacks of mail.

At first, the letters had upset her with their desperate pleas for help, the pitiable expressions of hopelessness of the infected, and the heart-wrenching goodbyes from people across the country who knew they would never see their loved ones again. But the lack of any mentally challenging work and the complete isolation had started to get to Becks. Her heart and mind were suffering in strange and unpleasant ways, so as painful as these *Letters from the Apocalypse* were, she *needed* them to still feel connected to the rest of humanity.

Before delving into the countless sacks of letters, however, she had gone into the sorting room to look for the mail set aside for Meadow Street, specifically for number 75, the Olson residence. There were four letters that had never been delivered, and Becks opened them in chronological order.

The first was from Burt's daughter, Elsie, in Virginia. She was frantic to find out how serious was her mother's infection, and if "the men in those white suits and masks" had taken her away to "one of those horrible facilities" she had heard about. Elsie did try to reassure her father that she and her kids were doing fine, and were "completely safe in the base housing." Her husband, Jim, was apparently in charge of troops sent to Washington, D.C. to "deal with the latest outbreak," but she expected it would "all be over soon" and Jim would "be back in less than a week."

Elsie ended the letter by asking her dad to "give mom a kiss" for her, "if it's safe," and to make sure he didn't leave the house. And above all, "don't try to do something heroic, like you always do."

The next letter was from his daughter, Chelsea, in Ann Arbor, Michigan. She related that things weren't as bad there as they were on the east coast, "but still, Bob and I think it's best to bring the family up to the lake house for a few weeks just to be on the safe side." Chelsea obviously hadn't heard that her mother had become infected, and even mildly

163

chastised her parents for not having email or cell phones. "Maybe I could have found out what was going on if you two had ever decided to enter the 21st century!" she wrote.

Chelsea also ended her letter in a similar manner to her sister. "And Dad, PLEASE!, just don't try to be a hero this time."

Burt Olson, defender of truth, justice, and the American way, Becks thought. *And I had to jab a knife into his brain…*

The third letter was brief, and from his son, Brian, in California, who didn't mention a wife or kids. Apparently, Los Angeles was "turning to shit real fast." Some friends had called and told him to join them "in the hills," but as the roads were "all fucking parking lots," and panicked people were "shooting at anything that moves," he couldn't get out of the city. His letter ended with a description of some aches and pains he was experiencing, and he apologized for the sloppy writing, but his "hands kept shaking." He was sure it was "just nerves," and promised to write again soon.

The last letter was from Elsie again. She hadn't heard from Jim in two weeks, and no one at the base had any information. Two of her kids were sick, but she didn't dare bring them to the clinic because she was terrified the guards would take them away. The base was still secure, but if she stayed, she wouldn't be able to hide her children's illness for long.

"Dad, I'm coming home. I'm leaving today. I'll stop in D.C. on the way and see if I can find Jim. I hope to see you real soon. With any luck, we will all be there before this letter arrives. Hope Mom is feeling better. Love you both so much."

Becks closed her eyes and imagined what she would find at 75 Meadow Street. Did Elsie ever find Jim, and did they all make it home, only to find that Burt was infected and his wife was dead. Or worse? It was like some addictive soap opera that was canceled mid-season. Becks' entire life was spent in the pursuit of answers, but this was just another AZA mystery that would probably never be solved. And as she knew there couldn't possibly be any happy endings to this story, perhaps it would be best if she didn't know. Still, if her journey back happened to cross Meadow Street…

And so the days dragged on with the heaviness and sorrow of the thousands of tragedies exposed in the letters. There was one day, however, where Becks actually laughed. At the bottom of one of the sacks, she found a bundle of letters from the Internal Revenue Service sent to about a hundred small businesses and self-employed people who had missed their quarterly estimated tax payments. The IRS actually had the balls to state that "Zombie infections, of either the taxpayer or a dependent, are not legal grounds for delay of payment."

However, the IRS was also quick to note that "Payments from infected individuals will not be accepted in person, and must be mailed by the specified date in order to avoid incurring additional penalties."

"Death and taxes!" Becks said to her sock monkey, Ginger, as she stuffed all of the IRS letters into the barrel and ignited them. "I'm surprised they hadn't come up with a zombie tax. Or would they have called it an undead surcharge?"

Physically, apart from being a bit undernourished, Becks was getting into the best shape of her life. Once her knee healed, which took almost three weeks, she started running—seriously running, not jogging. She had cleared a path through the packages that took her around the sorting room and both storerooms. She would then go over the counter into the lobby, and back over again. At first, she would just put her butt on the counter and swing her legs over. On the tenth day, however, she was able to jump up onto the counter and leap down. Two weeks later, if she got up enough steam, she was actually able to vault clear over the counter.

The basement and back entrance stairs also were part of her route. After a couple of weeks she enhanced that part of her workout, as she started carrying heavy bags of ice-melting salt up and down the stairs.

One ridiculously heavy package she had opened, which had been mailed at a cost of $112, contained some fancy barbells on a rack. Becks couldn't believe someone paid to ship a weight set, but she took advantage by working her way through progressively heavier barbells in conjunction with her calisthenics and running. From ten minutes of running with no added weight, to an hour carrying as much as fifty pounds on her back and another ten in her arms, she began to discover a level of speed and endurance, the likes of which she never thought herself capable.

Of course, this wasn't just some excuse to pass the time. It had a purpose; a deadly serious purpose. Becks was well aware that the ATV probably wouldn't be able to take her all the way back to the highway, especially since the last ice storm brought down many trees and limbs. In fact, from what she had seen just around the post office, she would be lucky to drive even a few blocks with all the trees, debris, and zombie corpses.

No, Becks knew her only chance of rescue was to literally *run* for her life. And for that, she needed protein and calories. She had recently found a shipment intended for Mr. Harvey Hornbecker of 18 Bridle Path Lane, which contained a 5-gallon plastic bucket full of "Emergency Meals." The meals were pouches of varieties of pasta dishes, to which you added boiling water. No matter what Becks tried, they all turned out like the consistency of wallpaper paste, and didn't taste much better, but at least they provided calories. But with her jerky gone, and none of her remaining supplies offering sufficient protein, she had to do something.

Deer never travelled in this neighborhood, due to all the zombies under the snow, but Becks had never been able to bring herself to shoot one, anyway, even on her many hunting trips with Cam. She had seen squirrels running from tree to tree, but they were just too damn cute to harm even a hair on their bushy little tails. Bunnies were also out of the question, and she hadn't seen any birds big enough to waste ammunition. That left only one thing.

"Rats!" Becks groaned, realizing that if she was to get the necessary protein she needed fresh meat, and lots of it.

Although she had pledged an oath to die before she ever ate raw rat, she did have fourteen George Foreman grills at her disposal, ordered by men and women all over town. There were several rat traps in the maintenance closet, and enough spoiled cheese spread sent from Minnie Connor to her sister, Maxie, (their parents obviously had a sense of humor) to use as bait.

"Maybe there aren't even any rats around here," Becks said as she set three traps in the parking lot late one afternoon. "Maybe they're all back in the storm drain and won't come out until spring."

As she went to bed that night, Becks couldn't decide whether or not she really wanted to catch any rats. While she had dissected her share of sanitized lab rodents in school, she didn't know if she could skin and gut a filthy street rat, and then actually eat it! At first light, she grabbed a bucket and went outside to see if she would have to find out just how strong a stomach she possessed.

Three traps, three rats—two dead and one huge one still squirming. Grimacing, she held down the body of the flailing rodent and quickly

166

pulled her hunting knife across its throat. She wanted to gag, and actually stood up to go back inside, but the lightheadedness she experienced upon standing made her determined to go through with it.

The first things to go were the tails—she was absolutely disgusted by rat tails. Then the feet were severed, followed by the two remaining heads. Peeling the dirty fur skins off the carcasses brought on the dry heaves, but that was nothing compared to gutting the little creatures. Heaping snow on top of the pile of rat organs and remains, so as not to attract zombies, Becks tossed the prepared bodies in the bucket and went inside to cook them.

Firing up the generator, Becks plugged in one of the 14 George Foreman grills, and while it was heating up, she grabbed the box that contained all the bottles of hot sauce she had found in the packages. There was quite a collection, and it seemed that each one promised to be more brutally hot and painful than their competitors. She always liked reasonably spicy food, but she wondered how her digestive system would react after months of eating small quantities of bland food.

Digging around in the box of bottles with colorful labels and clever names, she found one that was actually called Death by Zombie, Bitingly Hot Sauce. It seemed oh so wrong, yet right, all at the same time, so she sprinkled some on one of the rats and slapped it on the grill. On another one, she just sprinkled salt and pepper she found in the break room. For the third and largest rat, Becks coated it with some homemade Texas barbeque sauce that Angel Sanchez had mailed to his cousin Jorge, along with a photo of himself and some friends armed to the teeth in the back of a pickup truck. The truck had a sign taped to the tailgate which read, "Bring it on Zombie Mothafuckas."

Becks almost pitied the zombie population of that Texas town—if there were any still standing.

Once the aroma of the cooking meat hit her nostrils, her aversion to the idea of eating rat quickly dissipated.

"Well, it doesn't smell like chicken," she said to Ginger, "but damn, it doesn't smell bad!"

Letting the meat get well done to make sure the heat killed anything these rats may have been carrying, she set the table with the monogrammed china plates and silver-plated flatware meant as a wedding gift to Donald and Sheila Percy of Belmont Avenue. Placing the crispy rats on the plate, she paused with a "What am I doing?" moment, but her growling stomach drowned out her mind's protestations.

"Here goes nothing," she said, cutting off a hunk of BBQ rat, closing her eyes, and shoving it in her mouth.

Chewing as hesitantly as if there might be broken glass in the meat, she slowly opened one eye, then the other, and began chewing in earnest. It was gamey, with a distinct flavor—to say the least—but not a completely bad flavor. The one with the zombie hot sauce was way too hot for her taste, but she ate it anyway. The one with only the salt and pepper was too...ratty, so she doused it in the Texas barbeque sauce and sucked the meat off every tiny rib and vertebrae.

Waiting a couple of days to make sure she had no ill effects from the rodent meat, Becks then started setting five traps every evening. And rather than letting all the melted fat from the grill go to waste, she recalled that Civil War soldiers would break up their barely edible hardtack crackers and fry the pieces in bacon fat. In her Cold War/Apocalypse version, Becks ground up the Civil Defense crackers, added some spices, mixed in the rat fat to form a kind of dough, then grilled the little cakes. They weren't great, but they didn't suck, either, and she couldn't afford to waste anything that would give her the strength to run and fight.

After two weeks and dozens of grilled rats later, Becks was feeling strong. She joked to Ginger about starting to grow fur and whiskers, but she was grateful she had overcome her cultural disgust of the revolting vermin and had done what was necessary to survive. And with the temperatures routinely spending daylight hours in the forties now, she knew the snow would soon melt and it would be time to go.

The question remained, however, what would be the right time? If she left while there was still snow on the ground, it would be difficult to run, and she could literally step into a mound of zombies. If she waited for it to warm up enough for all the snow to be gone, the zombies who had survived being outside would all be fully mobile. All those who nested indoors would also come out. The answer was simple—there was no good time to head out on foot.

Unfortunately, the decision was taken out of her hands when a ferocious coastal storm pounded the area for 48 hours. Warm rain fell in buckets and eroded the snow pack like acid. By the end of the second night, the copious amounts of rainfall, coupled with all the melted snow, turned the post office street into a river—a river filled with rotting zombie corpses killed by the cold winter, as well as recently deceased zombies who drowned in the flood waters.

Those fresh corpses were what concerned Becks the most, as it had been found that bodies of water containing new corpses became breeding grounds for the parasites. She had read about one town in New Hampshire that was killing zombies and throwing them into a nearby lake. The parasite eggs made their way into streams and wells, and any survivors who didn't boil their water became infected. And infection would also occur if you waded through these contaminated waters and had any sort of an open wound, or the water splashed into your eyes, nose, or mouth.

In short, the flood waters in northern New Jersey had created one big ZIP kiddie pool, and there was no way Becks was about to jump in. But as soon as those waters receded, she would hit the ground running. On the positive side, the rushing waters had swept a lot of the bodies off the road and either into ditches or piled them up against fallen trees or cars. Any stretch of open pavement was a bonus, but how far that clear pavement stretched was the question.

Three days later the flood waters were gone from the street, but the ground was exceedingly soft and spongy. Testing the lawn in front of the post office, Becks found that walking was tricky, as every boot step slipped and sank in the muddy soil. If she left now, she wouldn't be able to get across yards and wooded sections with any speed or confidence. She would need to take the ATV on a reconnaissance mission of the nearby streets to assess her best route.

Gearing up one evening in her silverware armor and night vision goggles, and mounting her ATV steed, Becks appeared to be ready for some type of steampunk joust. She had utilized all the broom handles, knives, and potentially deadly objects she could find in the packages to make spears, clubs, and anything else she could wield to clear her path of zombies.

However, her favorite weapon wasn't one she had made herself. It was an "authentic reproduction" of a "15th century German flail" purchased at a cost of $380, plus tax, shipping, and handling, by Jason Weems of Century Road. There was a disclaimer in the box which stated that "the enclosed authentic reproduction is meant for entertainment purposes only, and is not to be used in any combat situations."

Becks wasn't sure what kind of entertainment the manufacturer had in mind, but she had certainly been amused by firmly gripping the stainless steel shaft and swinging the hefty spiked ball into the heads of all the worthless "collector dolls" from the Danbury Mint. Becks had checked the invoices in those packages and found they had all been ordered in the final weeks before the collapse. She couldn't imagine what went through these women's minds. With zombies running amok, shortages of food and fuel, and frequent power outages, they all decided that their time and money would best be spent ordering porcelain dolls!

In any event, the dolls had provided good practice for Becks as she prepared her defenses. Her pistols were still her primary arms, but when quiet kills were needed, she would be glad to have all of these primitive, but deadly, weapons at her disposal. She had used a bungee cord to strap a small garbage can to the back of the ATV to hold her hockey stick, spears and clubs, but the flail was in a holster she modified, right next to her beloved .44 Magnum.

The ATV was running a little rough, even though Becks had made sure she started it up and ran it for a while at least once a week. Perhaps the old gas from the mail trucks was the problem, but she didn't have a lot of options. It sputtered and protested for the first few minutes, but evened out enough to proceed.

Easing out of the parking lot and onto the road, she cautiously headed left toward the intersection—the same route she had taken that resulted in spending two nights in a storm drain. The melting snow had revealed hundreds of dead zombies, but the flood had pushed the majority of them out of the way. As it was dark, there weren't too many mobile zombies around, and because they hated water, those who didn't drown in the flood had shambled their way toward higher ground, which fortunately was to the east.

It was nice to see the full length of the sign posts this time as Becks pulled up to the intersection. The horror of "The Day the Earth Moved" still made her shudder, but she would never make that kind of mistake again, she thought, and then tapped on one of the broom handles so she didn't jinx herself. She may have devoted her life to science, but knocking on wood still had its value.

Turning left, she proceeded slowly down the hill into uncharted territory. At the bottom of the hill was some standing water, about an inch or two deep, but by driving at no more than walking speed, Becks was able to make sure none of the potentially contaminated water splashed on her.

There were more bodies in the road, and plenty more scattered across the front lawns. The odor of decomposing flesh was quite strong, but it was somewhat mitigated by the aromatherapy oils, ordered by Susie Compton of Lafayette Avenue, which Becks had rubbed onto her surgical mask before she left. It was a trick they used at the funeral home where she had worked, and then she regularly used it to observe autopsies or perform human dissections. But even with the heavily scented oil, the stench of death was everywhere.

Navigating around several fallen trees and numerous corpses, she was pleased to have made it a few blocks without incident. Unfortunately, two blocks in front of her was a large herd stretching the width of the street and spilling over into the tall weeds of the abandoned homes on either side. Even at this distance, Becks could tell they were reacting to the sound of the ATV engine, but as long as she didn't turn on the lights they probably wouldn't move towards her.

Working under that assumption, she moved forward to within about 100 feet to get a better idea of the size and condition of the herd. They were a thin and hungry-looking group of zombies, which was nothing new. Unfortunately, though, they weren't nearly as lethargic or had as much tissue damage as the zombies who had been stuck outdoors all winter. The relative cleanliness and decent condition of their clothing also spoke to the fact that this group had sheltered indoors, and had only recently emerged from their nests and came together.

Her assumption that the herd wouldn't move to the sound of the engine in the darkness was only partially correct. While the bulk of them just stood in place and turned their heads in Becks' direction, at least a dozen started moving fairly quickly toward her. She knew by their speed—which was still slower than a human's brisk walk, but fast for the undead—that they had recently switched, probably within the last month or two. That was both encouraging and troubling news, as it meant there was most likely a human population in the area—one that was still losing its friends and family members to infection.

Becks mentally filed away all this information as she turned to head back. When she had put a full block's distance between her and the herd, something caught her eye that made her stop. There was a rusted gas grill in the driveway of one of the houses, and it gave her an idea. Thanks to Eddie's inclination to set things on fire, Becks decided to see if the grill's propane tank still had anything inside. Disconnecting the hose from the grill to the tank, she turned the knob on the tank and heard the telltale hiss of escaping gas.

Assuming her best Olympic discus thrower pose, except she was using two hands, Becks spun 180 degrees and released her grip on the tank. The heavy container of propane flew up in an arc and came smashing down through the living room picture window, bounced across the floor and settled against a couch. Becks then carefully reached through the broken window and used her lighter to ignite the drapes. The flames were too bright for her night vision goggles, so she had to turn away. She drove back another half a block and then waited.

It took about fifteen minutes for the heat of the fully engulfed living room to be sufficient to explode the propane tank, but when it did, it was quite spectacular—although it did pale in comparison to the multiple tanks Eddie had used to destroy his house. The entire structure was soon ablaze, giving an orange glow to the entire neighborhood. This was more than just an amusing pastime for Becks—although she had to admit she was getting rather fond of blowing shit up and burning things down—this was an experiment to see if the zombies followed their previous behavior and moved toward the light of the fire.

Sure enough, the blast and ensuing conflagration drew the entire herd like moths to a flame. Actually, that wasn't the best analogy, as unlike self-immolating moths, zombies stopped just short of burning themselves—usually.

Becks had simply hoped to be able to use diversions like burning buildings on side streets to draw the herds off the main road, but something unexpected happened. While the front rows of zombies stopped a safe distance from the intense heat, those at the back of the herd kept pushing forward. Like a relentless tidal wave, the mass of undead flesh pushed those in front right up to the walls of the burning building, killing and severely injuring dozens. And the carnage only ended when the force of the herd was no longer sufficient to push the rapidly growing heap of sizzling, charred flesh.

With Plan A now jelling, Becks turned the ATV away from the zombie roast and headed back to the post office for what she hoped would be her last night there. However, she did make one slight detour.

A lone male zombie stood in the middle of one of the side streets. With flail in hand, she gunned the engine and made her approach. It looked a bit dazed and confused at the loud sound of something it couldn't see, and appeared unsure how to react. Becks resolved its dilemma as she lifted up off the seat of the ATV to get just the right height and angle to swing the spiked ball into the side of the zombie's head. A satisfying cracking sound accompanied the devastating blow that resulted in one of the long spikes penetrating deep into the cranium. The zombie dropped like a sack of medieval potatoes, and Becks imagined herself as the triumphant knight riding her mechanical steed back to her castle.

She would never admit this to another human being, but sometimes apocalypses could be fun.

Chapter 15

For a final splurge, Becks let the generator and heaters run all night. Surprisingly, the noise didn't bother her. In fact, the total silence of the post office, and especially the fallout shelter, had worn on her nerves, and it was good to have artificial sound again. Even in the relatively tranquil suburb of Nyack where she grew up, there were always phones ringing, passing cars, jets and airplanes, lawnmowers—something to constantly give you subconscious reminders that you lived in a technological world filled with people like yourself.

These months of complete isolation and quiet were constant reminders that the world had gone to shit and she was surrounded by creatures who were nothing like her. As Becks packed up and prepared to leave, she finally realized that if she had to be there much longer she would probably develop some serious psychological issues. Perhaps she already had, and just didn't recognize them.

"You've been a great friend, Ginger," Becks said to her sock monkey as she gave it a hug, "but I think it's best you stay here and look after things."

Propping up Ginger on the front counter, Becks pinned a note to her stuffed friend that described how she had ended up stranded in New Jersey. The note also talked about Sgt. Colaneri, Angie, and the Tasi family, as well as West Point and the Picatinny Arsenal, urging others to try to reach Interstate 287. She also mentioned the fallout shelter, and all of the new clothing she had separated into various boxes of men's, women's, and children's styles and sizes, along with countless other items she had grouped together according to their usefulness.

"Take whatever you need," she wrote. "I hope these things help you to survive."

She left one more note in the sorting room, where she had labeled the sacks of mail she had read and categorized according to subject. For example, there was the "I'm infected" sack, the "I'll never see you again" sack, the "I'll see you soon" sack, and even the "I hope you die" bag of letters, although thankfully they were in the minority.

"Please do not destroy these letters," she wrote on a big piece of cardboard with a red Sharpie. "They are the only memorials to generations of families that have been lost."

Perhaps all of her sorting, categorizing, and labeling had been a bit crazy, but without a lab at her disposal, her brain needed some sort of tasks to keep it from turning to mush. But now the task at hand was to prepare everything to make sure her brain didn't get eaten.

Becks separated all of her food and water so that she had a three-day supply of survival crackers in her pockets and bottles of water duct taped to her body, in the event she had to drop everything and sprint. Her backpack was crammed with about a week's worth of food—including the precious MREs she had set aside—and a couple of days of water. A duffle bag was stuffed with more food and water and strapped to the ATV. Realistically, she knew the ATV wouldn't go far, but she wanted to have more supplies than she thought she might need.

The same went for weapons. Her pistols, hockey stick, and sniper rifle were like parts of her body that she would not drop under any circumstances. The flail was in its holster, but due to its weight, she would jettison it if necessary.

Another important part of her arsenal was the pepper spray she found in a cabinet in the post office. Initially, the mail carriers must have used it to fend off vicious dogs, but as the infection spread, pepper spray became essential to temporarily incapacitate zombies. The eyes of the undead were just as sensitive to the potent irritant, and many lives had been saved as people had time to run or call the authorities—when authorities were still around to call, that is. Becks hoped she would never be in a position where her only option was pepper spray, but it was one of those things Cam always said, "It's better to have it and not need to use it, than leave it behind."

As twilight approached, she started feeling antsy and anxious. The post office had been her port in the storm, literally and figuratively, and she was about to leave that safe haven for dangers both obvious and unknown. She had certainly faced plenty of life or death situations before without being this nervous and she couldn't understand why she was so on edge.

"I must have eaten too many rats," she joked to Ginger as she placed the keys to the post office next to the sock monkey.

Just before leaving, Becks had unlocked all of the doors and had taped signs on the front windows indicating that there was food, water, clothing, beds, and a generator inside. As an afterthought, she took another piece of white cardboard from a priority mail box and simply wrote, "Becks was here." At first, she just looked at it as a playful whim, but then a thought crossed her mind as she recalled all the signs people had hung out their windows and nailed to the fronts of their houses. The next fire she set, she decided, she would leave a calling card.

Finally, it reached that hour when most zombies stopped walking because it was too dark. Those whose eyes had deteriorated to the point of blindness still walked night and day, but they were easy to spot as they bumped into everything and fell down a lot, and therefore were easy to avoid. With Becks' night vision goggles, she should be able to rule the night, and planned to travel only in darkness.

From what Eddie had told her, she estimated she was about five miles from 287. In a vehicle with minor obstructions, she could make it before the engine warmed up. On an ATV with a few herds of zombies, it could take a couple of days. On foot with many herds and a lot of obstacles, possibly weeks. Possibly never.

Trying to remain optimistic as she flipped down her goggles and started up the ATV, she took off for what she hoped was the last leg of her very long journey. As she pulled into the street, the ATV sputtered, jerked, and stalled.

"You have got to be fucking kidding me!" Becks yelled, not caring how many zombies heard her.

Taking a moment to compose herself, she tried the engine again. It started, coughed a few times, almost cut out, but then sounded strong and steady.

"Okay, let's try this again."

Stopping in the intersection, she carefully looked in all directions for any zombies. There were several at the base of the blind curve, but that was to the east, and she was heading west. There were a few stragglers here and there, but she made it uneventfully back to where she had torched the house and quickly realized what a mistake it had been to set the fire on the street she needed to traverse. The piles of burned dead zombies had drawn scores of the hungry undead, and they jammed the road from side to side as they struggled with one another to grab a piece of the feast.

It would be like trying to cut through a mob of little old ladies swarming the shrimp and crab legs station of a casino buffet, Becks thought. *Well, maybe not that dangerous...*

As the ground was quite flat in this neighborhood and the properties just seemed to blend together—uninterrupted by any fences she could see—Becks decided to try to travel through several backyards to her right, behind the herd. Turning into the driveway of a small Cape Cod style house, she eased her way into the tall weeds of the backyard. Fortunately, the vegetation was all dead and dry, so it easily snapped and crunched beneath the wheels of the ATV.

Driving through a maze of rusted patio furniture, tree limbs, swing sets, overturned barbeque grills, and tool sheds, she made her way slowly past house after house. There was one yard that had a short picket fence, but it was more decorative than functional and with a little nudging by the ATV, a 6-foot section of the flimsy wood broke and gave way. She gave it a little extra gas just to make sure she would not get entangled in the splintered pieces of fence, but gave it just a little too much and lurched forward. Hitting the brakes, she stopped just short of driving right into an inground pool.

"Oh no! I am not doing that again!" she said out loud, remembering all too well one of the worst nights of her life, when she had fallen into a pool in Nyack, and had then been surrounded by zombies.

Skirting the edge of the pool, she drove up and over a patio that had several corpses sitting in Adirondack chairs. At least, she thought they were all corpses. Out of one of the chairs, a young female zombie suddenly lunged forward and grasped Becks' left leg. Startled, Becks turned too sharply and almost veered back around into the pool. The zombie was small, but strong and determined, and Becks couldn't shake her loose.

Realizing that at least three more of the figures in the Adirondack chairs had now risen and were heading her way, she didn't want to stop and get into a prolonged fight so close to the big herd. Instead, she spun the ATV around and headed for the picket fence on the other side of the yard at full speed, hoping it would shake off her attacker. Dragging the clinging zombie through the tall weeds and then smashing straight into the fence, the tenacious zombie still had both hands firmly gripping Becks' leg. In fact, now she was even hanging from Becks' boot by her teeth!

The sound of the ATV was clearly drawing more attention, so Becks needed to do something on the fly. The careening vehicle was hard enough to control without removing one of her hands to grab a gun or another weapon, so she drove through three more backyards dragging the zombie before an opportunity presented itself.

Someone had gone to considerable time and expense to build an impressive outdoor wood-fired brick oven. BZA, this family must have been the envy of the neighborhood cookout scene. Years ago, Cam and Becks had gone to a party where they were making pizzas in a similar outdoor oven, and she never forgot the scrumptious taste of that crisp, smoky crust. Now, she was about to make another brick oven memory of an entirely different nature.

Going as fast as she dared, Becks aimed right for the brick edifice to America's love affair with backyard cooking. It was a tricky piece of steering and coordination, but with the correct timing and angle of her last-second turn, as well as having the strength to stick her occupied left leg out about two feet, the female zombie's body impacted with the bricks with a delightfully satisfying cracking sound. The shattered zombie let go of Becks and fell in a crumpled heap.

177

As relieved as she was to be free of the unwanted passenger, she was far from being home free, as more dormant zombies were rising up from yards and streets, spilling out of houses, and staggering blindly toward the sound of the engine. Even though she had put some distance between her and the main herd, she had underestimated the number of undead who had not joined the pack. While the ATV was powerful enough to knock down a few single zombies in her path, groups of three or more presented a real problem, and more groups were starting to form.

The night vision goggles saved her life time and again as she was able to zigzag through the growing crowd, but they couldn't help her if she became boxed in a backyard with impenetrable fences. When it looked as though a sturdy stockade fence was about 60 feet ahead, Becks made a sharp left between two houses, running over a prone zombie who was too weak to stand, but still feebly reached out to try to grab her. The aggressive treads of the tires and weight of the vehicle made hamburger meat out of the already half-decayed zombie, but Becks' only thought was that she was glad no chunks sprayed up onto her.

Zooming out onto the road, the way ahead was clear as far as she could see, so she took advantage and went as fast as possible. At top speed, however, the engine sputtered again and the vehicle bucked once or twice, so she had to back off on the throttle. Still, she kept moving at a good pace and had gone at least half a mile before the next obstruction loomed in the distance.

The two-lane road opened up to four lanes before a major intersection—an intersection jam packed with cars. There had been a major multi-car accident as people fled right after quarantine, and many other cars became blocked, unable to move forward or back. Herds of freshly switched zombies quickly surrounded the stranded motorists, and it became a deadly waiting game—a game that zombies almost always won.

The zombies just stood there waiting for days, as one by one, the stranded motorists got out of their cars and tried to make a run for it. The tale of the outcome of this ultimate game of cat and mouse was told by the hundreds of scattered bones and bits of tattered clothing strewn about the intersection.

There was no way the ATV could get through this scene of carnage, so Becks turned right down a side street, hoping to bypass it. She wasn't the first to try to do that, as another line of abandoned cars made for an interesting ride. Repeatedly bouncing up, over, and down the sidewalks, she snaked her way two blocks before she had a relatively clear left turn. The main street was clear of cars at this point, but dormant zombies in twilight states were everywhere, and with the roar of the ATV, they would become active very quickly.

As much as she wanted to keep heading toward 287, she didn't want to take any foolish risks. She had a clear path diagonally across the street to a fabric shop, so she made a beeline to the glass double doors. Withdrawing her pistol, she prepared to shoot the lock, but a quick tug on the handle revealed that it was unlocked. It was a bit tricky trying to hold the doors open wide enough to get the ATV inside, but before any of the zombies got within arm's reach, she was in the fabric store with the doors locked.

It took a few minutes to make sure the aisles were clear, and the offices and storeroom in the back were unoccupied. Then she made sure the growing crowd in the street didn't start pressing against the glass storefront, which could give way with enough weight. But fortunately, once the ATV was silent, they all lost interest and sank back into twilight.

Realistically, Becks had been hoping to make it at least a mile that night. (Unrealistically, she had hoped to be cruising down Interstate 287 by dawn.) She had only gone a bit under three-quarters of a mile, but it was a huge step to finally get out of the post office and really start her journey home. Granted, the large populations of zombies everywhere was going to make things more difficult than she had anticipated, but with patience, and starting fires to create diversions, she felt confident she could make it, even if it meant only traveling one block or just one building at a time.

"Slow and steady wins the race," her father used to tell her whenever she felt overwhelmed, referring to one of her favorite childhood stories. Of course, Becks always identified with the swift hare—and was always bewildered and annoyed that he lost—but she would now have to embrace the qualities of the tortoise; a tortoise with the fiery breath of a dragon.

Turning off her night vision goggles, Becks switched on a flashlight so she could have a look around. She had very fond memories of visiting fabric stores with her mother, who was an accomplished seamstress. Unfortunately, Becks was even worse at sewing than she was at cooking— which was saying a lot—but only with cloth. With flesh she was

179

something of an artist, deftly suturing blood vessels and closing up wounds. But give her a dress pattern and a couple of yards of polyester and it was an embarrassment. Once, Becks even managed to sew the sleeve of the shirt she was wearing to the material of the skirt she was trying to make!

Despite her failings in the field of fashion, she still loved the look and feel of all the different fabrics. From the soft comfort of fleece and flannel, to the slinky sensuality of satin and silk, she was enamored of all the plaids, flowery prints, neon colors, and subtle earth tones these materials had to offer.

Pulling down several bolts of blanket fabric covered with cartoon characters, she unraveled yards and yards of the fluffy material and layered it on top of sheets of foam rubber in the corner of an office to make a bed. On the road, she usually slept with all of her clothes on so she could be up and on the move in case of an emergency, but a bolt of 100% silk in a vibrant hot pink just made her melt. Becks never had the money or inclination to indulge in expensive lingerie, but this silk was just screaming to be wrapped around a naked body.

Peeling off all of her clothes—every last stitch—she used at least five yards of the fabric to create a half sari, half mummy-like outfit that probably looked bizarre, but felt divine. There were plans to be made and scouting missions to undertake, but all the horror of the outside world would just have to wait until morning. Snuggling in between several hundred dollars-worth of fleecy dinosaur, sheep, and alphabet block-patterned material, wrapped in even pricier silk, Becks drifted away to sweet dreams of happier times from the past, and better times ahead.

A strange sound penetrated her sleep around dawn. At first she thought it was part of her dreams, but as it grew louder, she opened her eyes to the wonderful reality—a helicopter! Sprinting to the front windows, which faced east, she was unable to see it. Racing to the back of the store, the alley entrance was locked, and before she could even begin to look for a key, the distinctive *whump whump whump* of the rotor blades faded to silence.

It was disappointing, yet also encouraging to know there were still aircraft in the area. Getting her bearings, she determined that the helicopter had been flying from north to south—another West Point to Picatinny Arsenal patrol? Trying not to jump to any conclusions that the

180

spring offensive was starting, and armored vehicles and soldiers could be coming down the street at any second, Becks nonetheless felt a surge of excitement. After an MRE for breakfast, she began to make plans to stick out like a sore thumb in case any other helicopters came by.

Locating the stairs to the roof, she really had to put her back into lifting the rusty trap door. The building was rectangular, with a flat roof covered with more than half a century of tar. There were a couple of obsolete antennas that no one ever bothered to take down, which were perfect for the pieces of neon orange, yellow, and green fabric Becks tied to them, like a warship returning to port with all flags flying.

Then she unrolled long bolts of red and white cotton, alternating two rows of each, and using upholstery tacks to secure them to the roof. With a can of black spray paint, she wrote on the strips of white material, "BECKS WAS HERE. HEADING WEST FOR 287. LOOK FOR FIRE."

That was the easy part of her plan. The other part involved the pile of cars back in the intersection two blocks away. Becks counted at least 80 zombies on the street, and at least half of them were between her and the intersection. She would use far too much ammunition eliminating them all, and the sounds of gunshots would probably draw many more—and possibly even hostile humans. She would need to get creative to thin the herd more quietly—but not completely quietly, she decided.

There was a an old boom box back in the warehouse that was battery operated, and she found enough D-cell batteries in a drawer to get it working. That was the good news. The bad news was that there was only one cassette tape, *Donna Summer's Best Disco Hits*.

"Ugh. Maybe I'd rather be eaten by zombies," Becks said, as she made sure the tape player still worked.

Next, she emptied a couple of coffee cans from the office and filled them with buttons she tore off of their little cards, concentrating on the metal and rhinestone buttons. Instead of replacing the tight plastic lids, she loosely covered each can with tin foil. Bringing the cans to the roof, she used all her strength to toss one of the them as far down the street to her left as she could.

The can made an impressive *clank* when it hit the blacktop, followed by the clinking sounds of hundreds of metal buttons scattering and bouncing. The noise, coupled with the rhinestone buttons glittering in the late afternoon sun, drew zombies from at least a block around. Tossing the other can to the right, it provoked a similar reaction, drawing most of the zombies toward it, and away from the front of the fabric store.

Armed with her guns, bladed hockey stick, and a boom box set to auto replay fourteen songs from the queen of disco, Becks ran out the front door and across the street to Sid's Laundromat. She had scoped out the building from the roof of the fabric store, and hadn't seen anyone inside. She hoped to change that.

To her dismay, the front doors were locked, but the butt of Becks' sniper rifle punched a nice hole big enough for her hand. Once inside, she made a quick sweep to make sure it was clear. Placing the boom box on a washing machine at the back of the long room, she turned it on and let *Love to Love You Baby* boom at full volume. Running to the front of the Laundromat, she propped open the front doors, and then raced back to the fabric store. Climbing to the roof, she waited to see if her plan would work.

As the first song droned on and on—*Doesn't this thing ever end?* Becks wondered—the zombies who had become disinterested in the buttons started turning around and shuffling toward the Laundromat. Before *I Feel Love* began, at least a dozen of them had gone inside. By the time the last beats of *Hot Stuff* echoed down the block, only six zombies remained within eyesight on the road.

Sprinting back across the street, Becks' heart was pounding as she released the latches on the front doors of the Laundromat to close them. But before she could reach inside the hole in the glass to lock the doors, a male zombie with some kind of terrible skin disease on his face, which obscured both his age and ethnicity, lunged for her, throwing his weight against the doors. Becks had to hunch down and plant her feet to keep him from getting out. With her arms, she swung the hockey stick around and thrust the blade up through the hole, catching the zombie just under the ribcage.

Even after being stabbed, the persistent zombie still tried to get through the doors, so Becks jumped to her feet and pushed forward with all her strength. Firmly caught on the blade, which was now buried at least six inches deep, the zombie staggered backward, but remained standing. The stick was just long enough to keep the zombie out of arm's reach and allow Becks to get her hand through the hole and turn the deadbolt. Once the doors were secure, Becks yanked back on the hockey stick to pull it free from his body.

The zombie stumbled forward again, and his hideous face slammed against the door. As he bled out, his face slowly slid down along the glass, accompanied by Donna Summer singing *Bad Girls*. Despite the peril of her situation—and the awful music—Becks actually stayed a few moments to examine the severely damaged flesh.

"Hmm, it's some sort of necrotizing fasciitis," she began out loud, as if dictating a diagnosis. "His left cheek has been eaten clean through to the teeth and gums, and sections of the skull are exposed. His left eye is completely gone. I do hope it's highly contagious to other zombies."

If she had access to a lab, she would cut a sample out of his face to determine what nasty microbe was at work, and find out if she could exploit it as a weapon against the zombies. As it was, Becks was just left watching, and pondering which was worse—flesh eating bacteria, or prolonged exposure to disco music.

Her moment of being a doctor again ended quickly as two of the remaining six zombies were now within a few yards. The already bloody blade of the hockey stick made quick work of them, and a third zombie fell to her deadly stickwork as she ran down to the intersection. Climbing up to the center of the mass of wrecks, she surveyed the surrounding streets and saw hundreds of zombies milling aimlessly about in small groups. Ignoring them, she dropped down under the cars and started her preparations.

Removing the two bolts of cotton gauze material she had strapped to her back, she cut off a couple of yards at a time and bunched up the fabric under at least a dozen gas tanks. Then with a hammer and screwdriver, she punched small holes in the tanks; just enough to create slow drips. As the gasoline soaked the fabric, she waited under an SUV until it was almost dark. Then, unrolling the last several yards of fabric, she twisted it like a giant wick, soaked it in gasoline, and then stretched it as far out from under the cars as it would reach.

Literally keeping her fingers crossed, she lit the fabric "wick" and then took off back down the street. As she approached the fabric store, the umpteenth rendition of *Love to Love You Baby* was still playing loud and clear, but the song was momentarily drowned out by the sharp report of something exploding back in the intersection. Billowing black smoke and intense flames were already reaching high into the sky by the time Becks dragged an office chair onto the roof to watch the show.

With dozens of cars fully engulfed, and the flames starting to spread to dozens more, explosions rocked the neighborhood every few minutes. Zombies from at least a half of a mile around made their way to the source of the sounds and light. And as happened before, once crowds gathered, the first ones to arrive were pushed relentlessly forward into the searing flames. Becks would have liked to stick around to watch them all burn, but she had to get moving once the street to her left was almost clear.

Just before she started the ATV, she ran back to the pink silk she had slept in, and used her knife to slice off a yard and stuffed it in her pack. Perhaps it was a foolish indulgence, but there were far too few pretty things left in this world, and Becks wanted something nice to hold onto for a change.

Turning on her night vision goggles and then pushing the ATV out the doors, it reluctantly started on the third try, and then dutifully roared off to the left, away from the expanding conflagration in the intersection. The first street on her left looked clear, and she raced past an appliance repair shop, two auto mechanic shops, and a classic old ice cream stand with all its windows smashed, and its fiberglass Eskimo fallen from the roof and hanging by its anchoring wires.

After a couple of blocks the businesses gave way to a mixture of small apartment buildings and houses, before the street curved back to the main road heading west. As the light of the bonfire faded behind her, the population of zombies increased. For another half a mile, though, there weren't any packs she couldn't avoid, but very quickly they became thicker. She still managed another quarter mile by driving over lawns and detouring back and forth along side streets, but after nearly getting cornered in a yard by a line of ten rather large and energetic zombies, Becks had to admit it was becoming too dangerous.

Barreling through a park and a playground, she came back out on the main road and decided to look for shelter. But just half a block ahead, she encountered another of those neighborhood barricades of furniture, garden statues, cars, and tree limbs, only this one was huge. Veering to the right, she could see a big herd ahead of her, so she turned into the first driveway and went around to the back of the house.

184

Turning off the ATV, she sat quietly for several minutes, hoping the herd wouldn't follow her. When it appeared as if the brief noise of her vehicle wasn't enough to rouse them from their twilight states, Becks tiptoed to the back door of the modest ranch house. The door was locked, but before she broke a window to get in, she tapped on the door for about fifteen seconds. She waited a couple of minutes, and then repeated the cycle of tapping and waiting two more times.

Hoping she had found a safe place for the night, she raised the butt of her rifle and knocked out a pane of glass from the door. But as the shattered glass fell to the floor, she thought she detected movement at the end of the hallway. Then there was the sound of something being knocked over inside, which made her freeze in place.

Footsteps and creaking floorboards throughout the house made it obvious that she almost walked into a very dangerous situation. Then as three, then six, then at least eight zombies squeezed down the hall toward the back door, Becks realized it would most certainly have been a deathtrap. Retreating from the back porch, she spotted a small wooden tool shed in the neighboring yard. Running over to it, she unlatched the door with one hand, as she grasped a pistol in the other. Jumping backward while yanking the door open, she was relieved to see nothing but gardening implements, some boxes, and a lawn mower.

Wheeling out the lawn mower, and removing a few other things to make some space, Becks threw down a dirty chaise lounge cushion for a bed. But before settling down with an MRE, she used some clothesline cord to secure the doors just in case any curious zombies came upon her hiding place. Thinking while she ate, she wasn't sure how she was going to get around the barricade or the herds, but a roll of landscape fabric and couple of containers of stump remover in the shed gave her an idea.

Chapter 16

Shortly after dawn, Becks was already hard at work. Rather than a diversion, this time she needed a deterrent to keep the main herd away from the barricade while she tried to climb it. Some group of people had obviously worked long and hard constructing it, so there may be something of value inside. If the barricaded area was completely secure, it could also serve as a base of operations while she did some recon to find ways around the herds and obstacles. If she was really lucky, there might actually be people in there willing to help.

Between her knowledge of chemistry, Cam's crazy ex-military survivalist friends, and way too many hours watching YouTube videos on how to blow up stuff using household products, Becks had a pretty good idea how to make an effective deterrent. Stump remover is made from potassium nitrate, which more than one YouTube video illustrated that, when mixed with sugar and wax, can produce a very serviceable smoke bomb. Mixed with sulphur and charcoal, it also makes gun powder.

There wasn't any readily available source of sulphur, but there was a bag of charcoal briquettes in the shed, and a couple of citronella candles. And she had the sugar packets from the MREs, as well as the hard candies from the fallout shelter rations. Using a sledgehammer and a piece of slate, she spent about an hour grinding up candy, sugar, and charcoal to fine powders, and breaking up the candles into tiny pieces. The top of a birdbath acted as a mixing bowl for the powders, candle wax, and the stump remover.

Next, she unrolled all of the landscape fabric and set it aside, because what she really needed was the long cardboard tube inside. At one end of the tube, she wadded in a pair of old rubber-tipped gardening gloves. Then with a trowel she added some of the chemical mixture. On top of that she added her own special touch—a can of pepper spray with its cap and nozzle removed. Then she added more of the mixture, dropped in another can of pepper spray, and then the rest of the mixture. After packing in several pieces of the landscape fabric in the open end, she carefully cut a couple of holes in the tube, squirted in half a can of lighter fluid for good measure, and inserted the wicks from the candles.

"Cam would be very proud of me!" she stated, admiring her own handiwork. "Now, if it will only work…"

The plan was to take the ATV as close to the herd as she dared, light the fuses, drop her homemade bomb, and then go right over to the barricade. She walked through every step she would take, over and over, trying to imagine what could go wrong—which was just about anything— and how she would react and where she would go for safety. She would need to travel light to be able to climb and run, so she would just carry

186

some survival crackers and the couple of bottles of water she taped to her stomach. And she would take her usual weapons, of course.

When she finally felt as prepared as she was ever going to be, she slowly opened the shed door a crack and peered out. No one was in the yard, but she glimpsed something moving by the house she had almost entered the night before. Opening the door a little wider, Becks saw that two arms were sticking out of the broken back door window. The flailing arms—obviously from two different zombies—either indicated they were desperately trying to get out, or they were stuck. Becks didn't care which it was, just as long as they didn't figure out how to unlock the door.

Getting on the ATV, she took a deep breath and said, "Okay, let's do this!"

The engine started to turn over, sputtered for a few moments, and then cut out. Trying again, it sounded like it was going to be okay, until there was this awful, grinding noise and it cut out for good. Becks was no mechanic, but she knew the sound of a catastrophic engine failure when she heard one.

"God damn it!" she growled under her breath, getting off the ATV and kicking it. Three times. "Okay, what's Plan B?"

Before she decided on a course of action, she crept along the side of the house until she had a clear view up the street toward the herd. They were still there, and numbered somewhere between 150 and 200—way too many to take on alone.

"Where's my Humvee and .50 cal when I need it?" she sighed.

Retreating back to the shed, she envisioned any number of scenarios, none of which ended well. She couldn't go right because of the herd. The barricade was straight ahead. And she didn't want to give up any ground and go back the way she came. Somehow, she needed to safely deliver her special smoke bomb. Opening the shed door again, she looked around for anything she could use, but there was only that lawnmower.

Too bad it's not a ride-on mower, she thought, but then had an idea.

It wasn't a ride-on lawn mower, but it did have power assist.

"Eureka!" Becks exclaimed, as Plan B was now in sight—if she could get the lawnmower working.

Fortunately, it was a Honda, and even in the midst of a zombie apocalypse it started on the first pull. Quickly shutting it off, she went back into the shed for an hour, just to make sure no one got all stirred up.

She also needed that time to shift supplies from the big duffle bag strapped to the ATV to two backpacks she could carry. She knew the time would probably come when she would have to go on foot—and had trained relentlessly for such an event—but it still sucked that she had to leave anything behind.

Space in the two packs and her pockets was at a premium, and food, water, and ammunition were obviously the top priorities. Twice she tossed aside Little Eddie's chemistry book, but twice she picked it up again. It was sentimental nonsense, and there was absolutely no room in her packs, but she simply couldn't leave it behind. Removing her silverware-covered jacket, she duct-taped the book to the inside lining on the left front. It was impractical and uncomfortable, but she did it anyway.

She then placed one pack on her back, and the other on her chest. Her rifle went over one shoulder, and the improvised quiver of broom-handled spears went over the other. Sadly, the flail was just too heavy and would have to stay. Surprisingly though, even with all the weight she was carrying, she could still run. But if she had to squeeze through any tight spaces, she would have to drop the quiver and front pack, at the very least.

As often happened these past few months, duct tape was the final step in her plan. Taping her bomb to the front of the lawn mower, she walked it up to the edge of the street. Giving it a pull, the engine roared to life. Wrapping duct tape around the power assist lever, she steered it into the street and aimed it toward the herd, which was only about 75 feet away. The herd was now well aware of her presence and moving toward her. Staying with the mower another 25 feet, Becks then let go and ran alongside for a few yards to light the fuses. Once they were both lit, she took off in a sprint away from the herd.

Fortunately, the mower went relatively straight, and the bulk of the herd's attention was now drawn to it. The "older" zombies—those who switched in the early days of infection—shied away from the loud noise and turned around, which was something she had observed previously with both loud sounds and bright lights. However, more than enough of the "younger generation" surged forward. When the front line of zombies was only about ten feet away from the mower, the two wicks ignited the lighter fluid. At first, Becks was afraid the whole thing would fizzle out, but then there were two bright flashes in rapid succession, followed by an ominous *phhhht* sound.

Thick, black smoke started billowing out of the two holes, just as the lawn mower rammed into a couple of zombies, causing it to stop moving, which was just what she wanted to have happen. The fact that numerous feet were caught underneath the mower and sliced to shreds was just an unexpected bonus. The herd stopped moving forward, but it wasn't sure which way to go as the smoke prevented them from seeing more than a few feet. But the best part was yet to come.

As the heat built up inside the burning tube, the two cans of pepper spray exploded, adding their fiery contents to the smoke. Becks actually laughed and clapped her hands as scores of blinded, choking zombies stumbled backward, trying to escape the irritating smoke, but each time the herd moved back, the lawn mower moved back with them.

Once she was certain the herd was well on their way down the street and away from her, she jogged over to the barricade and looked for the best way over. Taking a minute to examine the haphazard structure, she realized there was some method to the madness. Starting with the washer and dryer combo, she could then step up to the sectional sofa. From there the garbage cans filled with dirt were steps to the mattress and box spring at the top. Reaching the box spring, she slowly peered over the mattress, and almost fell over backwards at what she saw.

Peering back from the other side of the mattress was a little girl—maybe six or seven, possibly older, but probably stunted by malnutrition. She had dirty blond hair, emphasis on dirty, with numerous scars and sores on her face and arms, and she was wobbling back and forth on an old wooden ladder that was used as a lookout.

"Who are you? Are you here to help us?" she whispered.

"Yes. Yes, I can help you, honey. I'm a doctor," Becks responded, regaining her composure. "How many of you are there? Are your parents here?"

"Some parents are still here. Most are gone..." she said with a thousand-yard stare as her voice trailed away.

"I'm so sorry, dear," Becks replied, as she inched up a little higher to sit on the mattress and see over the barricade. There was another large barricade straight ahead, about two blocks down. The neighborhood looked like hell, but she couldn't see any other people. "Could you go tell one of the parents that I'm here, and I that would like to come in?"

189

"If you leave all of your weapons on the mattress, you can come in and we will give you something to eat. No one will hurt you," the little girl said as if speaking rehearsed lines.

None of her original innocence was now evident in either her words or demeanor, as her eyes darted to the right as if she was looking for someone. Becks had heard enough kids lying in the emergency room over the years to know that this girl was not being honest. Some of the most memorable lies had been from a boy who swore that, "I didn't push my sister off the roof of the garage," and the five-year-old girl who definitely "didn't light a pack of fire crackers in my sister's bed." The list went on and on, but the bottom line was that Becks knew something was fishy.

"Don't be afraid, sweetie" Becks said in her most soothing tone. "I don't want anything from you. I just want to cross your barricades and go home. Why don't you tell your friends to come on out so we can talk? I know someone is watching us."

The girl got a strange look on her face—kind of a wild look—and then shouted at the top of her lungs, "She's on to us!"

Just as the girl's head ducked down, a shot whistled past Becks' left ear. Flattening on the mattress, Becks pulled out a pistol with one hand, and with the other she reached over and grabbed the girl by her collar. Yanking her up onto the mattress, Becks sat up and put the girl in her lap to use as a pretend shield. She had no intention of hurting a hair on this girl's filthy, lice-infested head.

"Stop shooting, for Christ's sake!" Becks yelled. "I'm an Army doctor, I can help you. I was stranded a few months ago and I'm just trying to get back home. Please, let's just talk about—"

Before Becks could finish, another shot rang out. The bullet tore through the girl's body and struck Becks in the abdomen. It felt like a mule had kicked her and she gasped for air. Another shot sailed wide by just a foot, and Becks dropped the girl's body and rolled off the mattress, dropping hard onto the garbage cans below. She was covered in blood, but who's blood?

There was a bullet hole in the pack she had over her chest. Pulling it off, she searched for the entry wound. What she found amazed her.

"Son of a *bitch*..." she said under her breath.

After passing through the chest of the girl, the bullet had struck one of the spoons Becks had taped to her jacket. While it pierced the metal, the spent bullet stopped in the middle of chapter two, "Covalent and Ionic Bonds," of Little Eddie's chemistry book! But her joy at the discovery was quickly overshadowed by the fact that someone had murdered a child just to kill her. There was blood on Becks' hands, *But not as much as there's going to been when I'm through,* she vowed, as she slid her sniper rifle over her shoulder.

Becks assumed that whoever was firing had either lost sight of her, or presumed she was dead, as there were no more shots. Slowly repositioning herself, she was able to put the barrel of the rifle through the slats of a packing crate and see down to the ground below. Minutes ticked by, and then finally there was movement. One child emerged from a house, then another, and another, until there was a group of sixteen kids of all ages.

"What is this, *Lord of the Fucking Flies*?" she moaned, lowering the rifle.

"I think it's clear," one of the older boys shouted.

"Well, go and take a look," a 30-ish woman in a ski cap and yoga pants shouted, as she came out from behind an SUV holding a hunting rifle.

Ahh, we have the shooter, Becks thought as she centered the crosshairs on woman's right thigh. If this woman was the only adult taking care of all these children, she didn't want to kill her, but she couldn't let the woman keep shooting at her, either. Becks aim was impeccable, tearing through the meaty part of the woman's thigh, but not touching the bone. She would bleed a lot and have trouble walking for a couple of months, but she would live.

Shrieking in pain, the woman fell to the ground and dropped the rifle. Immediately, one of the older girls picked it up and sent two more rounds Becks' way.

"Well, that didn't work," Becks said, both angry and dismayed at the turn of events. Still not wanting to harm a child, she spoke up. "Stop! No more shooting!"

The girl answered by splintering one of the slats of the packing crate with another well-placed shot.

"Please listen to me!" Becks shouted, quickly losing her patience. "I just want to get across your barricades and get the hell out of here. There are army patrols on 287, and we can all get to a safe place to live."

"Liar! You want to kill us and take our stuff, just like everyone else," the girl yelled as she took aim for her next shot.

"*I don't want to kill anyone!*" Becks protested. "That woman just killed this poor girl."

"She was sick anyway," the woman on the ground bellowed like an insane person as she used both hands to press down on the wound to try to stop the bleeding. "We all have to make sacrifices to survive! She knew that. I have to keep *my* kids safe."

Becks wondered if the little girl had any choice in being the sacrificial lamb, or even had any clue her life was in danger when she was sent up that ladder. She also doubted that the woman saw the irony in keeping "her kids" safe by killing other children, and she wasn't about to waste her breath trying to talk sense into her.

"Look, no one else needs to get hurt. In fact, I can help you, I'm a doctor. Looks like everyone could use a doctor, especially you," Becks said, hoping the woman's self-preservation instinct would kick in, but it didn't.

"Kill her! Kill her, kill her, kill her!" the woman shouted maniacally, over and over.

The girl with the rifle started shooting again, as did two boys with pistols. The younger children actually ran and got rocks to throw.

Becks closed her eyes and let out a prolonged groan. She couldn't go back. She had to go forward. The only way forward was over this barricade, down the street, and over the next barricade, which she couldn't do as long as children were shooting at her.

No, they're shooters, not children, she said over and over in her mind, as the crosshairs settled on the girl's shoulder where the rifle butt rested. But right before she squeezed the trigger, Becks readjusted the target ever so slightly. The bullet struck the wooden stock of the rifle, shattering it to pieces, two of which drove into the girl's neck and chest, but she would live.

The two pistols were much smaller targets, and the shooters couldn't keep them still, as the kickback was more than they could handle. Their shots were spraying wildly about, but she still couldn't take any chances they might get lucky. The oldest boy took one of Becks' bullets in the forearm, but before she could take out the other shooter he ran out of ammunition. Removing her finger from the trigger, she waited to see if anyone else would pick up the guns.

When it seemed as though everyone inclined to shoot at her was out of commission, Becks hoisted herself back up onto the mattress and swung her feet over onto the ladder. But before she started to descend, she paused to close the eyes of the little girl whose pale, drawn face was splattered with her own blood.

Pulling out both pistols when her boots hit the ground, Becks was relieved to see that the unharmed children had scattered. The woman and the two wounded kids still lay where they fell, writhing in pain, and she actually took a half step toward them to at least consider binding their wounds, until the crazy lady started shouting again about killing her.

Suddenly a hail of rocks showered down around her, a few bouncing off the silverware armor, but a couple finding their mark. One even struck the side of her face sending a trickle of blood down her cheek.

Picking up the pace, she ran as fast as she could to the other barricade. The children ran too, carrying sticks and knives. In the middle of the second block, a little four-year-old boy came running out of the bushes, catching her by surprise and colliding with her. They both fell, but Becks was quickly on her feet to see if the boy was okay. As she knelt down to help him up, he thrust a pocket knife into her leg, just below the knee. He didn't have the strength to drive the blade very deep, but it still hurt like hell, and he wasn't finished.

As he raised the blade to strike her again, Becks blasted him right in the eyes with pepper spray. The little boy howled in pain and started running around in circles, crashing smack into a tree, which knocked him out cold.

"Serves you right, you little shit," Becks shouted, as she turned to sprint the last half a block to the other barricade.

The ladder here was even more rickety than the other one, but she couldn't take her time as rocks were already reaching her. Straddling a broken coffee table at the top of the barricade, Becks looked for some safe footing to the ground, but two of the kids were already ascending the ladder. A couple of bursts of pepper spray sent them reeling backward, but others quickly took their place.

Stepping down onto a wicker rocking chair, her foot went right through the brittle seat. Tumbling forward, with the chair shoved up to her hip, Becks bounced off a stack of old tube televisions, and down a series of file cabinets before slamming onto the pavement. It took a moment for her to flex her arms and legs to determine that she was battered, but not broken. Using her free foot to push the wicker chair down off her leg, she got to her feet and scanned the road ahead. It appeared clear for at least a block, but before she had time to move another rock hit her square on the left elbow—right on the funny bone—sending shooting pains down her arm.

"Owwww!" she bawled, spinning around and aiming her pistol at the ten-year-old boy who had just thrown the rock from the top of the barricade. "Get down right this second or I swear I will put a bullet in your face!"

The boy's eyes widened a second before he dropped out of view—which didn't prevent him from launching a piece of brick up and over the barricade, missing Becks' head by just inches.

"I should have shot you, you little fucker!" Becks screamed, completely incensed. She was tempted to climb back up the barricade and put a bullet into every one of those demon children, but deep down she admired their courage and tenacity—qualities she would need as she ran for her life.

Chapter 17

Becks wanted to sprint full speed down the center of the road, straight to Interstate 287 in no more than an hour, and much less if she dropped everything and ran free. She felt like a dog on a leash, always tethered, never able to go where she wanted, when she wanted. In fact, more than that, she just wanted to stroll down the sidewalk and admire the brilliant blue sky and white puffy clouds, and stop to smell the wild roses.

The reality was that the smell of rotting zombies filled the air, and she had to crawl alongside houses and cars, and creep through tall weeds. She was a fugitive from the undead, and every group of zombies was a posse looking for public enemy number one—Dr. Rebecca Truesdale, wanted for her human flesh.

It was an unusually hot day for spring and the sun was intense. Even though zombies thrived in warm weather—which was why the southern states had far fewer survivors—their eyes couldn't handle the super bright sunlight. Fortunately, the ZIPs controlling the bodies were not the best managers of the more delicate sensory organs. So at high noon, the majority of the undead stood under the shade of trees or any other shelter that was convenient.

Those left out in the open would simply close their eyes and face down. This behavior was not to be confused with a twilight state, where the zombie needed some time to "wake up." It was a distinction that survivors often failed to make, at the cost of their lives.

After getting a couple of blocks away from the hell of "Kidtown," Becks found an unlocked SUV to climb into and take a breather, and attend to her knife wound. Thankfully, it didn't need stitches, but any open wound was inviting infection in these unsanitary living conditions, so she slathered it in antibacterial ointment and applied a bandage. Using the rearview mirror, she checked out the cut on her cheek made by the thrown rock. It was superficial, although it bled profusely. More ointment and another bandage and she was good to go.

What wasn't good, in fact, was terrible, was the way she looked. Becks was shocked by her pale, sunken cheeks, the dark circles under her eyes, and could it be… the start of wrinkles!

"Stress lines," she assured herself. "That's all they are, just stress lines that will go away as soon as I get back and get some real rest."

Twisting up the mirror so she didn't have to look at herself any longer, she had some crackers and water, and then hit the road again. As she was crawling along the foundation of a house on the corner of a block, she noticed something two houses down a side street that demanded her attention. Tattered, fading, but still flying high, was a Washington Redskins flag atop a tall flagpole.

"Are you fucking kidding me?" Becks said, as her New York Giants blood began to boil. "A stone's throw from the Meadowlands and these people are Redskins fans!?"

Of course, in Becks' book, it wasn't as bad as being a Dallas Cowboys fan, but it was still treason, punishable by burning. She had wanted to send another smoke signal anyway, and this house would be as good as any to torch. Carefully making her way along a bank of out-of-control hedges, which reminded her of films of the impenetrable hedgerows of the Normandy invasion, she then darted toward the open garage of the Redskins' house. It was open, but it wasn't empty.

To get out of the bright sunlight, four zombies had taken refuge at the back of the garage. As Becks froze, they sprang forward. Not wanting to raise more of the undead with gunshots, Becks deftly wielded her hockey stick into the ribcage of the closest female, who was completely naked except for a toe tag from the morgue. The blade got stuck between her ribs, and with no time to spare, she pushed the stuck zombie back into the other three, causing them all to fall down. That gave her precious seconds to pull out one of her broom-handled spears and drive the long knife into the eye socket of a 40-ish male in a really nice hand-tailored suit.

Another zombie female, probably in her seventies, tried to stand up, but Becks put a boot on her throat and used her spear to send the old zombie to her long-awaited eternal rest. But as she tried to pull out the spear, the last unharmed zombie—a robust male in his twenties, wearing some sort of fast food uniform covered in too much blood and gore to identify — shifted the pile, sending Becks sidestepping to stay on her feet. The sudden movement and sharp angle caused the knife to twist and separate from the broom handle, just as the former burger slinger grabbed her foot.

Gripping the handle like a baseball bat, Becks began whaling away on the zombie's head, but still he hung on. Pulling himself out from under the three corpses, he got his other hand on her leg, right on her knife wound. Wincing in pain, she nonetheless continued her furious assault on his thick skull, breaking the wooden shaft. Spinning around the broom handle in her hands, she drove the sharp, splintered point into the back of his neck, clean through to the concrete floor. His hands trembled for a few seconds, but then he started to grip even more tightly—until she rotated the shaft in wide circles to inflict maximum tissue damage. Slowly, his hands went limp, his body twitched once or twice, and he was finally still.

As soon as Becks was sure they were all truly dead, she lowered her boot on the naked woman's chest and yanked the blade free. During the early days of infection, everyone stockpiled bleach, and this household was no exception. Grabbing one of the gallon jugs that lined a shelf, she doused the blades. Then she soaked a rag in bleach and went over everything she was wearing, as the messy battle had splattered drops of infected blood all over her.

Checking the garage for other useful items, she found a can of fluorescent orange spray paint. Removing her packs and the quiver, she slithered across the lawn through the high grass to the edge of the road. There were a few zombies a couple of blocks further down, but none really close. Taking a chance, she stood up and sprayed a short message on the black pavement. With an arrow pointing west, she simply wrote "BECKS." With an arrow pointing to the barricaded neighborhood, she wrote "KIDS NEED HELP."

Crawling back through the grass to the flagpole, she reached up with her knife and cut the rope. The Redskins flag fluttered lazily to the ground. Grabbing it, she hurried back to the garage and lowered the door so she wouldn't be seen. She had hoped to explore the house for supplies, but after tapping on the metal door leading into the kitchen, the racket that arose inside signaled it was too full of zombies to attempt to clear. On the plus side, a lot of Redskins fans would go up in smoke.

Some cans of kerosene and paint thinner would do the trick nicely. Stacks of newspapers that were never picked up for recycling would make it even easier to torch the house. (As she crumbled up the newspapers, Becks resisted looking at the increasingly alarming headlines, which spoke of the onset of infection and the ensuing horrors.) With the kerosene-soaked flag as a wick, Becks set her latest bonfire. What she didn't know as she began creeping and crawling westward again, was that sparks from the Redskins' house would ignite the house next door, which would set ablaze piles of dead brush that would eventually involve six more structures and several cars. With half of a suburban New Jersey block burning to ashes on such a clear day, the towers of smoke could be seen for miles around—especially by the patrols on the highway.

The westward road on which she had been traveling since New Ridgelawn finally ended at a T-intersection. It would have been a great dilemma as to which way to go, if it hadn't been for the most wonderful sight—a bright red and blue, shield-shaped, Interstate 287 sign pointing to the right. A black Volkswagen beetle had crashed into the sign and bent it almost to the ground, where Becks would never have noticed it, but fortunately it was just high enough for her to see. Not only did it mean she was headed in the right direction, it meant she had to be even closer to the highway than she originally thought.

And there was even more good news—the three dead passengers in the VW had taken a big box of food with them, and a pistol. They never got to eat the food because they had crashed due to a swarm of zombies, which then surrounded their car. Rather than try to make a run for it and be eaten, or die slow deaths trapped inside the car, they had chosen murder-suicide as their best option. The interior full of dried corpses and brain splatter didn't faze Becks in the least as she settled into the empty back seat and gorged on high-calorie snack cakes and Red Bull energy drinks.

The potent combination hit her stressed-out, malnourished body like a buzz saw, and when she started moving down the road this time, it was the fastest crawl on record. In less than ten minutes she had traveled two blocks and speared five zombies. She really only needed to kill two of them, but she was so amped up that she went out of her way to get the other three just for fun.

At this point, another Interstate 287 sign directed her to turn left, heading west again. Ahead was a long, tree-lined street that looked like a war zone. Houses had burned, cars were overturned and riddled with bullet holes, and remnants of corpses and countless bones were scattered everywhere. It was impossible to tell if survivors had fought zombies or other survivors, but the end result was that this neighborhood was toast. And it had obviously been picked clean by scavengers, as there weren't any weapons next to the bodies, and every car and backpack was emptied of food and water.

Maybe Becks' nerves were just on edge because of the sugar and caffeine rush, but this area made her very jittery and really gave her the creeps. For all the horror she had witnessed, for some reason, this was one of the most unsettling sights. She had seen death in many places, *but this is a place of death*, she thought. And the more she saw of the carnage, the more she got the sense that this had been humans fighting humans. Killing for supplies had been commonplace after quarantine, but this looked like it was a massacre.

"Fuck the tortoise," Becks said, forsaking her usual caution. "I'm going full on hare!"

No more creeping through bushes and between cars, she decided, as she stood up and just started running as fast as she could along sidewalks, front yards, and even in the street to avoid zombies, downed trees, and other obstacles. Perhaps it had been her survivor's sense, or some sixth sense, but she couldn't have picked up the pace at a better time, as several shots rang out behind her, near where she had first turned the corner.

Becks couldn't be certain she was the intended target, and she certainly wasn't going to slow down to find out, but she doubted it was a mere coincidence that just as she arrived in the neighborhood, someone decided to start shooting. And unless he or she had some kind of vehicle, there was no way anybody would catch the rabbit-swift Dr. Rebecca Truesdale as she raced block after block, lungs burning and heart pounding.

Her mad dash only slowed when the zombies became too thick to evade. There were a few close calls where her hockey stick and spears weren't sufficient and she had to use her pistols—drawing even more attention—so she knew she had to get off the streets as quickly as possible. A large neo-Victorian house to her left became her objective, as it had a high turret room that might afford a good view toward the west. To reach the porch of the house, she had to shoot and stab a pack of five zombies, who appeared to have been a family with two boys and a girl.

Other packs were coming together and heading her way with the makings of a significant herd, so she had to act fast. Banging on the front bay window, she tried to keep one eye on the street and one inside the house. As two zombies entered the living room, a dozen reached the end of the driveway. As three more zombies shuffled into the living room and pressed their ugly faces against the window, two dozen more approached the front yard from all directions. She could handle five zombies inside, but if there were many more it could become too dangerous. Unfortunately, the odds on the porch were about to get even worse. There was a third option, and she went for it.

Standing on the railing of the porch, she reached up and grabbed the gutters, and swung her right foot up into them. Luckily, they were strong, copper gutters—probably costing more than she used to make in a year—and she was able to hoist herself up onto the roof of the porch. From there, she was able to scale the slanted first-floor roof, scamper across the ridge to the bottom of a small porch off the second-floor master bedroom, and raise herself up and over that railing. Through the glass French doors, Becks could see that there were two bodies on the king-sized bed. Banging several times on the glass, the figures didn't move, so she could assume that they, at least, were dead. Becks contemplated entering the house from here and taking her chances, but she could do that later, as she wanted to get to the third floor.

That was a little trickier; she had to remove her packs, quiver, and rifle to be able to grasp onto the decorative Victorian-style moulding and swing her legs up onto the small section of roof below the turret. Standing up, she could see through the windows that the sunny room had an overstuffed chair with bright yellow upholstery, with a cozy handmade afghan draped over the back, a tea table with a floral china teapot, cup and saucer, and a small rack of books and magazines. This had obviously been a sanctuary for the lady of the house to escape for some peace and quiet during her hectic schedule.

Perhaps Becks would break a window and enjoy an MRE there in the evening, but first she turned to the west and brought her binoculars to her eyes. As much as she hated the winter, at that moment she wished it wasn't spring, as the leaves were already thick on the trees, obscuring the views. What she could see, was a frightening number of zombies in the surrounding streets. Travel from here would have to be only after dark, and with the night vision goggles.

Carefully scanning to the west, Becks had hoped to see a convoy of army vehicles within spitting distance. Unfortunately, a block away looked like more trees and houses, as did another block further down, and so on and so on. A cold stab of sick fear hit her stomach, as there was nothing to indicate how far she was from the highway. Logically, she knew it was out there somewhere close by, but emotionally it felt like it was a million miles away.

About to give up, she glimpsed something odd. At first glance it just looked like a rock wall to the southwest, maybe less than three-quarters of a mile away. Leaning up against the turret and holding her breath to steady the image, she stared between the treetops at the small section of rocks that were visible. It was definitely a manmade wall, as it was flat on the top and sides, but there was something strange about the way it was constructed—strangely familiar.

A breeze blew the trees back and forth, giving her brief extended views, and it finally dawned on her—this was one of those rock-filled, metal mesh barricades used on highways to block the noise from disturbing residential neighborhoods. Becks remembered seeing walls such as this on 287! If it had been an oasis in the desert she couldn't have been more excited. After all these long months, the end of her journey was literally in sight.

On the other hand, the end of her life was also in sight if she didn't figure out how to traverse that distance through hundreds, if not thousands, of zombies. It would take a lot of smoke and flames to draw these crowds from her path, and there was still the small matter of safely getting around in order to set the fires. She also had the option of using sound, but if she had to listen to another disco tape, she would start turning zombie herself.

All of that could be decided after she got some rest, as she suddenly began to feel very sluggish. What goes up with sugar and caffeine, must come down, and Becks was rapidly bottoming out. And as there didn't appear to be a lock on the turret room door, she decided for now to just stretch out face down, straddling the peak of the roof—as she had so often seen squirrels do at her home in Nyack—and enjoy the warm spring sunshine as she "rested her eyes" for a few minutes.

The next thing she knew, a rumbling explosion almost rocked her right off the roof. She had fallen fast asleep and hadn't been aware that dark thunderclouds were rapidly rolling in. Big, cold drops of rain began to fall and a flash of lightning appeared to strike just a few blocks away. Being exposed at the top of one of the tallest buildings around—wearing pants and a jacket covered in silverware—was not the wisest position to be in during an electrical storm. Not trusting her footing on the slick roof, Becks instead slid on her belly to the gutters, where she was able to drop down and swing back over to the mini porch.

The French doors were unlocked, so she was spared the noise of having to break glass. The plush carpet silenced her footsteps as she approached the bed and used her hockey stick to poke the bodies to make sure they were really dead. It was a man and a woman with gray hair, and they were holding hands when they died. A sweet picture of the loving couple was on a bed stand, next to several more frames of their large family of kids, grandkids, and even great-grandchildren. As touching as this scene was, it was also quite disturbing.

First, there were no obvious signs of trauma or weapons, so the couple most likely voluntarily took an overdose of something like sleeping pills—just as Becks' parents had done. She didn't know where in the house they had OD'ed, but imagining her own parents in a scene like this got her all choked up. Secondly, if all these people in the photos had taken refuge in this house, she was in for a hell of a time trying to clear it out.

Checking the bathroom and walk-in closet and finding no one else, Becks locked the bedroom door and slid a heavy dresser in front of it. She only needed a roof over her head right now, not an entire house, so as long as she was safe and dry—and not a prime target for lightning—she was content.

She could have rolled the corpses off the bed, but they looked so peaceful. They had also both been rather corpulent, and as the mattress must have absorbed a lot of decomp juices, she decided to curl up on the couch to catch a few hours of sleep. Her intention was to leave after dark and make a final push for the highway, but when she awoke, she found there was still a steady rain, so she turned over and went back to sleep.

Morning didn't present a much brighter picture, with a chilly, dense fog blanketing the area, and there were still occasional showers. Tiptoeing out onto the mini porch, she was pleased to see the crowd of zombies had dispersed, or so she thought at first. Leaning over the railing, she found that most of them were now crowded onto the porch for shelter and warmth.

So much for leaving through the front door, she thought.

She could spend the day twiddling her thumbs, sitting with two corpses, or she could clear the house and search for anything useful. Ten minutes later, after moving the dresser away from the door, she stood with pistols drawn, obviously opting for the latter. Her plan was to open the door to the hall, make a racket, and then pick off the zombies one by one as they came up the stairs. If there were more on the second or third floor, and things got too dicey, she could retreat to the master bedroom and abandon the plan, or try something else. Giving herself a three-count, she yanked open the door and came face to face with…an enormous piece of furniture.

That explained why the couple had not been eaten. When they had made the decision to end their lives, family members had the foresight to push a huge, oak, chifferobe in front of their door. Perhaps their children and grandchildren already knew they were infected, and couldn't bear the thought of switching and eating the beloved matriarch and patriarch of the family. In any event, Becks wasn't sure whether this would help or hinder her operation. Holstering her weapons, she gave the chifferobe a powerful shove, and it barely tipped an inch.

Son of a bitch...

Turning around, she braced her back against the stubborn piece of furniture and pushed for all she was worth. It leaned forward, almost to the tipping point, but she slipped on the carpet and it slammed back into the doorframe, which drew unwanted attention before she was in position. Sounds of footsteps came from both the left and right ends of the hallway. As the chifferobe was over six feet high, and was wide enough to cover the door from side to side, the only way for her to see what was going on was to drop down and look underneath, where seven-inch legs provided some viewing space. There were three adults, two males in sneakers and shorts—or maybe they weren't wearing any pants?—and a female in sweat pants, but barefoot.

"I suppose I could shoot you all in the ankles," Becks said, but then had a better idea that would conserve ammunition.

A spear she hadn't yet used—in fact, had almost not even made—contained a vicious-looking, serrated, Bowie knife with a twelve-inch blade, ordered by Charles somebody-or-other, she tried to recall, on Patterson Road. It took half a roll of duct tape to secure the beast to a wooden mop handle, and Becks had yet to use it, as it was too wide to thrust into an eye socket, and its weight made it cumbersome to wield. Still, she had brought it along, in case she needed to saw through anything. At the time, she envisioned that being a rope or branch. Now, she envisioned it tearing through at least six Achilles tendons.

The female was the easiest victim on which to start the process, as she was standing sideways at just the perfect angle. Positioning the wicked, razor sharp, stainless steel teeth perpendicular to the tendon, Becks started to saw away. Oblivious to pain, the zombie just stood there as the knife ripped into her like a shark. It only took a handful of back and forth motions until Becks heard that distinctive *pop*, as she had cut deep enough for the tendon to completely rupture. About a minute later, she had sawed through the female's other Achilles tendon, and the thick carpeting drank in the gushing blood.

Her next victim was the largest male. Becks thought she was in for a workout with him, but shortly after cutting into the tendon, it popped with no more provocation. The weight of the male apparently put more strain on the tendon, making it more susceptible to rupturing.

His other ankle was a little trickier, as he kept shifting positions as he tried to beat his way through the chifferobe. Becks missed the tendon three times, but was able to cut through muscles and blood vessels down to the bone on two sides of his leg. The third male was also shifty, but by the time she was done, Becks was able to saw through one Achilles tendon, hunks of muscle, many blood vessels, and a total of six toes. There was no way any of these zombies would be chasing her around the house.

As the saturated carpeting started pooling with blood, five more adult zombies and three zombie children began making their way upstairs. Sawing legs might incapacitate them all, but at some point she needed to put them down permanently. Using the revolver from the Volkswagen—which was a .22, for which she didn't have any more ammunition—she was able to use the last two rounds to eliminate the first pair of zombies trying to reach the second floor. It was a sweet piece of marksmanship, as Becks pointed the pistol under the chifferobe, between several bleeding ankles, and waited until the tops of their heads were just visible above floor level.

The first headshot sent the young female zombie tumbling to her left, plummeting over the railing, and slamming down onto the marble entryway. The second was a male with an enormous head —*They grow them big in this family*, Becks thought—who fortuitously fell backward onto the other six zombies, knocking them all down the staircase like undead dominoes. In the crush of bodies, one of the children had his neck snapped, another suffered a broken leg, and an adult female sustained a compound fracture in her arm.

The two fresh kills of family members drew the attention away from Becks and to a long-awaited dinnertime. Those who were able to stand and walk went either to the dead child on the floor, or stayed by the staircase and began tearing into Bighead. The Achilles triplets attempted to descend the staircase, which they all did, although it was face-first, causing a few more broken bones.

"Now if I can just move this monster out of the way," she said, getting to her feet and trying to think smarter, not harder. "Ah yes, we can go from Achilles to Archimedes."

Becks was quite pleased with herself as she recalled the famous quote from the brilliant ancient Greek, "Give me a lever long enough and a fulcrum on which to place it, and I shall move the world." Perhaps it was a sound principle for moving a planet, but she wondered if Archimedes had ever tried to move an oak chifferobe?

Pulling all the plus-size blouses off of one of the heavy-duty, metal closet rods, Becks then placed one end of the rod under the chifferobe at a low angle. Using a footstool as a fulcrum, she let her rear end do the rest of the work. By sitting on the other end of the closet rod, the lever dutifully tipped over the chifferobe. As an added bonus, the massive piece of furniture teetered briefly at the top of the stairs, and with a little kick of encouragement, it slid down the staircase, crushing two of the adults feasting on Bighead. Her hockey stick spear easily finished off the remaining zombies, who were either already badly wounded or occupied eating, leaving Becks free to scavenge the entire house.

At first, Becks was surprised that there wasn't much food left, but then she remembered the average size of the family members, as well as the number of mouths to feed, and it made perfect sense. Some canned peaches and granola bars were real treats, as were the canned green beans and carrots. Apparently, the family had consumed all the junk food first, and left the healthy items as a last resort. Becks was more than happy to eat their castoffs.

Next was a weapons search, which turned up lots of knives (which she didn't need), a tire iron, and not a single gun! Becks had to keep reminding herself that suburban New Jersey was not rural New York, where the per capita firearms ratio made life much easier for survivors. She also noticed one of the older males—who had probably been a teenager in the 1960s—was wearing a T-shirt with a peace symbol on one side, and on the other was a red circle with a line—the "No" symbol—over the NRA logo.

"And how did that work out for you?" Becks asked derisively to the corpse.

What would be of great help, were the four emergency radios she found, the type that could be powered by cranking a handle, or with the inset solar panels. These radios also had bright LED lights and a siren, making them ideal for distracting the herds.

Just out of curiosity, Becks checked the AM and FM bands to see if anyone was broadcasting anything. There was nothing but static on the FM band, and she was about to give up on AM until the dial reached down to 640. It was one of the old Emergency Broadcast System frequencies, Becks had learned, from some of the antique radios in her parents' store, which had the Civil Defense logo at 640 and 1240 AM, where the special stations could be found in a crisis situation. Apparently, some government agency in the area had chosen 640 to broadcast the ZAP ads—Zombie Action Program—that spouted endless propaganda about how everything would be fine, even as the world collapsed into chaos.

The station must still be functioning on solar power, as Becks spent the better part of an hour listening to all the bullshit about the "Military and civilian defense forces standing steadfast as a shield between citizens and danger." Then there was the one about the CDC assuring everyone that the infection was no worse than a "bad case of the flu." And she really got a laugh out of the piece played most often, recorded by the president himself, who promised that "no one's lives would be disrupted" if we just remained calm and went about our business.

"I got your business right here, Mr. President," Becks said, grabbing her crotch in an uncharacteristically crude gesture.

By late afternoon, more dark clouds blanketed the sky and it began to rain again. Becks was terribly frustrated that she would most likely be stuck here another night, but she resigned herself to make the best of it. Lighting some scented candles in the turret room, she snuggled into the comfy chair, draped the afghan around her shoulders, and dined on a surprisingly good beef with mushrooms MRE.

Her chair just happened to be positioned facing the direction of the rock wall on the highway, and as she was sucking down the last few grains of rice covered in gravy, she could have sworn she saw flashes of light coming from the other side of the wall. *The headlights of a convoy?* she hoped, and prayed.

Running back downstairs, she grabbed all of the emergency radios and raced back up to the turret. Cranking like mad, she charged them all enough for their flashlights to shine brightly. Positioning the tea table in front of an open window, she set down three of the lights at different angles, all roughly in directions where she supposed the highway was located. With the fourth, she flashed it on and off and waved it back and forth.

"One if by land, two if by sea, four if surrounded by zombies," Becks said, laughing at her own little joke.

It was a long shot that anyone would see her beacons, but if there was even a one in a million chance, it was worth a try. The friend of a friend's uncle had won the lottery when Becks was a child, and it had made a great impression on her young mind—longshots can pay off. With that thought, she cranked, and waved, and flashed the lights deep into the night, until with arms and legs weary, she just curled up on the floor, wrapped in the afghan. As she faded, so, too, did her beacons, slowly going dim and dark.

Awakening mid-morning, Becks actually screamed and stomped her feet when she saw that it was still raining. She spent a restless day pacing, ranting, and looking out the windows to see if the sky was ever going to clear. She had to close the front drapes over the bay window, as every time she passed by, the natives on the porch grew restless, too. The kids in the family had a few handheld video games for which she found fresh batteries, but they were more frustrating than fun, so she went back to pacing and rummaging around the house until nightfall. Then it was back to the turret again to use her signal beacons, until she was too tired to stand or crank.

Hours later, somewhere in the fog of half-sleep, Becks thought one of the flashlights was shining in her eyes, so she waved her arms in front of her, trying to bat it away, but found nothing but air. Turning over to avoid the light, the back of her head heated up quickly. Sitting bolt upright, she finally realized what was happening—sunshine, glorious sunshine, and not a cloud in the sky! Seizing the binoculars, she scanned the level of the rock wall from side to side for any sign of activity, but there were only trees.

What did I expect, a "Welcome Home" banner flapping in the breeze?

Turning her sights to the surrounding streets, her heart sank even further when she saw packs and herds of zombies still filling the streets and yards. Taking a closer look, however, she noticed something odd. Many of them, if not most, were not *standing* there on the pavement and grass, they were *lying down*. Unless this was some type of behavior Becks had never before witnessed, these zombies were dead!

Risking daylight movement, Becks was geared up and ready to go in minutes. The zombie convention was still in full swing on the front porch, but the back yard only had a couple of stragglers. Quietly dispatching them, she then used a lawn chair to help hoist herself over the stockade fence into the next yard. No one was in sight as she wended her way through several more yards to the next street over, and was amazed at what she found.

At least fifty bodies were sprawled across the road and amongst the tall weeds of a couple of lawns. About a dozen mobile zombies were chowing down on some of the juiciest corpses, and they paid no attention to Becks as she approached the nearest body. Having brought along the tire iron, she raised it and brought it down on the corpse's forehead in a shattering blow. Then using the prying end, she popped off the top of the skull like the shell of a hardboiled egg. Becks had not lost her mind; she needed to examine the ZIPs membrane that encased the brain. It was one of the prettiest sights she had ever seen.

Back when she was working at ParGenTech with Phil, as the infection was just beginning in the Hudson Valley, she had come upon the idea of introducing different strains of ZIPs to the zombies. This "competitive suppression" program worked, and it killed the zombies because the competing ZIPs fought one another to the death—leaving telltale dark lesions on the thick, white membrane that the parasites formed around the brain.

And here the lesions were again, clear as day, glistening in the bright sunlight inside the skull Becks had just bashed open. Someone was poisoning the zombies! Just to make sure, she cracked open two more heads and found the same beautiful lesions. As far as she knew, only the military had poison meat grenades, and Captain Lennox had mentioned that they were working on other delivery systems at the Picatinny Arsenal. Could the oft-rumored spring offensive to clear northern New Jersey really be commencing? Should she just go back to the house and wait for troops to come marching down the street?

That was certainly an option to consider as she crouched between corpses, admiring the lesion-covered membranes—until one of the not-quite-dead-yet zombies raised his head and bit hard on Becks' left wrist, right on the flesh exposed between the top of her glove and bottom of her jacket sleeve. Startled, Becks yelled and fell backwards onto another corpse, while her right hand reached for her .44 Magnum. The zombie's head blew apart like a water balloon, but the damage had already been done.

Several of the zombie's filthy teeth had punctured Becks' wrist, and blood was flowing freely. Of course, the bleeding was not her main concern, as ZIPs eggs were no doubt already coursing through her body looking for places to grow and multiply. And she had no Eradazole.

The clock was ticking.

Chapter 18

So close, yet so far, Becks thought, as she wrapped the piece of pretty pink silk around her wrist as a bandage. Time was now of the essence, and she didn't have the luxury of waiting for someone to rescue her. She had to save herself.

A dozen emotions were swimming through her heart and mind, and tears were in her eyes, as she stood up and started sprinting. With pistols blazing, without hesitation, she cut down anyone in her path. If cars blocked her way, she vaulted up onto hoods and trunks and leapt from vehicle to vehicle. If there was a downed tree blocking her path, she used her hands and feet like a monkey to clamber over it. If there was a street full of corpses, she weaved through them without slowing down.

Only a fraction of the zombie herds were still alive, but there were still enough of them to make every foot of ground she had to cover dangerous. At one point, about ten zombies began to surround her, but she climbed to the top of an SUV and calmly put a bullet in each of their heads. Reloading, she hit the ground running again, like a woman possessed.

No more hiding. No more creeping and crawling. No more silent kills. Let every zombie and scavenger for a mile around know that Dr. Rebecca Truesdale was a on a mission. And if you got in her way, you would die.

The landscape of modest, closely-packed houses morphed into opulent homes with large pieces of property. Zombies, both dead and alive, were fewer and farther between in the area, but still the roar of her .44 Magnum echoed for blocks around as she showed no mercy. It was as if all the months of pent-up fear, anger, despair, and frustration had reached critical mass, and *nothing* could prevent Becks from going nuclear.

A curving road led her to an intersection with at least twenty energetic zombies blocking whichever direction she decided to go. Using a tree to get to the top of a nearby garage, she pulled her sniper rifle over her shoulder. Sitting with her left elbow resting on her left knee, Becks supported the rifle on her arm for better accuracy. She scored eighteen head shots, two shots missed a little low in the throat, and with three others she settled for bullets to the heart, as tree branches partially blocked those targets.

The intersection clear, she sprinted past the bodies and took the road that appeared to go due west. As she headed up a steep hill, Becks thought she glimpsed the rock wall at the top of an embankment, just a few blocks away, but her attention was suddenly drawn elsewhere. At the crest of the hill, she stood and looked down on a sea of zombies, all looking back at her. With the hungry groans of hundreds of starving undead, they rolled like a tidal wave toward her. Spinning around, she saw that a hundred more were starting to make their way up the hill from the other direction, drawn by all the loud gunshots.

So close, yet so far, she thought again, as she looked for any way out. Each direction appeared more hazardous than the next, but there was a big, old station wagon on the western downslope of the hill that could provide refuge until the herd passed. *If* the herd passed.

It was a Country Squire station wagon with the fake wood sides and a tail gate that could swing open or drop flat for picnics or drive-in movies. Before Becks could become the main course for a zombie picnic, she ran to the tail gate, swung it open, dove in, and slammed it shut before the herd reached her. Lunging for all the door locks, she was safe—at least for the moment.

Fists and faces pressed against all the windows, like some macabre 360-degree drive-in movie. Becks scrambled over the seats to get behind the wheel, and although the key was still in the ignition, the battery was as dead as she would be if she didn't figure out something. And sooner rather than later would be helpful. Perhaps if she got on the floor of the passenger seat and remained still, the zombies would lose interest and go away. But after an hour, none of them had budged, and the temperature inside the car was reaching brutal levels. She could remain there another few hours, and possibly pass out from the heat—or worse—or she could try to do something.

Climbing back into the driver's seat, she put the transmission into neutral, and pulled like hell to turn the wheels straight, pointing down the hill. She hoped gravity would do the rest, but with the mass of zombies in front of the car, it was going nowhere. She scrambled back to the tail gate window and started banging and yelling. Aroused by the noise and movement, the zombies in the back started pounding on the car, while the ones in the front started moving toward the back.

"Come on, you ugly, motherless fucks, is that all you got?" Becks shouted, whipping them into a frenzy.

Suddenly, the station wagon lurched forward a few inches. Continuing her tirade, more and more zombies pressed against the back of the car, and it actually started to roll, ever so slightly. Then it picked up some real speed. Crawling back to the front seat, Becks attempted to control the massive vehicle, which was no easy feat without power steering. Zombies were pushed aside by the growing downward force of the mighty suburban assault vehicle, and those that didn't get out of the way became mere speed bumps beneath the wheels.

After about 100 feet, the station wagon broke free of the herd, and once there was nothing in its way, it picked up a frightening amount of speed.

"Uh oh! Shit, shit, shit!" Becks yelled, reaching with both hands for the safety belt while her boot pounded away at the unresponsive brake pedal, but it was too late.

Bracing for impact, the huge station wagon slammed into a fallen tree at the base of the embankment. Becks was thrown hard against the steering wheel and windshield, cracking a couple of ribs, opening a big gash in her forehead, and spraining her bitten left wrist. But the herd was already heading in her direction, so she didn't have a second to spare.

Getting out of the car, she felt a bit woozy and everything hurt, but she still managed to start crawling up the embankment as fast as she could. Three days of rain had turned the dirt to slick mud, and for every hard fought yard, she slid back two feet. The herd was closing in, but she fought tooth and nail to reach the base of the wire mesh and rock wall, which was much higher than she thought. Clutching onto the wire, she grimaced in pain from all her injuries as she began to ascend. Exhausted, she didn't know if she had the strength to make it.

Then she heard something in the distance that was unclear at first, but grew closer and louder. Was she hallucinating, or were voices calling out her name?

"Come on Becks, you can do it!"

"Keep going, Becks, don't give up!"

The blood running into her eyes from the cut in her forehead made it hard to see, but looking up, there were definitely faces looking down at her! Struggling to climb higher, the zombie herd had now reached the embankment, and when one of them slipped and fell in the mud, five more climbed over its body to get ever nearer to Becks.

Shots rang out from the top of the wall, taking out those zombies closest to her, but there were just too many of them. Then she heard a voice shout at her to stay still, so she froze and looked down at the hungry mob below. Suddenly, zombie eyes, ears, and noses started to bleed, and row after row fell dead to the ground. Becks had seen a weapon like this at work before—in fact, she had taken great delight in using it—at the Picatinny Arsenal. It had to be the "whale bone," or "sonic disrupter," as she had liked to call it.

With renewed strength and determination, she fought her way up the wall inch by inch, until a hand reached down to help, but it was just out of reach. Hanging on with just her sprained left wrist, which caused shooting pains that made her see stars, with her right hand she pulled off the yard of pink silk. Gripping it tightly, she used a whipping motion to send the other end into the helping hand, which grasped it like an iron clamp. With one mighty pull, she was yanked to the top of the wall and into a strong pair of arms that held her tight.

"My dearest, dearest Trues, baby," a very familiar voice said, as she was clutched even harder. "Oh my god, look what's happened to you!"

Wiping the blood from her eyes and looking into Cam's face, she replied, "Yeah, well you should see the other guys."

Chapter 19

As Army medics swarmed over Becks, Cam, Captain Lennox, and several familiar faces from Cam's compound stood by, each one blurting out pieces of how they had found her, and how some had given up hope, while others never lost faith.

Becks learned that the photos the helicopter had taken of Eddie's house in flames had first given them a glimmer of hope that she had survived. But then the long months of winter with no signs of life brought them to despair. Then spring arrived and they spotted more fires, each being successively farther west toward the highway, bringing them back to hope, which grew to belief that she was out there somewhere—a belief confirmed by more aerial photos of the messages she had left behind.

For days, a desperate Cam and his men kept up 24-hour patrols along a several mile stretch of 287, while Captain Lennox and his men launched new aerosol dispensers into the herds of zombies to spread the competitive ZIPs. The three days that Becks had been delayed because of rain turned out to be a lifesaver, as the poisoned zombies had time to die, be eaten, and infect others, giving her a clearer path. Her gunshots had narrowed their search, and the crashing station wagon pinpointed her location, directing all forces to come to her aid and defense.

"But I guess you have a few stories to tell, too," Cam said, gently taking her right hand, which was just about the only part of her not damaged. "Save your strength, though. You can tell us all about it after you've had time to rest at the hospital at West Point."

While she couldn't get back to West Point a minute too soon, Becks refused to get into the ambulance until they gave her a map of the area.

"This is where someone was shooting at me. Looks like a massacre took place, so there could be some bad characters in the neighborhood," she began.

Retracing her steps, she next pointed to the area where all the feral children and the crazy lady lived behind barricades. She found the post office were she spent the winter, and Sparrow Lane where Sgt. Colaneri and the others had lost their lives, and she handed Captain Lennox the sergeant's dog tags, which she had worn since the day he died.

Then Becks pulled out the chemistry book taped to her jacket and showed everyone the bullet still lodged in chapter two, and told the story of how Little Eddie had died. She told them about Isabel Tasi's death, and the courageous Eddie Tasi, who may or may not still be alive, and Angie, Jennifer, Donnie, and the Rovers, and New Ridgelawn, and all the people there who needed help. She even mentioned Buttons and Smidgey, and the Doberman who sheltered them. And she made Captain Lennox promise that once they got boots on the ground for the spring offensive, they would add Kidtown and New Ridgelawn to their list of objectives.

Only then, after she made sure help would soon be coming to those who needed it, did Dr. Rebecca Truesdale get into the ambulance and finally head for home.

After two weeks in the hospital, Becks was hounding Phil for complete updates on all the projects, and begging to get back to work. She had played cavewoman with her spear for too long, and needed to breathe the rarefied air of a laboratory again. Phil obliged her first request with stacks of project files just to keep her in bed a few days longer, but he knew Becks was an unstoppable force and promised to let her start working the minute the doctors gave her the okay.

Cam barely left her side for those two weeks, and many other friends and acquaintances stopped by. Becks became so sick and tired of recounting her story over and over, that she actually welcomed a reporter from the new single-sheet newspaper, *Hudson Valley Survivor*, so all the details would be in print and she wouldn't have to keep rehashing the unpleasantness any longer.

Becks thought the far more interesting story was what had happened in the Hudson Valley since she left so many months ago; not the least of which was that someone was printing a newspaper again!

Farms were springing up everywhere. In an ironic twist, housing developments that had been built on farm land, were now having their once finely manicured yards plowed for crops, and their houses and garages used for livestock. Parks were turned into tomato and vegetable farms, and golf courses were becoming waving fields of wheat, barely, and oats.

One of the few smart things the government had done in the Hudson Valley before everything collapsed, was to send a special team to the

Indian Point nuclear reactors with orders to keep them operational *at all costs*. Not only did this dedicated crew prevent a meltdown which would have made the region uninhabitable, but it now meant that power was being restored to the east side of the river, with plans to run a cable across to the west side. The nuclear plant that had once been so reviled, became a shining beacon of resurrection for communities trying to piece themselves back together.

With power came some manufacturing, and despite decades of everything being made in China, people found that Yankee ingenuity had not been lost. Some cars were getting back on the road, although a full day's labor on a farm or in a factory would only get you one gallon of gas. But at least now there was some work available, and something to work *for*. The towns along the river were becoming trading centers again, and the river, an avenue of commerce. A couple of one-room school houses had even opened, and a few hospitals tried to at least establish emergency clinics for basic treatments and Eradazole distribution.

Of course, except for the areas with electricity, the Hudson Valley now resembled more of the early 1700s than it did the 21st century, both in terms of its small population and living conditions. But the region that had been ground zero for the apocalypse and was initially the hardest hit, was the first to start getting back on its feet.

Much of the credit for that belonged to people like Cam and his men, who had formed the Civilian Action Patrol, or CAP, whose branches spread the length of the river. Unlike the useless ZAP organization, CAP helped survivors with food, shelter, and protection. Their handmade flyers could be seen on sign posts and telephone poles from Albany down to the border of New York City.

"Warning to all zombies," they read, "We gonna CAP yo asses."

That was all the good news. All the other news was bad. No one had to tell Becks that New Jersey was a hell hole. New York City was even worse. Everything basically south of the Mason-Dixon line was considered to be a total loss. Little news was available for the Midwest and west coast, but the general picture was that cities and towns in warmer regions were decimated. However, those in colder climates, as well as isolated communities, were hanging in there, but just barely.

Beyond the borders of the United States, Canada was doing quite well with its frigid weather, but past that, it was anybody's guess. The majority of the countries around the globe had gone dark, with no word from anyone for months.

It was a grim picture of the end of humanity. But as Becks looked out her window at West Point at the green trees and the sparkling Hudson River below, she knew that there was something about the human spirit that was indomitable. If there was one chance in a million for survival, a person would fight, body and soul, for that chance.

And if Becks had to face a million zombies alone, she would find a way to kill them all.

The first novel in the series, *HVZA: Hudson Valley Zombie Apocalypse*, is available in paperback and e-books.

"...heart pumping, page turning action..."

"...gripping, on the edge of your seat read from beginning to end..."

"This book has just the right mix of science, horror, action, tragedy, humor, and (ultimately) hope."

ISBN: 978-1-937174-15-6

The graphic companion to the *HVZA* novel,
eight different teams of artists explore the characters and events
of the zombie apocalypse.

"A truly imaginative Zombie Anthology. Full of stories for every appetite."
-- Paul J. Salamoff, Writer/Producer (Discord, Logan's Run: Last Day)

"One of the coolest collections of independent comic book writers and artists
take on the world of horror with this collection of unique tales!"
-- Darren Davis, publisher of Bluewater Comics

"Not since peanut butter and chocolate has there been as perfect a combination as
zombies and comics! What's better than one zombie story? How about a whole
brain-eating collection of zombie stories?!"
--Jim Salicrup, Editor-in-Chief, Papercutz and former Marvel Comics editor on
"The Avengers," "The Amazing Spider-Man," "The Uncanny X-Men" and "The
Fantastic Four."

ISBN 978-1937174-18-7

For more information, video, blogs, and podcasts, go to:
www.hvzombie.com

and

http://drtruesdale.wordpress.com/
http://voiceofthehudson.wordpress.com/

Which do you prefer?
Vote for your favorite at **www.hvzombie.com**

Linda Zimmermann: Zombie Killer

Linda Zimmermann: Zombie

About the Author

Linda Zimmermann is no stranger to the undead. She is the author of the popular *Ghost Investigator* series of books which chronicle her actual ghost hunting adventures. In addition, she is the award-winning author of science and history books. She enjoys lecturing on a wide variety of topics, and has spoken at the Smithsonian Institution, Gettysburg, West Point, and national Mensa events. Linda has also made numerous appearances on radio and television.

When she isn't glued to her computer writing books, Linda goes cycling, kayaking, swimming, cross country skiing, and snowshoeing. She is a lifelong NY Mets and NY Giants fan, so don't even think of trying to call her when a game is on.

As a vegetarian, if Linda ever turned into a zombie, she would have to subsist on brain-flavored tofu.

www.gotozim.com

www.ghostinvestigator.com

www.badsciences.com

Linda Zimmermann's books are available from her websites, Amazon, Barnes & Noble, and most major retailers. They are also available for Kindle, Apple, NookBook, Kobo, and other E-book formats.

www.ingramcontent.com/pod-product-compliance
Lightning Source LLC
Chambersburg PA
CBHW020413180626
46812CB00003B/959